The Necessary Murder of Nonie Blake

ALSO BY TERRY SHAMES

A Samuel Craddock Mystery

The Necessary Murder of Nonie Blake

Terry Shames

SEVENTH STREET BOOKS®
AN IMPRINT OF PROMETHEUS BOOKS
59 JOHN GLENN DRIVE • AMHERST, NY 14228
www.seventhstreetbooks.com

Published 2016 by Seventh Street Books®, an imprint of Prometheus Books

Cover image © Media Bakery
Cover design Grace M. Conti-Zilsberger

Inquiries should be addressed to
Seventh Street Books
59 John Glenn Drive
Amherst, New York 14228
VOICE: 716–691–0133 • FAX: 716–691–0137
WWW.SEVENTHSTREETBOOKS.COM

20 19 18 17 16 • 5 4 3 2 1

Library of Congress Cataloging-in-Publication Data

Shames, Terry
   The necessary murder of Nonie Blake : a Samuel Craddock mystery / by Terry Shames.
        pages ; cm
   ISBN 978-1-63388-120-4 (paperback) — ISBN 978-1-63388-121-1 (e-book)
   I. Title.

PS3619.H35425N43 2016
813'.6—dc23

2015030329

Printed in the United States of America

*To Sam and Ada Gaines and their descendants,
who filled my head with stories*

CHAPTER 1

Although none of the Blake family has caused the police in Jarrett Creek any trouble for a long time, I'm not surprised that people are in an uproar when they hear that Winona Blake is back in town. Most people don't even know her real name—she's always been called Nonie.

"She was a dangerous girl and she'll be a dangerous woman." Loretta Singletary, my good friend and neighbor down the street, has stopped in to bring me a hefty slab of coffee cake along with her opinions. She gets up early and bakes every morning and dispenses her goodies like she's trying to fatten up all her friends. Along with her coffee cakes and sweet rolls, she usually brings me the latest news-about-town.

I can't help groaning. "Loretta, I don't want to hear this. They wouldn't have let her out of the mental institution if they thought she was a danger to anyone. And besides, if her family isn't worried, why should anybody else be?"

"You know as well as I do that they're always letting people out of mental hospitals, and then they go crazy and kill somebody." I'm trying not to stare at Loretta's new permanent that has her white hair in tight curls all over her head. I don't know whether to mention the hairdo or not. I've had the experience of complimenting her on her hair only to find that she's unhappy with the way it looks, mad at her hairdresser, and by extension mad at anyone who notices it.

"No, I don't know that. And if you didn't watch all that TV you wouldn't believe it either."

"It's not just me." Her feathers are ruffled. She doesn't like to be called out for watching what I think of as alarmist TV. "Patty Larson is putting together a petition to have Nonie escorted out of town."

Now I laugh out loud. "Loretta, I hope you don't sign it."

"And why not?" She's like a banty rooster when she gets mad.

"Because anybody with any sense will look at the list of signers and know that they're looking at the silliest people in town."

"Says you," she grumbles. "For your information I had no intention of signing it anyway. I know you can't run somebody out of town. But I think as chief of police you ought to at least go over there and find out what she's up to."

"That's not going to happen," I say. "If a bunch of you are so all-fired interested, why don't you get a welcome wagon together for her?"

My suggestion wasn't serious, but the gleam in her eye tells me that she is considering the idea. Everybody will be itching to get a look at Nonie. Twenty years ago, when she was fourteen years old, she tried to kill her younger sister. At the recommendation of a psychiatrist, the family sent her off to an institution near Dallas, and she had been there ever since. At least that's the way I heard the story. I wasn't chief of police at the time it happened. I was working as a land man for an oil and gas company, and I traveled all over the state and so sometimes missed getting the whole story of events that happened in town.

Now I'm chief of police again more or less by default. Jarrett Creek went bankrupt and couldn't afford to pay anybody. I didn't need the salary, so they asked me to step in. Even though it had been many years since I was in the job, people still called me chief, and it seemed natural enough for me to say yes.

Loretta says she's got to go, and by the excitement in her voice I'm afraid that by suggesting a welcome committee I've started an idea that will take on a life of its own. From what little I know about the Blakes, though, they'll find a way to deflect the curiosity seekers. A few families, no matter how long they've lived in Jarrett Creek, are never really part of it. The Blakes are like that. Nonie's actions set the family apart, and since then they've never made much of an attempt to fit in.

For the next few days, Loretta doesn't mention Nonie Blake—

in fact, she's obviously making an effort to keep me out of the loop on what the ladies are up to. That's fine with me. It's mid-August and hot as blazes, which seems to bring out the orneriness in people, and I have a few dustups to settle. Plus the kids are back in school, and the high school boys like to protest by spending the evenings drinking and racing cars along the dam road. I have to shut them down every couple of nights.

It's a shame that school starts up so early, before summer is over. When I was a youngster the best days of summer were late August when you could lie around with a fishing pole and while away the afternoon. At least that's my nostalgic recollection—it probably didn't happen very often.

So I've pushed Nonie Blake out of my mind when a call comes in to police headquarters a few days later. It's Charlotte Blake, her voice trembling.

"Chief Craddock, something has happened. My sister Nonie has drowned and I don't know what to do."

"Drowned where?" I ask.

"In our pond out behind the house." She starts to cry.

"I'll be right out there. Don't move anything or mess with the body."

"We already moved her. We had to get her out of the pond. We couldn't just leave her there."

"I understand. I mean, leave everything the way it is now."

I call an ambulance to come from Bobtail. Then I call Bill Odum, one of my two deputies, and tell him I need him to come out to the Blakes' ranch as soon as he can. He says he can leave right away, that he and his daddy have just now finished clearing a field. When he isn't working part-time as a cop, he works for his daddy on their farm.

The Blake place is on the north side of town, out past the cemetery and a few miles down a gravel road. I barrel down the road, kicking up a lot of dust. Not too many houses out this way. Every one of them is situated on a couple of acres of land. People got in the habit of calling these places "the ranches," but for me it doesn't fit. When I think of a ranch, I think of acres and acres of land stretching farther than the eye can see, not some scrubby couple of acres.

I don't know why anybody would want to live out here. There's something desolate about it, even though there are plenty of trees. But there's also scrub brush and big patches of land with nothing growing on them, not even weeds. It's worse this time of year when we haven't had enough rain and the sun is at its hottest. If you walk around in this area, you run across a lot of fire-ant beds. Makes my ankles sting to think about it.

I head up the gravel driveway to the house and park in front of the garage. I pause before I get out, sizing up the place. It's massive, both tall and wide with a big wraparound porch, generous windows, and an oversized front door. But it's unadorned, no carved trim on windows or doors, no embellishments, and it's painted a gloomy gray. If the house ever goes to ruin, no doubt people will soon say it's haunted, not only because of what happened out here twenty years ago, but also because it looks unapproachable.

Charlotte said the pond was located out back of the house. The backyard is as scrubby as the front, with exhausted patches of grass barely holding their own in the red dirt. There's a big hulk of a barn set several yards back that has seen better days. The heat shimmers off the tin roof, the glare piercing even though I'm wearing sunglasses. As I get closer to the barn, I hear a child's voice, high and loud, and a woman crying, the sound coming from behind the structure. A trick of acoustics makes it seem like the air is full of voices.

The pond is set a short distance back from the barn. The family is gathered near the banks next to a heap on the ground. As I walk up, I see that the pond is half-obscured with brown algae and dead leaves. A putrid smell hangs in the air. I don't see how the family can stand the odor, although I suppose with Nonie lying there they aren't noticing much else.

I had forgotten that Loretta had told me that Charlotte has a five-year-old boy, and I'm surprised to see him crouched beside the body looking at it intently. Squatting next to him, his hand on the boy's shoulder, is a scrawny young man with his back to me.

Adelaide Blake; her daughter Charlotte; and a man of about fifty, with a thick body and curly gray hair, have their eyes on the two crouched there. Adelaide Blake is sobbing into a handkerchief. I'm curious why Adelaide's husband, John, isn't with them.

At the sound of my footsteps, they turn to me with an air of relief. Only the child doesn't look up, keeping his attention on the body. Children are fascinated by death and can seem heartless because they don't really understand the full import of it.

Charlotte walks toward me, and the scrawny young man who was keeping vigil with the five-year-old stands up. His thin, pale face is streaked with dirt and the trace of tears, and his black pants and T-shirt look damp. The Blakes have four children, one of them much younger than the other three. This must be him. He's around twenty. There's an older brother who doesn't live in Jarrett Creek. He has made a bit of a name for himself riding the rodeo circuit.

"Mrs. Blake, Charlotte." I take my hat off and nod to them. Adelaide turns away, weeping, and Charlotte puts her fist to her mouth.

I walk over next to Nonie Blake's body and say to the child, "Mind if I take a look?"

Charlotte says, "Trey, come over by me."

"No, Mamma, I'm watching Aunt Nonie," the child says.

The young man takes the child's hand. "Come on, Trey, let's go."

He whines in complaint, but he lets himself be led away.

It's obvious that Nonie is dead, but I lean down to put my fingers on her artery nevertheless. I wonder how long she was in the water. It must have been several hours. Her skin is wrinkled and white. She's wearing a brightly flowered dress and slippers that don't look like the kind of thing you would wear to come outdoors unless it was only to step outside for a moment.

Physically, Nonie doesn't look like her mother and sister. They are both tall and slim, and she's only about 5'5", and although she's not heavy, she has more weight and shape to her. Her head is canted to one side. I reach over and center it, and then peer closer to be sure of what I'm seeing. I can say one thing. Nonie Blake didn't drown. The side of her head has been bashed in, crushing her cheek and jaw. Surely the family must have noticed this when she was pulled from the water, but Charlotte said she drowned.

Everybody is quiet while I am observing the body, as if they're hoping I can perform a miracle. I straighten back up and shake my head. "Ambulance will be here soon," I say, although I realize that now I'm going to have to put off having the ambulance take her away until the Texas Rangers or the highway patrol get here.

I walk over to Adelaide. She has stopped crying, but her expression is stunned. She's in her midfifties. Her hair is tucked into a large gray bun. "Mrs. Blake, I'm so sorry," I say. "Does anybody have any idea what happened?"

She sniffs. Her voice is strangled. "Can you ask Charlotte? I need to collect myself."

"Of course. Why don't we move away from the pond?"

She takes a few steps back but can't take her eyes off her daughter's body.

I turn to Charlotte. Her face is pale. She's not a pretty woman, her face long and thin with a sallow complexion, and her eyes bulging slightly. But she has sleek brown hair and a trim figure. She's wearing a short-sleeved yellow blouse and white slacks.

"I don't know that we've met officially," I say. "I'm Samuel Craddock."

"Thank you for coming so quickly," she says.

The man with her puts his hand out. "I'm Les Moffitt," he says. "I'm a friend of the family."

"And this is my brother, Matthew," Charlotte says, indicating the young man still holding the five-year-old's hand. "We call him Skeeter. And that's my son, Trey."

Trey slips his hand out of Skeeter's and runs back to the body. Charlotte has her eyes in his direction, but I don't think she really sees him.

Skeeter wipes his hand on his pants before he shakes mine. His hand is damp and surprisingly cool.

"Charlotte, can you tell me who found your sister's body?"

"That was Skeeter." She reaches over and puts her arm around her brother's shoulders and pulls him to her.

He swipes dirt off his face with the back of his hand.

"Skeeter, why don't you tell me how you happened to find your sister," I say.

"Everybody was in an uproar about Daddy. I came out here to the pond to get out of the house for a few minutes. When I got to the pond . . ." He stops for a minute and swallows. "I saw this shape and I thought it was a fawn that might have fallen in the water and drowned, so I went around the side to pull it out. When I got close, I saw . . . I saw the dress and I knew it couldn't be . . . you know what I mean."

Adelaide moans. Charlotte is gnawing at her lip.

Charlotte's little boy suddenly jumps to his feet, runs to his mother's side, and grabs her hand. "Mamma, Mamma," he says. "I saw Aunt Nonie move. You said she couldn't move anymore, but I saw her."

Charlotte draws a sharp breath. "Les, could you take Trey inside?"

"I saw her! I did!"

She kneels down next to the boy. "Honey, it was some water settling in her body."

The child looks back at Nonie, frowning, not wanting to believe this information. Charlotte takes his shoulders and moves him around to face her. "Trey-Trey, would you like Uncle Les to take you inside and give you a cookie?"

The boy sticks a finger in his mouth. "Two cookies."

"Okay, two cookies. And you can watch TV."

That seals the deal, and Les Moffitt leads the child away.

I turn back to Skeeter. "When you say everybody was in an uproar over your daddy, what do you mean?"

Skeeter looks at Charlotte. She says, "Daddy has had Parkinson's for several years and now he's got some dementia with it. He gets agitated sometimes."

"I see. Skeeter, you pulled Nonie out of the water by yourself?"

"Yes sir."

"When you got her out, did you happen to notice the wound at the side of her head?"

"What wound?" Charlotte's voice is high with tension.

Skeeter looks down at his feet, nodding slightly. "I thought maybe she had hit her head on a rock." He looks up at me, his eyes as weary as an old man's. "But there's no rocks around the pond that I know of."

All the air goes out of Charlotte. She closes her eyes and clenches her teeth.

I look to Adelaide to see how she has taken this news, but she's looking out over the pond as if she either didn't hear it or doesn't want to process it.

"Why don't you all go back to the house and I'll be there in a minute to talk to you," I say.

Charlotte and Skeeter start to walk toward the house, but Adelaide stands her ground. I lock eyes with her, wondering if she has something in particular to say to me, but she looks away quickly and stares at the body. She clears her throat. "I'm going to stay here for a minute," she says. "If that's all right."

"That's fine. I have to make a couple of calls."

"She's not going anywhere," Adelaide says.

I walk a little distance away to put in a call to the Rangers and the highway patrol, telling them I'm going to need some help here and giving them directions.

When I walk back, Adelaide hasn't moved. With a sigh, she says, "She didn't have a chance to get back into life."

"It's a shame," I say.

I stand there with her a few minutes longer. I'm thinking that although Skeeter brought Nonie out of the water here, she may have gone in anywhere along the shoreline of the pond.

I hear vehicles crunching up the gravel driveway, more than one. When I hear doors slam, I say, "Mrs. Blake, it would be best if you go inside. I'll walk with you."

"All right, then." We head toward the house. She goes inside, and I walk over to talk to Bill Odum and the ambulance drivers, who arrived at the same time.

I tell the drivers that things aren't as straightforward as they seemed when I called them, and it'll be a while before they can take the body, so they may as well settle in.

Then I tell Bill Odum to come with me. "I want you to take a look," I say.

At the pond, he crouches down to get a closer look. "Uh-oh," he says, seeing the way the skull is damaged. "We're going to have to notify the state."

"I already put in the calls." I tell him I'm going to go back to the house to talk to the family, and I want him to walk around the pond and see if he can figure out where Nonie's body went in. "And keep a look out for a weapon. I don't know whether somebody hit her here at the pond and shoved her in, or if they might have done it somewhere else and dragged her body here. You know what to look for."

I'm wishing we could put a sheet or something over the body, but the last time I did that, I caught hell from the coroner for interfering with the body temperature and making it harder for them to determine the time of death.

Odum looks out over the pond and shudders. "Snaky kind of place. I'm going back to the car to get me a tire iron to poke around with." He doesn't move right away. "I went to school with Charlotte. I don't remember her very well, but I do remember my mamma was pretty shook up by what happened. She wanted to keep me out of school, but luckily Daddy convinced her that didn't make any sense. You don't suppose Charlotte did this, do you?"

"It's a little early for that kind of speculation." I start toward the house, Odum walking beside me. "By the way, Doc Taggart's going to be here soon. Would you ask him to come to the house when he arrives?"

CHAPTER 2

Les Moffitt answers the Blakes' door. He is jowly, with pale-blue eyes and high color in his cheeks. His smile is a little uncertain, as if he's been left to his own devices and isn't sure what his place is. "Charlotte is upstairs putting her son down for a nap," he says. "She asked me to hold the fort until she comes downstairs. This is a hell of a situation."

"Where is Adelaide?"

"She's checking on John. She'll be down soon, too. Why don't we go on in the living room?"

I'm struck by the contrast between the starkness of the house's exterior and the sumptuous living room. A plump sofa and armchairs in rich colors are grouped around a massive fireplace. Elegant side tables in some kind of antique European style—French? Italian?—hold all manner of expensive-looking knickknacks. The walls are covered with art in the same style, elegant scenes of boats in harbors and quaint villages and pastoral paintings. Knowing something about art, I note a couple of fine bird watercolors and a large oil painting that could be an Onderdonk. Not my taste, but a handsome representative of his landscape paintings. I don't know that I've ever been in a home around here that displayed such splendor.

I can't help wondering how they keep things intact with a five-year-old in the house. But then I see that one large corner of the room is given over to a play area—an elaborate train set is the centerpiece, with boxes of plastic building blocks and toys shoved up against the wall. There's an entire bookcase filled with children's books.

Moffitt seems at home in the setting and gestures for me to take one of the armchairs. I sink into its plush cushions and think how nice it might be to get something like this chair in my house. I can imagine Loretta's reaction if she showed up one day and I was taking my ease in it.

"Can I get you a soft drink or a cup of coffee?" He looks anxious, as if he feels like he ought to ask but hopes I won't request anything he can't lay his hands on easily.

"Thank you, but I'm fine."

When Moffitt sits down, I say, "What's your connection with the Blakes?"

"Uh, I . . . well, that is, I'm a friend of the family." He nods again. "You know, good friends. I've known the family a long time."

"You live around here?"

"Over in Bryan."

"What kind of work do you do?"

"I'm an investment counselor. That's how I met the Blakes. I help them with their investments."

You don't hear much about people in Jarrett Creek needing the services of an investment counselor. Most people are more the type to let what money they have collect interest in a savings account. It's another way in which the Blakes set themselves apart.

"Were you here when Skeeter found Nonie's body?"

"No, I happened to get here right after they called you. I was going to take Adelaide out for an early dinner."

"Not John?"

He frowns. "You're not aware of the situation with John?"

"I heard he has some dementia. It's gone too far for him to go out with you and Adelaide?"

"That's right. Matter of fact, that's what Adelaide and I were going to discuss, whether or not it's time to have him sign over a power of attorney to her."

"I see. So when Skeeter said things were in an uproar . . ."

"John gets a little agitated. He . . . uh . . . needs a lot of care." He narrows his eyes and speaks almost in a whisper. "If you ask me, he'd be better off in a facility somewhere so he could get away from . . ."

"Here you are," Charlotte is smiling, but her eyes are tight as she zeroes in on Moffitt.

He leaps to his feet. "Did you get Trey to sleep?"

"Not yet. Skeeter's reading him a story. Soon as he goes to sleep, Skeeter will come down." She's still standing and turns to me. "Did Les offer you something to drink?"

I tell her he did. "Is your mamma coming down soon? I'll need to talk to her, too."

Charlotte frowns. "Trey riled Daddy up with his noise, and she has to get him settled down. It might be hard for her to join us right away."

With Charlotte here, Moffitt edges toward the door. "If you don't need me, I think I'll be on my way." He hands me his business card. "This is where you can reach me if I can help with anything. Charlotte, tell your mamma I'll call her in a day or two to reschedule."

Charlotte sits down on the sofa, tucking her feet together primly. "Now what were you telling Skeeter—something about a head wound?"

"Charlotte, did you get a close look at Nonie's body?"

She shakes her head. "Makes me queasy just thinking about it. I don't know how Skeeter could stand to . . . to touch her, much less pull her onto the shore."

"It looks like Nonie was attacked before she went into the water. It'll be up to the medical examiner to find out if she died before or after she went in, but the blow she sustained to her head was substantial."

"That means . . ." She shivers, although it's warm.

"It means somebody killed her. I don't know an easier way to say it."

"That's absolutely crazy. Who could have . . ." She manages a wan smile. "I guess that's the question, isn't it. Who?"

"You have any idea?"

"Do I have an idea? No, not at all. I mean, I guess one of us would be the obvious suspect, but . . ."

"We'll discuss that directly. Let me get a few details straight. Exactly how long has Nonie been back?"

She puts a hand to her chest. "She came August tenth, to be exact. And today is the eighteenth? Is that right?"

"Yes, it's the eighteenth. Remind me how long it was since Nonie went away?"

"Too long. It would have been twenty years this fall. I hate that phrase 'went away.' Like she was on vacation." She's twisting her hands and she sounds like she could cry any minute. "I don't know why people feel the need to tiptoe around the matter and sugarcoat it. We've all lived with Nonie's situation for a long time—too long, if you ask me. I thought she ought to come home, but my parents didn't agree with me." She tilts her chin up a little, defiant. I remember suddenly how young she is, probably late twenties. Somehow, she gave the impression of being in charge of things, and it made her seem older.

"I'm surprised you were willing to have Nonie back given what she tried to do to you." Nonie had tried to kill Charlotte by hanging her. Nonie was fourteen and Charlotte was eight.

"We were children when all that happened," Charlotte says. "Mamma and Daddy sent her to a psychiatrist, and he seemed to think she did it deliberately, but I don't care what he said, I don't believe she really knew what she was doing."

"Why did they release her after all this time?"

"Mamma said there was some new medication she was taking and they didn't think she needed to be there any longer."

"How did you feel when you heard she was coming back?"

She gets a funny look on her face. "The fact is, I didn't know she was coming back. She showed up here out of the blue and Mamma said she knew she was coming."

"Why didn't your mamma tell you? Seems like she would have, given the history between the two of you."

Charlotte shakes her head. "I know it sounds crazy. Mamma said she didn't know how to break the news to me. She should have known I'd be okay with it. I've made my peace with what happened."

"You have?"

"Maybe not as much as I thought I had. It's been a little strange with her here."

"Your brother seemed pretty upset. Had he gotten friendly with Nonie since she got home?"

"They hit it off. I don't think they spent a lot of time together, though."

"Did anybody else come here in the past week to see her?"

She shakes her head. "Les is the only person who has been here this week. He came by one day, but they didn't have any conversation. He'd just met her. So we're the only people she saw, unless . . ."

"Unless what?"

"I suppose somebody could have visited her after we went to bed."

"Did she ever go out?"

"Not that I know of."

We hear footsteps on the stairs at exactly the same time the front doorbell rings. Charlotte jumps up and heads to the door. I hear Doc Taggart's voice. "Craddock here? He wanted to talk to me."

I go into the entry at the same time Skeeter comes down the stairs. Charlotte goes over and grabs Skeeter's arm and brings him to the front door.

"How you doin', Skeeter?" Taggart says, stepping inside. His demeanor is too hearty, given the situation.

Skeeter grins.

"I'm doin' okay. Except, you know." He points outside.

I tell them that I'm going to confer with Taggart and that I'll be right back with them.

"We'll wait in the living room," Charlotte says.

"What in the hell happened?" Taggart says when we're alone. "How did she manage to drown?"

"You didn't look at the body?"

"Bill Odum intercepted me and said you wanted to see me."

"You'd better come take a look. Somebody bashed her head in before they threw her in the pond."

Taggart and I head for the pond. The west is full of threatening clouds and heat lightning, and in the late afternoon sun, with shadows from the trees beyond the pond, the air is almost lavender. The mosquitoes are in full force when we get near the scummy water. I slap at my arms and legs.

Taggart stoops down and examines Nonie. "Oh, my Lord." He blows out a breath. "I guess if it's a homicide, they'll have to take her body over to Bobtail where T. J. can take a look at her." T. J. Sutter is the county coroner and justice of the peace.

"I already called him and the Rangers."

"Okay then." He sighs. "This is a mess. I had heard they let Nonie come back. What made them decide to bring her home now?"

"I'll have to ask them that."

"I'll bet it went over big with Charlotte having her back here."

"Charlotte said she wanted to bring her home."

"After what Nonie did to her?"

"Yes, she said they were just kids and she didn't believe Nonie knew what she was doing."

"Charlotte doesn't know what the hell she's talking about. Nonie was crazy. Flat out. I wouldn't have trusted her."

I have no idea how he knows this. He's a country GP, and as far as I know he wasn't trained in psychiatric care. "Did you have a hand in assessing her after she tried to kill Charlotte?"

"No, of course I didn't. They left that to the big cheeses. I forget where they took her. Houston, probably. But I was the family doctor and you could tell from the time she was little that there was something not right going on with her."

Taggart has always irritated me as being a know-it-all, and this sounds like one of those things he's pontificating about that may or may not be true.

"Who found her?" he says.

"Adelaide's younger son, Skeeter."

"Poor kid. Has to be a shock."

"You know anything about John Blake? He seems to be giving the family some problems."

"He's been going downhill for several years. They used to bring him to me, but they've started going to a specialist in Houston. I told Adelaide they needed to get him into a facility, but she said she married him for better or worse, and she was sticking with it. Poor devil."

When he says "poor devil," I don't know whether he means Adelaide or the old man.

He sniffs. "Parkinson's is a rotten disease. I guess you have to admire Adelaide for wanting to take care of him. I knew John when we were kids. Never could figure out what he saw in Adelaide. She never had much to say and when she did, it didn't mean much. She must have been a tiger in bed, is all I can say."

I'm not quite sure how to reply to that.

"Unless you need me for anything else, I'll go on home now," he says. "I can't do anything. It's up to the medical examiner now."

When I go back into the house, Adelaide has joined the others in the living room. She looks like she's at the end of a long, hard day. A couple of strands of hair have escaped from her bun and are trailing over her shoulder, and her face is practically gray. I remind myself that it's her daughter lying out there dead, even though Nonie hasn't lived under her roof for a long time.

"I've had a few words with Charlotte," I say to Adelaide and Skeeter, "and I need to talk to the two of you as well. But first, I'd like to take a look at the room Nonie was staying in."

CHAPTER 3

The room where Nonie Blake spent her last few days is small but nicely furnished with an old-fashioned rag rug on the polished oak floor, a double bed with a carved mahogany headboard, and a flowered bedspread. There are a few more antique pieces in this room—the dresser topped with a mirror, a carved nightstand, and a spindle-back rocking chair. The top of the dresser contains a few personal items: a hairbrush, a small photo of a young girl in a cheap frame—maybe Nonie when she was very young—and a cup with a little dark liquid in the bottom. I sniff it and it smells like chocolate.

On the bedside stand there's a worn paperback romance novel called *Heart of Stone*. The cover shows a bare-chested man with a mane of blond hair holding his hand out to a woman dressed in a tight skirt with her chest almost busting out of her bodice. I open it and see a penciled marking that indicates the book was used and cost fifty cents. Next to the book there's a small tube of Jergens hand lotion and a box of tissues.

The closet is tiny but plenty big for the few clothes hanging there—two pairs of slacks, three blouses, and a dress. There are a pair of sneakers and a pair of sandals on the floor.

The top dresser drawer contains underwear, a nightgown, and a couple of T-shirts. There's a small zipper case with a thin chain with a cross on it. The other drawers are filled with household items—linens, candles, stationery, and framed photos, which means the room was used for storage before Nonie came home.

I step into the center of the room and try to figure out what's troubling me. Then I realize her belongings are sparse. Even being in a mental institution, she would have accumulated more in the way of clothing and personal items over twenty years. Maybe she left some items at the facility with the idea of having them sent. I feel like I can't really get a handle on her from the small impact she made on this room.

The bathroom is down the hall from her room. There I find minimal toiletries—toothbrush and toothpaste, deodorant, shampoo and mouthwash, and a few cosmetics. In the medicine cabinet, in addition to aspirin and Tums, I find a prescription bottle, but it's not Nonie's prescription. It's for someone named Susan Shelby, filled at a pharmacy in Tyler, Texas. That's the only medication I find.

I go back into the bedroom and look in vain for the medication Charlotte mentioned that supposedly got Nonie out of the hospital and back into normal life. Maybe Adelaide can tell me.

I consider closing off the room with crime-scene tape, but there's really nothing to see here.

"That's strange," Adelaide says when I go back downstairs and ask her if she knows where Nonie's medication is. "I don't know that I ever saw it. I assumed she would take it if the doctor said she had to, but I never asked."

I address Charlotte and Skeeter. "Did either of you ever see her take any pills?"

"Let me think." Charlotte pauses and then shakes her head. "I don't believe I did."

Skeeter says the same.

"When I was looking for Nonie's medication, I found some pills in the medicine cabinet with the name Susan Shelby on it. Who is she?"

Adelaide darts a glance at Charlotte.

Charlotte shrugs. "I don't know anyone by that name."

"I don't know where they came from," Adelaide says. "What kind of pills were they?"

"It's called Levoxyl. Used for low thyroid, I believe."

"Yes, I take it myself," Adelaide says.

"The prescription was filled in Tyler. Anybody visit you recently who lives in Tyler?"

She shakes her head slowly. "I think the last person who used that bathroom was my son Billy, when he was home last time."

"That's your older son? When was he here?"

"Not in a while. Several weeks. He's out on the rodeo circuit."

That doesn't explain why he would know anything about the pills. "Is he planning to come home soon?"

"We're trying to reach him," Charlotte says.

"I guess we can ask him what he knows about the pills when he gets here," I say.

"Nonie didn't have much in the way of clothing or personal items. Do you know if she had planned to send for some later?"

Adelaide's mouth tenses, and she runs a thumb along her lower lip before shaking her head. "I don't know anything about that," she says. "I assumed she traveled with her belongings."

Another assumption that Adelaide didn't bother to ask her daughter about. It doesn't add up. I have an uneasy suspicion that Adelaide is lying, but I can't imagine why. I'll probe a little deeper when I talk to her alone, but first I want to question Skeeter about the details of finding the body while they're still fresh in his mind.

Adelaide protests that she wants to be with Skeeter when I question him, but I confirm he's twenty years old. "He's old enough for me to question him alone," I say.

I take Skeeter onto the front porch to talk to him, and I see that a highway patrol car has arrived and parked behind the ambulance. It's dusk now, and the porch lights cast a dull yellow glow into the yard. There's always a lot to be done with a crime scene, and people slip to and from the back of the house in the shadows, like ghosts. I tell Skeeter to wait, and I walk over to the patrol car to find out if they know when they plan to take Nonie's body away. I'd as soon the boy not have to see that.

Turns out the medical examiner has come and gone, declaring that it was a waste of his time to come out when Taggart could as easily have pronounced her dead. Before the highway patrol can authorize the ambulance to remove the body, they're waiting for the Texas Rangers so they can decide who has control of the case. I can't tell from the way the patrolman talks whether they want control or if they're itching to turn it over to the Rangers. Could go either way. Jurisdiction in a small-town suspicious death is sometimes murky. Theoretically it's up to the highway patrol to investigate if they determine that the town police force isn't up to the job, but often they hand it over to the Rangers, who have more resources.

When I get back on the porch, I sit down in a wicker chair next to Skeeter. "Skeeter, I'm sorry about your sister. She hasn't been home long, but Charlotte tells me you and Nonie seemed to like each other."

"She had a funny way about her. Different. Finding her in the pond like that was terrible."

"I know it was. Tell me, how were things after Nonie arrived? What did you think of her? Did she get along with everybody in the house?"

"She seemed nice. Charlotte told me what Nonie tried to do when they were kids, but as far as I could tell she was a regular person. Quiet. Kept to herself most of the time."

"Had you ever met her before she came home?"

He stares at me. "I was a baby when she left."

"They never took you to see her?"

"Far as I know, none of them ever went to see her at all."

That's an interesting bit of information. Seems unlikely, and I wonder if they went to see her and simply didn't tell Skeeter.

"Since she got here, have there been any arguments, or problems?"

"Not with her. But Mamma and Charlotte argue a lot."

"What about?"

"You name it, they can argue about it. If Mamma says she's making pancakes for breakfast, Charlotte says eggs. But they mostly argue about Daddy and what to do about him."

"You mean whether to keep him home or send him to a nursing home?"

"That's right. Charlotte wants him to go into a home, and Mamma says over her dead body."

"You have any opinion on the matter?"

"Me? I don't know. I guess if he was out of the house, things would be a little easier around here. But I hate to think of him being taken care of by strangers."

"Did Nonie get into any of the arguments with your mamma and sister about that?"

He thinks about that. "I'm not sure they argued in front of her. I think Charlotte and Mamma were trying hard to make it look like things around here were more friendly than they are."

"So there weren't any arguments between Nonie and them?"

He puts a hand up. "I didn't say that. She got riled up a time or two."

"What was it that upset her?"

"Silly things. She didn't like some kinds of food. I mean, I guess everybody has some food they don't like, but I don't think most people go all ape about it." He snickers. "She didn't like beans. She said they made her pass gas." He laughs harder. "I thought that was the whole point of beans."

I can't help laughing with him. "When you say she went ape, what do you mean?"

"One day she threw a vase. Not at anybody. Just threw it on the floor and broke it to smithereens. And a couple of times she yelled. Like I said, she was mostly quiet, but when she got it into her head to yell, she could make a good racket."

"Anything in particular that set her off?"

"She . . . she seemed to think she should be getting . . ." He stops, as if confused.

"Getting what?"

"She seemed to think she was owed."

"Owed money?"

"I don't know. Charlotte is the one to talk to if you want to know more about that."

"Fair enough. Why don't you tell me the circumstances when you found Nonie."

"Well, that." His voice flattens. "Daddy was in a state this morning and when Charlotte went to take Trey to school, Daddy got pretty wound up. I was in my room and I heard him talking loud and wandering around the house all morning. He had been kind of riled up since Nonie got here and I wondered if she would hear him. I decided to lay low in my room until lunch. When I went downstairs, Charlotte and Mamma were sniping at each other, and Daddy was squalling. So I made a sandwich and took it back upstairs."

"Did you wonder where Nonie was?"

He cocks his head. "I guess I figured she was upstairs in her room, the same as I was."

"What time did you go out to the pond?"

"After lunch. I'd been inside too long and needed to go out and get some air. So I went out to the pond."

"Did you notice the body right away?"

He scratches his head, the yellow light from the porch making his face ghastly. "No, not right away. I sat down under a tree and I guess I fell asleep for a while. When I woke up, I got up and walked around, and that's when I saw her."

"You didn't call out for anybody?"

"Like I said, I didn't realize at first that it was a person. I thought maybe it was a deer. It was around the other side in the shade of that tree that hangs over the water."

"So how did you get her body over to where you brought her out?"

"I waded in and walked around to this side of the pond. It isn't that deep except right in the middle." He shakes his head and blows out a breath. "It was spooky."

"Was she face up or face down?"

"Face down."

"How did you know it was her?"

"I recognized that flowered dress she wore around the house."

"You didn't think to call for help then?"

"I was in a hurry to get her out of the water. I was thinking something might get at her, like a snake or something."

"Must have been hard dragging her out of the water. Wasn't she heavy?"

"In the water she wasn't. Hoisting her onto the bank was a problem. I guess I shouldn't have moved her, should I?"

"It's all right. We all have an instinct to try to get somebody onto the land, even if it's clear we're too late."

He sighs.

"When you pulled her out, that's when you noticed the wound on her head?"

He's quiet so long I'm beginning to wonder if he heard me, but finally he speaks in almost a whisper. "Yeah, I saw it."

"But you didn't tell anybody."

In the light of the porch, I see him shake his head. Finding the body rattled him, but there's more to it than that. I'm wondering if he thinks he knows who killed her and he doesn't want to say.

"Did you hear any unusual commotion outside last night or this morning?"

"No sir, but I'm a pretty good sleeper."

A car drives up and switches off the lights. Probably one of the Rangers.

"When was the last time you saw her alive?"

"Last night. We had dinner at six—Nonie didn't like eating so early, so sometimes she ate later. But she ate with the family last night."

"Did she seem okay? Did she say she was going out or anything?"

"Out? Where would she go?"

That's the question, isn't it? "Skeeter, do you have any idea who might have done this?"

He jerks his head around to look at me. "Has to have been a stranger. Nobody here would have done that."

"Samuel?" A voice comes from the darkness. "Is that you on the porch? You have time to talk to me?" The voice is one I recognize, Luke Schoppe, a Texas Ranger a few years younger than me who is part of our jurisdiction.

"Yeah, I'll be right there."

I stand up, but Skeeter continues to sit there.

"Skeeter, I want to ask you something."

"Go ahead."

"Why aren't you in college?"

"I was over at A&M for a year and a half. I flunked out last semester."

"What were you studying?"

"I hadn't figured that out yet."

"Do you have a job?"

"How can I get a job? I can't do anything." His voice sounds bleak.

"Sure you can. You could work on a farm, or go on over to Bobtail and find a job. You ought to put up a notice at the café."

"Mamma doesn't want me to go to work."

"Why is that?"

"She said I don't need to."

"You're old enough that you shouldn't need her permission."

"Yeah, but even if I got a job, how would I get there? I don't have a car. And Mamma won't let me use ours." He stands up. "You better get on down there. That guy's waiting for you."

"Who told you Nonie needed to take medication? Was it Nonie herself?" I ask. Luke Schoppe has come with me to question Adelaide.

Charlotte has gone into the kitchen, and I hear her banging pots and pans louder than necessary.

"Oh no, it was the woman from Rollingwood—where Nonie had been living. She said it had been determined that Nonie was well enough to be released. She was very nice when she told me."

"Was she a doctor?"

"I don't know who it was. A woman. She might have told me who she was, but I was so flustered when she told me Nonie was coming home that I forgot everything else."

"Charlotte said that she had no idea Nonie was coming and that later you told her you knew. Why did you keep the information from her?"

Adelaide's cheeks grow pink. "I know I'm going to sound awful, but I knew if Charlotte heard they were releasing Nonie, she'd insist on going up there to get her. I didn't want Charlotte to do that. With John in the state he's in, and Trey to be taken care of, we can't simply pick up and leave on a moment's notice. It would have taken a whole day to drive up there and back. I thought if Nonie was well enough to come home, she was well enough to take the bus."

"Humph," Schoppe says. Like me, he must think that's pretty harsh.

There's something odd going on here. I can't imagine a mental hospital keeping someone for twenty years and then simply calling to say they're letting her out and not making any arrangements for her transportation or to explain how she needs to be cared for.

"Did Nonie's doctors keep you updated on her condition over the years?"

"What?" She's looking past me, as if she expects someone to appear in the background. "Oh, I suppose they did. For a while anyway." She waves her hand in a vague gesture. "You know how doctors talk. Half the time I can't understand what they say."

"What do you mean, 'for a while'?"

"I honestly can't remember the last time I talked to her doctor. I figured if they weren't calling, everything must be all right."

What mother wouldn't press a doctor to tell her in straight terms what was going on with her daughter? But maybe Adelaide didn't want to know. Maybe, unlike Charlotte, she had never forgiven Nonie for what she tried to do.

"You told me you never actually saw her take her medication."

Her jaw tightens. "Yes, I told you that."

"Did you notice anything unusual in Nonie's behavior the night before she was killed?" I'm thinking that one reason I may not have found any medication is that Nonie decided she didn't need it and threw it away. I know that sometimes happens with mental patients. Right after they stop taking the medication, they seem fine. But before long, the holdover from the drugs wears off, and they start to act up again.

"Mr. Craddock, or Chief Craddock, I guess I should say, and . . . I'm sorry what was your name?"

"Luke Schoppe."

"Yes, now I remember. Listen, if she acted strange, I wouldn't have known it. I'm so distracted by John that I hardly know what goes on in this house anymore."

"When was the last time you visited Nonie in the institution?"

"I'm not sure." She tugs at a stray piece of hair and tries to tuck it up into her bun, but it falls out again. "I don't know what that has to do with anything. As I said, it's difficult to get away."

"When was it?" I see Schoppe's eyes narrow, assessing Adelaide.

"It's been a while. We went up a few times, but the doctors said our visits upset her. I don't know why visits from her family should upset her, but when the doctor said I shouldn't come back for a while, I decided I didn't have to go if she was going to be that way."

Her eyes are suddenly angry. She sits forward at the edge of her seat "I know you judge me for not going to visit her. I know a lot of people would. But do you have any idea what it's like to know that you have a daughter who tried to kill her sister? I never got over it. I admit that. I wanted to do the right thing and bring Nonie home, and Charlotte kept saying she wanted Nonie to come back, but I never really wanted that. I'd have been happy to forget she ever existed. There, I've said it." Her mouth starts to tremble and her eyes fill with tears.

"When you first heard that Nonie was dead, what did you think had happened to her?" Schoppe says.

"I didn't know. I don't think that pond is dangerous, but maybe that's because I'm used to it. When you told us that the side of her head was bashed in, I hoped it was a mistake and that she really just drowned, pure and simple."

"No, she didn't drown. Somebody hit her with something."

Adelaide kneads her temples between her thumb and forefinger. "It was such a shock to see her lying there. Poor child. She was a wrong one from the beginning, but she didn't deserve to die that way. It makes no sense. Who would kill Nonie?"

"I'd like to ask you the same thing. Do you have any idea?"

"Of course not!"

"How did John react to her being here?"

Her cheeks are flaming red already, so I don't know if the question flusters her more. "He was fine. As fine as he can be, anyway."

Schoppe says, "You say your husband has dementia. Could he have gotten it into his mind that she was a danger and killed her?"

"Oh, good heavens no," Adelaide says. "He can't make his hands work well enough for that, even if he had that kind of nature, which he doesn't."

We don't get any more out of Adelaide. I tell her I'll be back in the morning. Schoppe and I go outside. The ambulance is gone, but there's still a highway patrol car in the driveway.

"I asked the highway patrol to have somebody stay here for the night to keep an eye on things," Schoppe says. He shakes his head. "I don't know that that's necessary. Whatever happened here, I suspect no one else is in danger."

"I agree, but somebody needs to stay here until I can do a more thorough search of the grounds."

We walk back to the pond and find a young patrolman walking around. He's slapping at mosquitoes, and I ask him if he'd like some bug repellent. He says he's already sprayed some on him. "It's dark. The bugs will be gone before too long."

I give him my phone number in case anything comes up.

When Schoppe and I get back to the front of the house, we both start to say something at the same time. "Go ahead," I say.

He says, "You want to look into this and call me if you have problems?"

"I was going to say I'll be glad to turn this over to you."

"Why's that? You're usually ready to jump right in."

"I don't know these people, and I don't have a good handle on what they might be up to."

"Anybody I assign to it won't know them any better than you do. You know how to investigate a crime."

"I suppose."

Schoppe and I go back to when I was chief of police the first time around in Jarrett Creek. At that time I had managed to break a case that involved a bank robbery with a hostage situation, and my reputation has stayed with me. I wonder if he isn't putting more on my ability than I can come through with.

"I'll give it my best," I say.

"Can't be all that many suspects," he says.

It's after ten o'clock when I get home. When I sit down to take off my boots it occurs to me that just as there was no reason to assume Nonie was killed in the daytime, there was also no reason to assume she was killed on the property. Maybe somebody lured her out of the house in the night and attacked her while everyone was asleep and then brought her back to dump her in the pond.

The last thing that flits through my mind before I go to sleep is that I don't think the Blakes are being completely honest with me. Too many little things don't make sense.

CHAPTER 4

Loretta is fuming when she pops by first thing the next morning. She usually has a feisty disposition, but I've rarely seen her as angry as she is today. It seems that somebody cut several of her late summer roses in the night.

"They must have needed a nice bouquet for a special occasion," I say. I can't help teasing her. Seeing her riled up is a sight to behold. Her eyes would set kindling on fire. Her cheeks are bright pink, and she's prowling around my kitchen as if she's looking for trouble. Even my cat, Zelda, has slunk out of sight.

"You're not taking this seriously," she says. "You're the chief of police. It's your job to protect us citizens. It's not right for somebody to come onto my property and cut those roses. How would they like it if I waltzed into their kitchen and stole a cake they made?"

"I don't think anybody would like that. Listen, I know it's a crime, but I don't know how I'm going to find who did it."

She narrows her eyes and taps her finger on her lips, speculating. "I don't know either, but I've got half a mind to sit up all night with a BB gun and wait for somebody to come by. Let them get a dose of pellets. Or I'll get Carl Orley to lend me his big dog." Orley has a Doberman, and I happen to know that Loretta is deathly afraid of it.

"That would be in the category of keeping an eye on the henhouse after the fox has been and gone."

"Don't make fun of me." And suddenly she looks like she's going to cry, and I feel bad.

"I'm sorry. I didn't mean to hurt your feelings. I've got other things on my mind. I guess you heard what happened out at the Blakes.'" Of course she's heard it.

"Oh, my stars, everyone knew it was a bad idea for that girl to come back. Is it true that somebody bashed her head in?" I guess it's her bad mood that makes her sound a little cold-blooded.

"I'm not going to tell you the details right now."

"A lot of people thought with Nonie coming back Charlotte ought to be sleeping with one eye open. Maybe after a few days she decided she couldn't put up with it."

"Loretta, all that happened twenty years ago! Think back twenty years ago in your life. Haven't you changed? Haven't we all?"

She gives me a snippy look. "I haven't changed so much that I'd ignore a killer sneaking around my house. If I were to bet, I'd bet on Charlotte."

"I wouldn't waste my money, if I were you. Do you know the Blakes at all?"

"Not really. They keep to themselves. I don't mean like they think they're better than anybody else. Just that they don't mingle much."

"Have they always been like that, or did they get standoffish after what happened with Nonie?"

"Always. At least Adelaide was. I might not be the person to ask, because I'm a good bit older than she is. But I don't remember her ever having a lot of good friends. John was friendly enough, but once they got married they kind of holed up out there at their place and kept to themselves."

"What church do they go to?"

"As far as I know, they don't attend church."

That explains why they aren't well known. Most social life in town revolves around either gathering at the Town Café for breakfast or lunch, or going to church activities.

"You know John Blake has Parkinson's, and he's a little off in the head."

"I do know that. But even before he was sick, whenever I ran into him in the past few years he seemed a little strange."

"Strange how?"

"Like his thoughts were always somewhere else. If you said hello to him, he'd look at you like he didn't know who you were at first. Then he'd speak to you, but it was like he didn't know he was in the same room with other people."

When I park in front of the Blakes' place, John Blake is out on the front porch by himself, standing with his arms out as if he's blessing an unseen audience. He used to be a tall, substantial man, but now he's thin and a little stooped. I get out of my truck and walk up to him. His hair is sparse and stringy and doesn't look like it has been washed in a while, and he's got at least a three-day growth of beard. He's wearing faded jeans so loose on him that they look like they could fall down anytime and a plain white T-shirt. For all the time the Blake women say they put into taking care of him, he doesn't look well cared for.

"Hey, John, what are you up to?"

I'm reminded of what Loretta said about John's thoughts always being elsewhere, because he looks startled, as if he wasn't even aware that I'd driven up. "Ho!" he says. His voice is gravelly. "Who is that?"

"Samuel Craddock. I haven't seen you in a while."

A crafty look comes to his eye. "You're the big chief," he says. At least he's got some mental capacity; although for all I know he thinks I'm part of a Native American tribe.

"Is Charlotte around?"

The screen door opens and Charlotte comes out. "There you are, Daddy. I wondered where you'd run off to. Hello, Chief Craddock. You been having a chat with Daddy?"

"I just got here."

"Sneaked up on me," Blake says. "I'm surrounded."

"Why don't we all come inside," Charlotte says. "It's hot out here and it's time for you to take some medicine."

"I don't like medicine," he says to me.

"Nobody does," I say. "But sometimes you have to take it."

He nods and strokes his chin. "I suppose you're right." He shuffles inside as she holds the door open for him.

Charlotte shoots me a grateful look. I follow her inside, and she turns and says quietly, "Could be you kept us from a showdown over the medication."

"I tell you what," I say. "Why don't you take care of him while I go in the back and tell the patrolman he can leave. Then let's meet back on the porch and we can talk in private."

I tell the patrolman he can go. He tells me everything was quiet last night. "Except for the mosquitoes at daybreak. I think I killed at least a thousand."

I settle in the same chair I sat in last night when I was talking to Skeeter. I'm glad the porch has an overhang to keep the sun off; otherwise the heat would be unbearable. I hear raised voices inside before Charlotte comes out and eases herself down into the other wicker chair. "Sometimes it's such an ordeal to get him to take his medicine. He has it in his mind that we're poisoning him." She looks less haggard this morning.

"Doc Taggart seemed to think your daddy would be better off in a facility."

"Then let Doc Taggart pay for it," she says dryly. Then she sighs. "I shouldn't say that. It's not the money. Mamma won't hear of it. I've tried to convince her, but she's determined to keep him here at home." She shakes her head. "But you didn't come here to talk about Daddy."

"That's right. I'm opening an investigation into your sister's death, so I need to ask you to go into more detail about her stay here."

She cocks her head at me. "You sound awfully official. I guess it's true then, Nonie didn't fall, hit her head on a rock, fall into the pond, and drown. I was hoping it was all a bad dream."

"No, it's real. I need some answers from you."

"I thought that man who was here with the Texas Rangers last night was going to investigate."

"It's officially his job, but he asked me to get started on the case."

"That's all right with me. I'd rather talk to you anyway."

"Good. I'd like you to describe to me how things went after Nonie got home. The more specific you can be, the better. Starting with how you found out she'd be coming home. You said your mamma didn't tell you."

She sniffs and looks off in the distance. Like her mother, she's stuck with a long face, a pointed nose, and thin lips that make her look like she'd be sharp-tempered.

"The first I saw of her she was standing on the front porch with a suitcase in her hand. She asked to talk to Mamma. I asked what she wanted, and she said, 'I'm your sister, Nonie. You didn't hear I was coming back?' I almost fainted. She said she had come on a bus to Bobtail, and from the bus station she got somebody to bring her home."

"Charlotte, I find it hard to imagine that the institution would simply let Nonie out and send her on her way without an escort or having some way to be sure she would be all right. You know how she got here from the bus station in Bobtail?"

"She said a couple saw her standing on the curb outside the station and they asked her if she wanted a ride. They were coming out this way, and they said it wasn't a problem to let her off here."

"She seemed okay with that?"

"Yes, she was very matter-of-fact."

"Did anybody call the facility to be sure she hadn't walked out on her own?"

"It did occur to me at first. But then I figured if she walked out with a suitcase, they couldn't have missed her, and if they'd done a bed check and she was gone, they would have called. And then, of course, later Mamma told me she knew Nonie was coming back. She just didn't know when."

"Did Nonie have any papers from the doctor?"

"If she did, I never saw them. Maybe she gave them to Mamma."

"What was the family's reaction to her coming back?"

"Like I told you last night, I had wanted her to come home for a long time, so as far as I was concerned, she belonged here."

"You're a liar!" John Blake's voice booms out the front door. We both look around, startled.

Charlotte grimaces "Daddy, come on out here."

"I'm staying right where I am."

"All right, then keep quiet." Her voice is mild.

"Not if you're telling lies."

She throws her hands up, gets up, and walks inside. "Where's Mamma?"

"Where's Mamma," he mocks her.

"Mother!" Charlotte calls. When there's no reply she tells me she'll be right back, and I hear her go up the stairs. In a minute she comes down with Adelaide, who insists that John go back up with her. Her voice is as harsh as Charlotte's was smooth.

"Sorry about that," Charlotte says when she comes back out. "He gets these things in his head."

"I understand. I was asking you to describe everyone's reaction when Nonie got home. She and Skeeter seemed to have gotten along. How about the rest of you?"

"It was mixed. Daddy didn't like having her here. He doesn't like change, and we tried to keep her out of his way. I knew it would be okay once he got used to her."

"And Trey? By the way, where is Trey?"

"He started kindergarten this year. And he loves it. I knew he would. He's a busy guy."

"Did he and Nonie do okay together?"

She hesitates, a frown puckering her forehead. "Nonie did the best she could, but I could tell Trey got on her nerves. She wasn't used to kids."

"Skeeter mentioned that he got the impression Nonie thought the family owed her something. He said you might know what that was about."

She considers the question. "I know what he means. She kind of had an attitude, like she expected us to cater to her."

"You know why?"

"I figured it was because she'd been institutionalized for so long that she thought we ought to make up for it."

"Were there any blowups about her expectations?"

"Not really. She could be a little pushy, I guess you'd say, but I thought it would smooth out once she got familiar with us."

"Did Nonie have any interaction with anybody outside the family since she got back?"

She hesitates. "I'm not sure."

"What do you mean?"

"There was an incident a couple of nights ago. It was odd. Nonie got agitated at times." She raises an eyebrow at me. "The doctor may have thought she was all right to be on her own, but she still had some quirks. Anyway, that night she was pacing the floor in the kitchen. I heard her and went downstairs to find out what was going on."

"What time was this?"

"Maybe nine o'clock. I had just put Trey to bed. Anyway, when I came down she said she had to go see somebody and wondered if she could take the car. I was surprised and told her I didn't know she had a driver's license. Would you believe it turned out she didn't?" She shakes her head and gives a bark of laughter.

"Did she say who she wanted to go see?"

Charlotte looks out over the yard. It's so hot you can almost see the sparse grass burning up right in front of your eyes. "No, she didn't say. I told her I would drive her wherever she needed to go. But she said it was private, that she needed to clear something up with somebody."

"She didn't say whether it was a man or woman?"

"No. I remember Mamma used to fuss at Nonie for being too bold with men. It made me wonder if she had some relationship with a man before she left here. She was fourteen. It's possible that some older man was . . . well, you know."

"Did she say anything that might have led you to believe that?"

"No. It was just from what Mamma said."

Who could Nonie have wanted to talk to? Twenty years is a long time to hold a grudge, so it must have been something pretty significant that happened. Could have had to do with a classmate, a teacher, one of her parents' friends. "Did she ever end up going out?"

"Not that I know of."

"I wonder if she called whoever it was on the telephone? Did she have a cell phone?"

"I never saw one. Where would she have gotten it anyway? I doubt that they hand them out to their patients at the hospital."

"Do you know if she might have called on your house phone?"

She looks blank. "I suppose she could have. There are plenty of times she could have used our phone and nobody would have known."

"And you don't know if she ever went out."

"No, but it's possible she did. She could have gone out after I went to bed. Maybe somebody picked her up. Maybe that's what happened and she was killed. You could ask Mamma. She doesn't sleep all that soundly, and she could have heard Nonie if she went out."

"Did anything unusual happen the day before she died? Anything that made you wonder if everything was all right?"

She sighs and pushes her hair back. "I've asked myself that over and over and I don't remember anything. The whole situation of her being here was unusual, so I'm not sure I would have noticed."

"Do you have a job?"

"No, I have the good fortune not to have to go outside the home to work. Our family has some investments and we do pretty well with them." Les Moffitt must have done all right by the family.

"And your brother Skeeter doesn't have a job either."

"No, he flunked out of school last semester. I'm trying to persuade him to do some independent study. He isn't good at applying himself. Nothing I say seems to matter. And Mamma might as well be talking to a brick wall—he doesn't listen to anything she says either."

"How about your older brother, Billy. Did you ever get a hold of him?"

For the first time, her face brightens. "Billy? I called him as soon as Nonie showed up here. He wasn't thrilled that she was home."

"Wait. Hold on. You didn't say anything about this earlier when we were talking. You said you were trying to get in touch with him about her death."

Her faces flushes. "That's right. The thing is, I didn't want Mamma to know I had called him to tell him Nonie was back."

"Why not?"

"Don't take this the wrong way, but after what happened when we were kids he never had any use for Nonie. I was afraid he might come home unexpectedly and find her here."

"So you did know where to reach him."

"I have his cell phone number. Sometimes he doesn't answer right away. Anyway, I called him last night to tell him what happened. It took a while, but I finally located him in Denton. I'm so glad for cell phones. I never used to be able to find him, but now I can usually track him down. He'll be coming home right away. I'll be really glad for him to get here."

"You two are close?"

"As close as two people can be when they never see each other. Billy is four years older than me, and he was always my hero. You know he's the one who saved me when Nonie . . ." She swallows and brings her hand to her throat. "What I mean is, if it hadn't been for him, I wouldn't be here."

I hear the screen door open. "Are you two almost done talking?" Adelaide says.

"Give us another few minutes," I say.

The door closes, and Adelaide's footsteps recede.

"Something that I want to check out with you. Skeeter said none of the family ever visited Nonie. Is that true?"

I don't tell her that her mamma had verified it. I want to hear what she has to say. Her lips are pinched into a straight line. "Skeeter talks out of place sometimes. He doesn't know anything about it."

"So the family did visit?"

"Mamma and Daddy went up there a couple of times early on, but the doctor assigned to Nonie said it agitated her when family came. So they stopped going. I suspect they planned to go back, but you know how things are. You think you're going to do something and suddenly a year has gone by."

She's right in most instances, but it's hard for me to imagine a parent never going to visit a child in a mental institution. Despite Charlotte's supposed good intentions, if she really wanted her sister to be brought home, it seems like she would have taken it on herself to at least go visit her in the hospital.

"There is one more thing. What's the situation with your son's daddy? He around?"

"No. He's been gone a long time, since right after Trey was born. He headed off to Montana. He said he wanted me to go with him, but I had the feeling he didn't really want me to go. I don't think he really wanted to be a daddy."

"Ever hear from him?"

She snorts. "If you're hinting around that he might have had something to do with Nonie's death, you're way off base. Last time I heard from him he was living in Bozeman, working on a ranch, and fixing to get married again. I can't in my wildest dreams imagine him coming back here and killing my sister."

CHAPTER 5

I walk around back to take another look around. Adelaide told me that the ranch is bigger than most of the others and that it extends back several acres behind the house. As far as I can see it's mostly scrubland dotted with post oak trees. I'm pretty sure they never kept cattle out here. A big area to the right of the barn has been fenced off. At one time it was a vegetable garden. There are still a few scraggly cornstalks, and I can barely make out where there were raised rows of plantings. It's mostly dirt now, so it hasn't been farmed in a long time. It makes me wonder why they bought this place—what they had in mind.

I walk back to the pond where Nonie's body was found. Most people around here call a pond a tank, from when all these small bodies of water used to be for watering cattle. Both Adelaide and John grew up in this area, so where did they get their fancy idea to call it a pond? The word *pond* conjures up an image from a storybook—a shallow pool of water with lily pads and nicely kept-up banks and cute little animals playing in the grass.

This small body of water is surrounded by weeds most of the way around. There's an old stump on the far shore next to a big sycamore tree whose branches hang out several feet over the water. Water moccasins like to lie in shady areas under trees like that one, or even in the low branches. There must not be any in this tank, or they would likely have latched onto Nonie's body. I shudder to think of Skeeter wading out in the muck to tow the body in. Young men can be impulsive.

Weeds have been trampled around the side where Skeeter dragged Nonie out and the ambulance drivers picked up her body. I walk gingerly around the rest of the bank, keeping an eye out for snakes but also for disturbed areas that might indicate a scuffle of some kind. I phoned

Odum this morning, and he said he didn't see anything, but it never hurts to double-check.

The graveled driveway leading to the house from the road isn't that long, maybe 250 feet. Nonie could have walked down to the road and met someone. They might have driven off somewhere and gotten into an argument, and she ended up dead. Then whoever it was brought her back here to dump her. If that was the case, they would have needed to drive close up and either carry her or drag her here. There are no footprints to verify that—not surprising, given the drought-ravaged land around the tank. There's barely any indication of all the foot traffic that was here last night.

Still, the most likely scenario is that someone in the family killed her. I can make up a far-fetched idea of a stranger or someone from her past, but more likely she met someone from the family outside in the yard so they could have it out, and whoever it was became enraged and killed her. Does the whole family know who actually did it and they've closed ranks? Is that why I feel that they are hiding something?

And what of the murder weapon? What became of it? I'll have to have somebody look for it. I stare at the pond, thinking it's very likely it ended up in the water. I hate to think of having the pond drained, but it may come to that.

No sooner am I back at headquarters when the coroner's office calls me from Bobtail. There's no question that Nonie Blake's death was a homicide. The blow to her head was hard enough to kill her before she was dumped into the water. "Probably done by a man," the coroner says. "Takes some strength to hit somebody that hard."

"What's your time of death estimate?"

"That's a moving target. If she'd been on land, body changes would have occurred fast because it's hot outside, but being in the water slowed things down. From the condition of the body, I think she was put in the water pretty soon after she was killed. Best I can estimate is a couple of hours either side of midnight."

"That'll do. Can you give me any idea of the size and type of weapon that was used?"

"I can't be exactly sure, but I'd say it was something not too big around—maybe the handle of a tool, like a spade or a hoe. Or maybe a tire iron."

"Not a rock?"

"Definitely not a rock unless it was an especially smooth, skinny one."

I ask him to send me a copy of the full report when he sends one out to Texas Ranger headquarters.

Zeke Dibble, Jarrett Creek's other part-time cop, is in the office with me, and when I get off the phone I tell him the coroner's findings. Dibble retired from the Houston Police Department and moved here so he could spend his time fishing. He hadn't been retired long when he realized he couldn't put up with retirement, partly because full-time fishing wasn't all it was cracked up to be, and partly because his wife kept finding household chores for him to do. So he joined our department. He may not have the fire of a young officer, but he makes up for it in experience. He listens to the coroner's assessment and says, "You and I both know, Craddock, that in the right circumstances a woman could hit somebody hard enough to kill them."

"Yeah, but I was hoping to eliminate half the population," I say dryly.

The bigger question is, why would anybody want to kill Nonie in the first place? What kind of threat did she represent? And if not to the family, then to whom? How in the world am I going to find out if she actually met someone the night she was killed? And if so, how did she arrange to meet them?

I pull the phone to me and call Charlotte Blake. "Charlotte, I need to find out all the phone calls made from your house line during the time Nonie was there. Do you have a current bill?"

"Our last bill was at the beginning of the month. Can't the police call and get that?"

"They'll want a court order or a consent from you. It'd be easier if you ask for it."

Les Moffitt's secretary says he's in his office, and after she consults with him she says that he'll be glad to make time to see me this afternoon.

Bryan-College Station is only thirty miles away from Jarrett Creek, but it could be a thousand. It's not what you'd call a city, but it's a big, thriving town dominated by the Texas A&M campus. It's where I went to school a long time ago, and I hardly recognize the place anymore. When I went there it was a sleepy university in a sleepy town. Now the town bustles with activity. Its streets are lined with restaurants and clothing stores, and in the past several years the buildings have grown up rather than out.

Moffitt's office is downtown in a building that houses a bank on the ground floor. The roster of businesses in the building tends toward financial dealings of one kind or another, except for one floor taken up with a law firm.

I've never used a financial advisor other than the Fort Worth banker that my wife's family always depended on. The money Jeanne and I inherited from her family was tied up in mutual funds and some solid real estate holdings. I found no reason to change that. It all brings in more money than I ever would have made in my lifetime. It isn't a huge amount in the financial world, but it's enough, and in a vague way I've always been a little uncomfortable about it. It seems odd that eventually the money will go to my nephew, Tom, who is no blood relation to Jeanne's family. But all of her immediate family is gone, and all the money ended up with her, then with me when she died.

The doors to Moffitt's office are glass leading into a pristine outer office with plush rugs, fine furnishings, and the kind of nondescript art on the walls that says it was selected for how it goes with the décor rather than for its artistic worth. The middle-aged secretary I talked to on the phone earlier is dressed as professionally as her voice indicated she might be, in a crisp white blouse, with not a hair out of place. She sets me up with coffee and says Mr. Moffitt will see me as soon as he finishes up his phone call. This takes several minutes, during which the secretary has to answer a surprising number of phone calls. Moffitt appears to be very successful.

Moffitt looks different here on his own turf, more self-assured and businesslike. He has a warm smile, but a habit I noticed from when I met him at the Blakes' of meeting my eyes and then instantly sliding his gaze to the right. It makes him look nervous.

He takes me into his inner office, asking his secretary to bring him a cup of coffee, too. His desk is massive, with stacks of papers and a very nice bronze sculpture. There's a large picture frame on his desk, turned toward him so that I can't see the photo. I wonder if he has a family.

He sits back in his chair and steeples his fingers. "How can I help you?"

I'd like to tell him I have a fistful of questions that will get straight to the heart of what I'm after, but I don't. This is a fishing expedition. I'll have to cast my net wide and hope for information that will lead me somewhere. "We didn't have a chance to talk much Monday, and I thought you might be able to fill in a few blanks."

"I've known the family a long time," he says.

"You said you're their financial advisor."

"That's right, and together we've made some decent investments. I'd have to say we're mutually satisfied with the results of working together."

"When did you first start working with the Blakes?"

He leans forward and opens a fat folder close to hand. "I pulled out their file when you called because I figured you'd want some specifics." He flips all the papers over until he's at the back of the stack. He picks up a letter and hands it over. "This is our initial agreement. I was a young man starting out, working for Bryan State Bank at the time, and I was drumming up clients. John Blake came over to talk to me, and as you can see we decided to do some business."

The letter is as he says, referencing a formal contract that they signed.

He picks up a fat bunch of pages. "This is the contract that the letter refers to. I'm happy to let you go through it if you want, but personally I'd rather have my fingernails pulled out than have to read this stuff."

"I don't think it's necessary."

On the way over to Moffitt's office, I was trying to remember what I knew of Adelaide and John. John's family had a farm outside of town, and I only knew Adelaide's mother as a mousy woman who kept to herself, much the way the Blakes do now. But I also know that she worked her whole life and didn't appear to be well off. If either of the families had money, I don't know where it came from. Like my money, it must have been inherited.

"The family money is John's, I take it?"

Moffitt hesitates. "You understand there's only so much I can tell you about their finances. It's a private matter, but I guess I'm not crossing any lines if I tell you that the money was Adelaide's, not John's."

"And since you started working with them, you've become a friend of the family?"

"I was John's friend, really. Still am, as far as that goes. It's a damned shame what's become of him."

"How often do you visit them?"

Moffitt squirms in his seat, the first time he's shown any real uneasiness. "I try to get out there once or twice a week."

I try to picture the circumstances. Does he call first and set up a time to go, or does he drop in? Who is he really there to see?

"You go to keep an eye on John?"

He meets my eyes, and again his gaze slides off. "And Adelaide. To make sure everything's okay. And Charlotte, of course."

It finally comes clear. He has a crush on Charlotte. "You like her son?"

"He's a cute kid."

"Ever had any kids of your own?"

He sighs. "They're grown. I have a boy in the military service and a girl who just got married. I don't know them very well. My wife and I split up a number of years ago and she moved off to Houston and remarried. Nice man. We're all cordial with each other. I didn't keep up with the kids the way I should have, though, although it doesn't seem to have affected them too much."

"So Monday you said you were dropping by and happened to get there right after Skeeter found the body?"

His answer takes longer than it should. He pats the stack of papers in front of him from the Blake file. "They called me."

"You mean they called to tell you that Nonie's body had been found?"

He nods and runs his hands along his mouth as if he doesn't want the truth to escape. "Yes, and they wanted me to come over. I had to cancel a couple of appointments, but Charlotte sounded upset."

"Why did they call you? What did they expect you to do?"

He frowns. "I told you, I'm a friend of the family. I think they didn't quite know what to do, and I like to think I have a soothing effect on them."

"How long had you been there when I arrived?"

"Not long. Ten, fifteen minutes."

This is new information. It would have taken him thirty minutes to get to the Blake house. I was there no more than fifteen minutes after they called. "Did you tell them to call me?"

"Yes, I did. I told Charlotte to call the law the minute she got off the phone with me. Like I said, they didn't seem to know what to do. When I got there I asked if they had called an ambulance or the police, and they said they still hadn't. I told them they ought to call you and you'd take care of the rest."

"The girl was dead. How hard could it be to figure out that they needed to call the police?"

Moffitt holds his hand up to settle me down. "I know, I know. I'm trying to figure out how to describe the situation. They were scared."

"Scared of what?"

He sits forward, his face screwed up. "They were afraid they would all be suspects."

Suspects. So they knew Nonie had been murdered. They all acted like it was a big surprise, telling me they thought she had hit her head on a rock. What Moffitt is telling me is that they knew somebody killed her, and they were worried.

"They called you first because they needed to get their story straight?"

He grunts. "Not exactly. More like they needed to figure out if they ought to call a lawyer before they called you."

Their hesitation still doesn't make sense to me. Then I remember Schoppe's questions last night, and suddenly I understand. "They thought maybe John did it."

He nods. "I think it crossed their minds. John is . . . how do I say it? He's unpredictable. I don't think he'd hurt a fly, but he didn't like Nonie much. We couldn't tell whether it was because she disrupted the routine or if there was some other reason."

"But in the end, they decided to call me. Which side were you on—calling me or getting a lawyer?"

"You have to understand, I'm a businessman. I never think it hurts to have a lawyer standing by to help you deal with unusual situations."

"Who made the decision not to call a lawyer?"

"That was Charlotte. She said if they didn't have anything to hide, why bother with a lawyer? I guess I see the wisdom of that now that I've met you. You didn't jump to any conclusions."

I may not jump to conclusions, but I'm disturbed that they all knew Nonie had been murdered and pretended they didn't.

"You say you were out there at the house a couple of times a week. Did you meet Nonie?"

"I did. Just once. Can't say I had much of an impression of her. I met her, and right afterward she excused herself and took off upstairs to her room. They said she was a little shy and didn't want to be around people too much."

"Besides John, did you get the impression that the family was upset with her being there?"

Moffitt considers. "I'd say of them all, Adelaide was the most disturbed about it. It's like she didn't know what to do with the girl. Now whether that was because the situation upset John, or because Adelaide herself had a problem with her, I couldn't tell you."

"I have to go up to Rollingwood and find out more about Nonie's last weeks there," I tell Ellen Forester that night. It's the third time she has asked me to dinner at her house. She's a pretty good cook, although it's always a vegetarian meal. I like the food fine, but the other two times I ate at her house, when I got home I felt like I had to rustle up a roast beef sandwich. No wonder she stays so petite.

"This is the most awful story," she says. She's preparing the meal and has relegated me to a stool at the counter. I tried to get her to let me help, but she says it makes her nervous to have someone else working in the kitchen with her. A lot of things make her nervous, which I blame on her ex-husband. He's a big brute of a man who treats her like she's worthless but doesn't seem to want to let her go. Ellen won't say much about him, but I gather that she took a lot of bullying from him, if not outright abuse, before she finally got the courage to leave him. She moved here to Jarrett Creek after her divorce and opened an art gallery where she also gives art classes. After she moved here, he continued to hassle her, which brought him unwanted attention from the Jarrett Creek police a while back.

"The Blakes are a strange family," I say. "After what happened between the two sisters, it seems like they closed in on themselves—although I think they were not exactly friendly before that."

"You said none of them works. That would be horribly boring. What do you suppose they do with their time?"

"Charlotte has a five-year-old, and John Blake, the daddy, has some health issues that seem to keep the family on their toes. For all I know they have hobbies that keep them going, but I don't know what those might be."

She nods. "A five-year-old could be a full-time job. Do you have any idea where they get their money?"

"Someone told me that Adelaide came into some money, but I knew her mother, and she never had anything she didn't earn."

"I don't know how you even begin looking for who killed that poor woman," she says. "If someone in the family did it, they'll protect each other. Are there clues? I'm serious. How do you figure these things out?"

She tilts her head at me. Her face is serious and full of wonder, and I suddenly feel a pleasant sense of warmth that I haven't felt in a long time. She's so different from Jeanne, and Jeanne was the love of my life. But Ellen is a genuine, fine person. She's stood firm against her ex-husband; determined not to be bullied by him any longer, determined to be her own person. I admire her and I like her. And at this moment with her looking so intently at me, there's a little more than that. I'd like to put my arms around her while I tell her what she wants to know.

But I don't feel free to make a move yet. Our relationship has been full of little conflicts. Maybe I've been a little too forward in handling her ex-husband. Maybe she still loves him, despite what he's done. Or maybe she isn't attracted to me the same way I am to her.

"What are you thinking about?" she says. "You have the funniest look on your face."

"It's a tough case," I say, feeling my cheeks burn. "You asked how

I plan to figure this out. There's no magic to it. It's a matter of paying attention to details and listening for inconsistencies. It'll take time."

"Dinner's ready," she says. "I hope you like this."

At her announcement that dinner is ready, her hybrid terrier, Frazier, hops up from his bed, where he's been watching us and trots to the stove, looking expectant. "Frazier, how long is it going to take you to learn that you aren't going to get my dinner?" Ellen says.

The dog's ears prick up. "I think it's the word dinner he's responding to," I say. Frazier turns his head to look at me.

"Oh, I know it. I'm getting to be like a maiden lady who talks to her animals." We both laugh.

We sit at one end of her massive dining table. I find it touching that she has such a big house and a lot of furniture, as if she is holding out for some kind of future where she entertains and the house is full of laughter and friends, and maybe grandchildren at some point. Her two children have only partially forgiven her for leaving their father—she was determined not to tell them how abusive he was to her, though how they could fail to see it is beyond me. Jeanne and I never had children, but it strikes me sometimes that kids can be awfully selfish and unaware that their parents are people, too, deserving of love and a good life.

"This looks very good," I say. There's a lot of brown rice involved and vegetables, with cheese. I taste it and tell her it's great.

Her whole face lights up when she smiles. She has dark-brown eyes and brown hair streaked with gray. "People think vegetarian food is boring," she says. "I'm going to convince you that it can be really delicious."

"I wouldn't be surprised," I say. A little white lie.

Ellen is easy to talk to, and we spend the rest of the evening talking about art. I've told her how I gradually came to appreciate art through my wife, and now I explain how hard it was at first for me to get a handle on modern art. "But once I did, it really grabbed me." I try to keep mention of Jeanne to a minimum. It feels like Jeanne belongs in another part of my life, and I don't want Ellen to have to confront my deceased wife every step of the way; the same way I don't want to have to have Seth Forester's name popping up every few minutes.

Ellen tells me that she loves teaching art. "It's amazing how many people enjoy it who never knew they had the least bit of talent."

I know she means Loretta Singletary in particular. Loretta's son's family took her on a trip to Washington, DC. Having been dragged through several art museums by her daughter-in-law, she came back with a mind to try her hand at watercolors. The surprise was that she showed a gift for painting, including composition, which is what seems to stump a lot of beginners. Loretta insists that it's nothing more than a hobby she has found a passion for late in life. And she despises being compared to Grandma Moses.

"She asked me the other day if I would teach her how to do oil painting," Ellen says.

"Are you going to do it? That's a whole different type of painting. You need ventilation and you have to be careful with it." I don't know this from personal experience, but I remember talking to George Manning, the Houston gallery owner where Jeanne and I bought a lot of our art, and him telling us that these days artists know to be a lot more careful with oils.

She looks amused. "Samuel, I'm an artist. You don't think I know that? You've never seen my studio here at my house. I had Gabe LoPresto convert part of the garage to a studio. I like to paint with oils, so it's well ventilated. I'm considering whether I want to give Loretta lessons out there. Why don't I take you to see it?"

Frazier follows us out to the backyard, as if he thinks he's the host, and stands guard while Ellen shows me her personal studio. One of the difficult things between us is that Ellen loves to paint, and her painting does nothing for me. I like a strong, dynamic type of art, and she likes to make art of animals and fantasy landscapes. Dreamy sorts of things. Not my taste at all. But she does know what she's doing, and I expect she can teach Loretta what she needs to know about oil painting.

CHAPTER 6

"Rodell, I could kill you," I mutter, starting yet another stack of files. Killing him isn't an option, since he died a few months back, but that doesn't keep me from sending murderous thoughts in his direction. Rodell was the chief of police for several years, and not a particularly satisfactory one due to a significant drinking problem. When he was in his last stages of illness, he stopped drinking and came in to headquarters to help a couple of times a week. There at the end I discovered a man I could have liked, who had a sly sense of humor and a sharp mind. But he died before he could complete the filing he was trying to catch up on. I'm still fighting his so-called filing system.

It's the morning after my interview with Les Moffitt, and I'm looking for the file on Nonie Blake from twenty years ago. It's not often that I need to look into old cases, but I want to take a look at the file to brush up on details before I ask any more questions.

Hearing that she was trying to have a meeting with someone here in town, presumably about something that happened before she went away, makes me wonder what was going on with the girl before she attempted to kill her sister. Was she having trouble with someone in her life that, as a fourteen-year-old, she wasn't equipped to deal with? Did it have something to do with her attempt on her sister's life? I'll feel on more solid footing if I read the file.

While I search, I alphabetize the folders. I'm thinking of putting Zeke on the filing, but he's not a man who takes kindly to busy work, and I don't want to aggravate him. The town is doing better financially, but we still can't afford another full-time cop. Zeke is worth holding onto as long as he'll stay on.

Finally I run across a batch of files from the correct year and in that batch find the folder itself. It's fatter than I thought it might be, and I'm impressed that Rodell kept all this. Then I realize this wasn't when Rodell was chief—it was one of the four years that Ennis Whitehall held the job. He was a quiet man but, from the looks of it, efficient.

Just as I'm settling in to read, the phone rings, which is pretty much the way it always works. The man who is calling identifies himself as Floyd Curtis, a name I don't recognize.

"I live over here in Caldwell," he says. "And I heard the news about that woman that was killed."

"You're referring to Winona Blake?"

"That's what the local paper said her name was. I told my wife you might not want to know about this, but she said I ought to call anyway." He talks in a slow and deliberate cadence, as if he's written his thoughts out.

"Why don't you try me out? It doesn't hurt for me to hear it."

"All right, then here it is. My wife and I had occasion to go to Bobtail. This was about a week and a half ago. When we finished with our business, we were passing by the bus station and there was a young woman standing outside on the sidewalk, hitchhiking. She had a suitcase in her hand. Now I don't hold with picking up hitchhikers, but my wife said this was a woman and we couldn't leave her standing there, something might happen to her. My wife is a good Christian, and she believes in doing good deeds. So I stopped, and my wife asked the young woman where she was headed. She said she needed to get to Jarrett Creek, and I told her we'd be going right through there on our way home and we'd take her where she wanted to go."

"I appreciate your calling," I say. "You're filling in a gap for me. What can you tell me about your experience with her? What was she like?"

He pauses, as if gathering his thoughts. "Well, sir, she was an unusual type person. My wife asked her who her people were and what brought her to town. She said she was the daughter of the Blakes out north of Jarrett Creek, and that she had been gone for a while and was coming home. But then my wife asked her where she'd been when she was away, and that was the wrong question. She got snippy. She said nobody needed to poke into her business. My wife apologized and said she hadn't intended to pry, that she was only being friendly. But the woman stayed kind of surly after that. Kept grumbling that people ought to mind their own business. Kind of talking to herself, like."

"Doesn't sound like she was appreciative of the help you gave her by giving her a ride."

"No, she wasn't. I didn't pay much attention myself, but my wife said she didn't even thank us. Not that we did it for thanks. We store up good works that our Father in heaven will appreciate in due time. But it did seem like she was lacking in manners. Hold on a minute. My wife wants to tell you something."

I hear him say, "Don't go on and on. He'll be busy."

"Hello?"

"Yes ma'am. I appreciate you and your husband calling. What is it you want to add?"

"It's a silly thing, but I remember thinking at the time that she was asking for trouble. So when the paper said she was killed . . . what?" I hear her husband whispering to her. "Oh, okay. My husband says I ought to let you go."

"I'd like to hear what you were going to tell me."

"It wasn't important."

"Mrs. Curtis, you never know when something is going to be important."

"All right. What happened was, the girl told us she knew a thing or two about some people's business, and that people would pay good money for her to keep her mouth shut. I thought to myself, 'Young lady, you are asking for big trouble.'"

"Did she mention anything specific?"

"No, like I said, she was hinting around. I don't mind telling you, it made me nervous. I don't hold with people talking behind people's backs. I never heard anybody talk like that before except on TV. I was glad when we saw the last of her. I guess she did get herself into trouble."

If Nonie followed through with trying to blackmail somebody, it looks like the family might be off the hook. I wonder who Nonie was referring to, and how she found out incriminating information about them. I'm hoping that in the police file there's some mention of people she might have had problems with—something to lead me to figure out who she was talking about.

Ennis Whitehall's report was never typed up, but he wrote it out in small, neat handwriting that squares with the kind of man I remember him being—precise and unflappable.

"I was called out to the Blake household by Adelaide Blake, who said her son Billy had just saved her younger daughter Charlotte from being hanged by her older sister. Upon arrival, I found Charlotte (eight years of age), traumatized, with rope burns around her neck. The family physician, Doctor Taggart, had been called in and he arrived shortly after I did. I talked to the son, Billy Blake, twelve years old. He seems like a boy with some sense.

"He described coming into the backyard near their stock tank to find his older sister, Winona (they call her Nonie), fourteen years of age, looking up at a tree limb. There he saw his younger sister standing on a chair with a rope around her neck. The rope was slung over the tree branch. For a minute he thought they were fooling around, but then he heard Nonie tell Charlotte to jump off the chair—and Charlotte did it.

"Billy said the only thing that saved Charlotte from breaking her neck is that when she jumped she held onto the rope. The girl didn't weigh much, so I believe he's correct. The boy said to me that he never moved so fast in his life. He said Charlotte wasn't that far off the ground, so he was able to grab her legs and take the pressure off her neck. He told Nonie to bring over the chair so he could stand on it and get Charlotte out of the noose, but he said Nonie was screaming at him to let Charlotte go. She tried to push him away so he couldn't hold onto Charlotte, but he kicked her and she ran off. He hollered until his daddy came out to see what the commotion was, and together they managed to get the girl down. Doctor Taggart confirmed that the girl would likely have died a very painful death by strangulation had the boy not saved her. Charlotte wouldn't have been strong enough to hold onto the rope for long.

"I tried to interview Nonie, but she was in a wild state and said she did what she did and it's nobody's business, and she wouldn't talk to me. Taggart tried to calm her and eventually gave her a sedative. I spoke with Adelaide and John Blake, and they divulged to me that Nonie had become increasingly difficult to handle, and they agreed to have her evaluated by a psychiatrist. It's a bad business."

Addendum:

"Pursuant to finding out more about Nonie Blake's state of mind, I interviewed her teachers, who confirmed that Nonie had become intractable in the classroom. She misbehaved, making wild claims and generally being disruptive. No one could account for her disturbance, although Lottie Raines, her English teacher, said she had a sister who became unstable in her teenage years, and that her family was told that the teenage years are when mental illness makes itself manifest. The school had brought the Blakes in and discussed the matter with them, but they had not taken any steps to corral the girl."

Addendum 2:

"I conferred with doctors at the hospital in Bobtail, and they recommended a psychiatrist in Houston. As a result of Nonie's actions and the psychiatric evaluation, and at the expense of the family, Nonie has been sent to the Rollingwood Institution in north Texas for further evaluation. Due to this action on their part, I see no need to further involve the law in the matter."

I lean back in my chair. Despite its strangely archaic language, Whitehall's report is thorough, for which I'm grateful. When I first heard that Nonie Blake was back, it seemed to me that twenty years was a long time for someone to be in an institution. Back when I was a youngster, you would sometimes hear about "crazy" people being put away and never seeing the light of day. Reading the details, I realize that she had major problems. Still, with the kinds of drugs they've developed since then, and more enlightened policies, I don't believe people spend that much time in institutions anymore. So why was she there for so long?

There's nothing in the report to indicate that Nonie was involved with someone outside her family, but the fact that she was having behavior problems in school might have some significance. If she knew a secret about somebody, it could have troubled her or given her an idea about blackmail. I'm going to have to go back into the past to find out what it was she might have known.

The last thing in the folder is a formal letter of evaluation from a psychiatrist in Houston, Dr. Richard Buckley, recommending that Winona Blake be sent to a psychiatric facility for further evaluation. He states that he administered standard mental tests as well as a physical examination. He refers to a complete evaluation for the details. There's no such evaluation in the folder. It's possible the chief didn't ask for it, since the family agreed that Nonie should be sent to Rollingwood.

Texas law regarding psychiatrists sharing patient information has probably changed since I was last chief of police. It was pretty haphazard as I recall, especially with regard to minors. I don't know what the current law says about obtaining records of either a minor offender or an offender who has died. My vague recollection is that if someone was accused of a crime, and the state ordered an evaluation by a psychiatrist, the evaluation could be shared with law enforcement. But this was all pertaining to court proceedings, and Nonie's case never went to court.

It's also possible that Dr. Buckley has retired by this time and his records destroyed if they've passed the statute of limitations. But even then, since Nonie was being evaluated at the behest of the state, the state would have copies of the evaluation. I could probably find out what the current law is regarding all these questions, but before I go to that trouble, I'll try a direct approach.

I call the telephone number on the letter from the psychiatrist. A recording with the doctor's soothing voice asks me to leave a message, which I do. So at least he is still practicing.

When I hang up, I pick up the folder again and read Whitehall's first few lines. There's one puzzling detail. Why did the family even notify the law about what Nonie had done to her sister? They surely would have known that calling in the police was going to bring down a world of problems on their family. Some families would have tried to hide it. The fact that they called in the law means that the Blakes must already have had a sense that Nonie was too big a problem for them to handle. The school had already called them in to discuss Nonie's bad classroom behavior, and this must have been the last straw.

I'm still mulling this when the phone rings. It's Charlotte Blake. "I was on the phone with the telephone company for an hour trying to get our phone log."

"Did you get it?"

"Yes, it turns out I can look online anytime and find it. Who knew? Anyway, I took a look and there was only one number I didn't recognize. So I called it and it was a company I forgot I'd contacted to get car insurance rates. So Nonie didn't make any phone calls that I can see."

CHAPTER 7

When I telephone Lottie Raines, she tells me she was only a schoolteacher for five years before she got married and later started having kids, and she never went back to teaching. She says she's always involved in school events, though, since she has a pack of children in the school system. She and her husband live not too far from me. I know her to say hello to. She's a talker—a skinny, jolly person, always surrounded by people whenever I see her.

I tell her what I'm after, and she says she'll be glad to tell me whatever she can remember about Nonie Blake. She says I can come over right away. "I was cleaning my house. Weekends, things get pretty torn up around here. But I'd rather talk to somebody than clean house any day."

Her husband has a good job as an engineer with the county, and they have a sprawling house with a big fenced-in yard. From the street you can see a tree house in the backyard and various climbing structures. The front yard is well kept, and when I step inside I can tell right away that Lottie was exaggerating about the mess made over the weekend. It's obvious that she's house-proud. Kids' toys are kept in bins instead of strewn all over the place and the entry floor is gleaming.

"I'm going to get you some coffee, and we'll sit in the living room," she says. She shows me in and disappears. It's one of those rare living rooms where a lot of living gets done. There's a big TV and lots of chairs of various sizes and a whole wall of family pictures. The furniture is sturdy—meant to be used.

She comes back in carrying a giant-sized mug of coffee, for which I'm grateful, and a plate of sugar cookies. She sets the plate of cookies in front of me and plops herself down with a big sigh. "I don't know how we ended up with five kids. I love 'em dearly, but they keep me running from morning 'til night." One of the effects is that she doesn't have an ounce of fat on her. But she looks happy, with laugh lines around her eyes.

"You look like you're up to the task," I say.

"Some days, yes, some days, no. Now. You wanted to ask me about Nonie Blake. I can't believe what happened to her. Such a sad story. I mean, what she did way back then was awful, but it seems to me she had paid her dues. I'll help any way I can. What do you want to know?"

"I'm going through her files from back then, and I found a reference to you as a teacher who thought she showed signs of mental unbalance."

She nods. "That puts it mildly. She was a little hellion. I bet they didn't say that I recommended to the principal that he tell the parents they ought to send her for psychiatric evaluation."

"It says in her file that the school did talk to the parents."

Her eyes narrow. "Oh, they might have hinted around that she could use a little discipline, but the principal would never have suggested a therapist. Perish the thought! He told me that the parents would be better served by taking the girl to church. He said she had been overindulged at home and all she needed was a guiding hand. That was plain hogwash."

"The file did say that you told the police that you recognized similar behavior to your sister's."

Her face clouds over. "Poor Allie. At least she had the benefit of my folks, who recognized that there was something wrong and took her to a psychiatrist. Of course we lived in Sugarland and it wasn't so hard to find someone close by. The doctor put Allie on some drugs and recommended a special school for her, but they couldn't afford it."

"What happened to her?"

"My mamma home-schooled her and she seemed to get better for a while. But when she was in her twenties she took her own life. I know this is going to sound awful, but in some ways it was a relief. She was a sweet girl, but when she was depressed she was hard to be around. A burden to my mamma in particular." She shakes her head as if to rid it of her thoughts. "Anyway, I was so caught up in her problems that I took a few psychology courses in college, thinking I might want to be a therapist. Turned out not to be a good fit for me, but I did learn a few things, and one of them was that it's the teenage years when some of these problems start to manifest themselves. I believe I saw that in Nonie."

"Do you remember anything in particular?"

"She exaggerated things. I wouldn't say she deliberately lied, but she said things that couldn't possibly be true. Kids made fun of her behind her back. I remember once she said her mamma was going to buy her some kind of fancy car—I can't remember what kind—when she was sixteen. Another time there was some rock concert in Houston that all the kids wanted to go to, and she told everybody that she went to it. They were silly things, but they added up. One of the problems for her teachers was that she refused to do what she was told in school. She flat out would not do homework. She told me her parents told her she didn't have to—which I knew wasn't true."

"That doesn't sound like such a big behavior problem."

Lottie leans across and takes a cookie and shoves the plate closer to me, so I take one, too. She nibbles the cookie and says, "You're right. I cut her some slack because I figured it wouldn't do any good to make a federal case out of it. But some teachers can't deal with a child who won't follow the rules. And they have a point. The problem is it sets a bad example. If one student gets away with refusing to do homework, pretty soon others think they should be able to get away with it, too. Nonie made good grades, so it didn't matter if she did homework, but if a student was struggling and decided to follow Nonie's example, it could hurt their grades."

While she talks, I take a bite of cookie, and it's delicious. "Did you call her parents?"

"Of course I did. But they didn't seem to be able to control her."

"Did she refuse to take tests, too?"

"No, in fact she liked them. I think it gave her a chance to show off."

She sees that I've polished off the cookie. "Have another one."

I take another cookie. "How did the other teachers handle it?"

"The math teacher—what was his name? Alvin something— graded her down for not turning in homework, even though she made one hundreds on her tests. He said she told him she didn't care, she wasn't going to do it."

"So no homework. Anything else?"

"Refused to go to assemblies. Said it was a waste of time. Instead, she'd go to town and get a soda or something and wait outside until it was over. Refused to go outside during fire drills . . ." Suddenly her hand comes up. "Wait. I remember one of the things she said that I found a little disturbing. One day I came into class and I heard her telling some girls that she had a way to get a lot of money. They called her a liar and she said, 'You wait. I know something that somebody is going to pay me not to tell.' They were impressed by that and wanted to know what she knew and who it was. Of course she wouldn't tell. I didn't think there was anything to it."

"Did anything more ever come of it?"

She sighs. "No. I had a class full of rowdy teenagers and I let it go. I probably should have taken her aside privately and tried to get her to tell me what she meant, but I imagine even if I'd done that she wouldn't have told me."

She picks up a manila envelope from the table and hands it over. "I don't know if this is anything you'd be interested in. After you called, I went and fished these out of my files. I kept the class picture from each class I taught—five years in all. I taught Nonie two years—I had her in sixth grade and then again in eighth grade."

I take out two eight-by-ten black-and-white photos. She points out Nonie in both of them. You can't tell anything from either photo.

Nonie is a face hidden among eighteen other youngsters, and not a particularly memorable face either. In both, she's standing in the middle row, and you can only see her face. In the eighth-grade photo, she's scowling, but so are several other students.

"Did you ever hear anything that might indicate why she tried to kill her sister?"

"Not anything credible. Once the kids found out what had happened, they made up all kinds of things—that she was a Satan worshipper or that she wanted to get in the newspaper and that's why she'd done it." She snaps her fingers. "Oh, this was a good one. There was a rumor that it was actually the brother who had tried to kill Charlotte, and he blamed it on Nonie. And my personal favorite, that Nonie was a vampire and that her sister found out and Nonie had to kill her."

We both laugh, but I do take note of the idea that Nonie's brother might have been to blame and he put the blame on Nonie. But there would have been no reason for Nonie to go along with it. Besides, there's plenty to indicate that Nonie was troubled and perfectly capable of doing what she did. What I want to know is why she told the doctor who examined her that she had done the deed deliberately. She must have known it would mean that she would be in terrible trouble.

"How did all of Nonie's trouble affect her siblings? With all the rumors, did they have problems in school afterward?"

"They suffered from all the talk, but not for long. Charlotte was a sweet girl, and eventually all that died down."

"And her brother?"

She smiles. "He reminds me of my middle boy, Dan. Quick with his fists. Not that I hold with boys fighting, but sometimes that's the most efficient way for them to settle their differences. What can you do? Anyway, Billy had a couple of fights and after that he was right back in with his friends. It didn't hurt that the idea of him being something of a hero made him a subject of great admiration among the girls. Girls are so silly at that age."

She catches the look on my face and laughs. "Yes, I know what you're thinking. Some of them stay that way."

We both laugh.

"Did Nonie have a boyfriend?"

"Not that I know of. That doesn't mean she didn't. It's amazing what kids can get up to, no matter how much you try to keep an eye on them." She narrows her eyes, caught up in the past. "I'm thinking back, and I can't say that Nonie was one of the precocious ones sexually. Some of these girls . . ." She shakes her head. "Let's just say there are a couple every year who could do well with a chastity belt. I pray that my girls aren't in that category."

I like Lottie. She's outspoken but without a hint of malice. "Any idea how Nonie would have had contact with any man outside her family or her classmates?"

"I don't know in particular. But I know some of the girls babysit at that age. And of course there are the men teachers."

When I get up to leave, she tells me to wait. She leaves the room and comes back with a plastic ziplock bag full of cookies.

"I'll take it," I say. "They may be the best cookies I ever ate." I hope Loretta doesn't hear that I said that.

I thank her for her help. She really has been helpful, especially with her suggestion that Nonie might have known something she claimed somebody would pay her to keep quiet. That fits with what the Curtis couple told me. More than ever I want to get my hands on that psychiatric evaluation. If Nonie bragged to her fellow students, she might also have bragged to the psychiatrist—maybe including names.

CHAPTER 8

Nonie's school records indicate that she had two male teachers—the math teacher, Alvin Haley, and the science teacher, Otto Schneider.

"Alvin is still with us," Jim Krueger, the school principal says, "but Otto left halfway through that same year."

We're in Krueger's office. I've told him I want to find out who Nonie's male teachers were. Krueger is a good principal, popular with students and teachers alike. To look at him, with his paunch and a sparse crop of hair that he combs over, you might think he could be the object of ridicule, but he's known as a fair man, and that goes over well.

"Why did Otto Schneider leave?"

"He said it was either get out of teaching or end up murdering one of the kids. He said he realized right away that he wasn't cut out for teaching. I wasn't principal at the time. I was a coach, and we used to talk some."

"You know where he went?"

Krueger settles back in his chair patting his remaining strands of hair, thinking. "That's been a while. I seem to recall he went to work for a chemical company down on the coast. I don't remember which one. Kind of left the school in a lurch for a teacher. I ended up taking one of his classes, though the only science I knew was what I got in my year of 'jock science' when I was in college."

Krueger tells me he doesn't know anybody who might have kept up with Schneider. "He was from Bobtail and took the job here because we were hiring. Maybe somebody from there knows what became of him. Why are you asking about Nonie's male teachers? Is there some suggestion that she was interfered with?"

"Not as far as I know. It's something I'm following up on."

"I was going to say, if you looked to Schneider for that, I think you'd be better off looking elsewhere. If I'm not mistaken, he played for the other team, if you know what I mean."

That gets my interest. "Is there any chance that Nonie found out he was gay and tried to use it against him?"

Krueger ponders the question and shakes his head. "I don't know how she'd find out. He was a quiet guy, kept to himself. He wasn't here that long."

"Any rumors that he might have been interested in any of the boys? If she'd found that out . . ."

"Look, you know as well as I do, if there had ever been the slightest hint, there would have been an uproar."

Not only that, but if Nonie had been intending to blackmail him when she returned home, she would have been disappointed, since he'd been gone from Jarrett Creek for a long time.

Before I leave to go talk to Alvin Haley, I tell Krueger I'd like to get a look at Nonie's school records.

"I'll have her file ready for you tomorrow. Older records are kept in another building," Krueger says.

Alvin Haley's last class ends at four o'clock, and I find him in his classroom, sitting at his desk, head in his hands.

"Excuse me."

His head jerks up. "Yes? What can I do for you?" He's a small man with an old-fashioned crew cut and wire-rim glasses. I can tell he's trying to figure out where he knows me from.

I introduce myself. "Wonder if I can have a minute of your time?"

"What's this about?"

"I want to ask you about one of your former students, Nonie Blake."

"Oh yes. I heard what happened. Let me get a chair for you," he says. "Those student desks will break your back." He's back in a minute with another chair like the one he's sitting in. "I don't know what I can tell you," he says, fussing over the position of the chair as if it matters. "I hardly knew the girl."

I sit down and cross my ankle over my knee. "You had her in your math class when she was in the eighth grade?"

"That sounds right."

"As I understand it, she refused to do homework. You recall that?"

He looks startled. "Who in the world told you that? I'd completely forgotten."

"Lottie Raines remembered it."

"Of course, it stands to reason she'd remember."

"Why is that?"

"She quit teaching when she got married, so she only had four or five years of classes to remember. When you've taught as long as I have, the students start to blend into one big wriggling mass of chaos in your mind. Except for the exceptional students, of course, and they're rare."

"So nothing about Nonie stands out for you?"

"Now that you mention the homework situation, I do remember because it was unusual. Sometimes you get students who won't do the homework because they're ashamed to admit they can't do it, or because their home situation is a problem. But as I recall she wouldn't do it because she got it in her head it was beneath her."

"Do you remember how it came up?"

"She announced it the first time I handed out a homework sheet. I remember she said it loud enough so all the students could hear her, that she wasn't doing homework. I told her that was fine, but she had to understand that it was part of her grade and if she didn't do it, I'd grade her down."

"What did she say to that?"

"Said she didn't care." He takes off his glasses and pinches the ridge of his nose. "This is coming back to me. I remember being surprised. Something like that hadn't happened to me before—I was a new teacher. I didn't know whether to take her seriously. I didn't know her, so I thought maybe she was trying to impress her classmates. I asked some of her teachers from the previous year, and they said they hadn't had that problem." He puts his glasses back on. "But she was serious. Never turned in homework. 'Course she was only in my class for a few months before she . . . well, you know."

"I understand she was a good student."

He nods and lets out a sound of exasperation. "Like I said, I was new to teaching. If something like that happened nowadays, I'd probably ignore it until I tested her. Then when I saw that she tested out on the material, I'd let the homework slide."

"Did she defy you in other ways?"

He rubs his hand back and forth across his jawline, thinking again. "If she did, I don't recall it. I've learned that there are a couple of students every year who have trouble following the rules or need to act out for one reason or another."

"Did you ever have a talk with her outside of class?"

"I'm sure I must have asked to speak to her after class about the homework issue, but if you mean outside of school, no."

"One of the other teachers mentioned hearing her brag about things that other students didn't believe. Do you recall noticing anything about her relationships with other students?"

"Like I said, if I did at the time, I don't remember."

When I get back to what we grandly call headquarters, which is no more than a big front room with two jail cells in back, Bill Odum is still there. He usually leaves at five. He's got a funny look on his face.

"What's up? Why are you still here?"

"A call came in that I thought I ought to tell you about in person."

"Uh-oh. Who from?"

"From Sheriff Hedges in Bobtail."

I sit down at my desk. It's odd for Hedges to call me. I worked with him on a case a while back and liked him, but I haven't had any business with him since. "What did he want?"

"He said the state is doing this program where they're assigning rookie cops to small towns. He thought since we're shorthanded we might like to have the help, so he put in a request for one of them. He said it was a long shot, which is why he didn't tell you anything in advance. He was calling today to say we're getting one of the rookies. A woman."

"Woman?"

"Yes sir, and . . ." He screws up his face. "The thing is, it's an attempt to get more minority cops in small towns. She's a Mexican. I mean, Hispanic, I guess they call it."

I'm struck temporarily mute, and Odum and I stare at each other. As sheriff of the county, Hedges has the right to appoint the police chiefs of the towns in his jurisdiction, so I guess that means he can assign deputies, too.

"That will be interesting," I say. "When did he say she'd be here?"

"Next week."

I cast an eye around the room. Somehow I think a woman is going to find it less than eye-catching. The spare desk is stacked with the filing I haven't had time for, with boxes against one wall full of the same. There are no pictures in the room, just framed documents from the state and an official photograph of the governor. I start laughing.

"What's funny?" Odum says.

I tell him my first response, that the state of the room would be unacceptable to a woman.

"You know that's sexist, don't you?" he says, grinning, with a twinkle in his eyes.

I sigh. "So if I don't tidy up, I'm a slob, and if I do, I'm being sexist. I guess we're going to learn a few things from this experience. Did Hedges say how long she was going to be with us or how her salary is getting paid?"

"He said the state is funding the program, but he didn't say how long she'd be here."

"Did he tell you her name?"

"He didn't say, and I didn't think to ask."

"That's all right. I'll call Hedges and have him fill me in." I nod toward the spare desk. "At the very least we ought to clear that desk so she feels welcome."

I'm home, and it's almost six o'clock when my cell phone rings and the caller identifies himself as Dr. Richard Buckley.

"You left a message on my phone about an old case?"

"Yes. I'm the police chief in Jarrett Creek and I need some information from you. Twenty years ago you evaluated the mental health of a fourteen-year-old girl by the name of Winona Blake who tried to hang her sister. You remember that?"

"Hmmm." That's the only thing he says for so long that I wonder if he's still on the line.

"Dr. Buckley?"

"Yes, I'm here. I'm trying to recall the case. I remember it vaguely."

"The girl was subsequently sent to a mental hospital in Rollingwood."

"That jogs my memory somewhat. I think there was something about the family that troubled me, but it isn't coming back to me. Why are you asking about her?"

"Well, sir, she recently got out of the institution, and after a week she was murdered."

"What do you mean, recently got out? You said this was twenty years ago? That can't be right."

"That's what I thought. I'd like to know if I can get my hands on her original evaluation."

"I can get you that. I'll need an e-mail or fax from you asking for the records, and I'll probably send it right along. I can't think of any reason to withhold the information."

I tell him I'll send him a request tomorrow morning. Then I head next door for my weekly wine date and conversation with Jenny Sandstone, my next-door neighbor. For a few weeks earlier in the summer, we didn't get together much. When she was involved in traumatic events after her mother passed away, I got a little too close and personal. Although she knew I was trying to protect her, her instincts to hide behind her boundaries is so ingrained that she had to retreat for a while. But now we're back to getting together weekly, although Jenny is more subdued than she was. It's a subtle change—she's a little more formal and doesn't laugh as easily. I hope eventually she settles back into her regular self.

I tell her the particulars of Nonie Blake's murder. Jenny's an attorney, and I feel like I can tell her pretty much anything, knowing she isn't going to blab about it. I value her opinions, which are many and freely given. "Twenty years. She shouldn't have been kept in the institution that long," Jenny says. "That's nineteenth-century crap. There's something fishy there. And the mother said they didn't visit her? Sounds like they may have had a court order declaring her incompetent so they could keep her institutionalized indefinitely."

"All right, that makes sense. I wondered how she could have been there so long, and the psychiatrist seemed to think it was odd," I say. "If they did have a court order, I wonder how and when it got lifted. I'm thinking I need to go up there to the facility and talk to them."

"You know they're not likely to tell you much, if anything. Patient confidentiality and all that."

"I suppose I can get a court order."

"I'd call them first. You might get a friendly person who'll be willing to stretch the law a bit, especially since Nonie was murdered."

I ask her how things are going at work. These days I'm always careful what I ask her, not wanting to bring up subjects she doesn't want to get into. Work is a safe subject. She launches into a description of a case she's working on that involves a divorce proceeding that's gone off the rails. She's with the prosecutor's office, and it's unusual for her to be involved with divorce cases. "These people need a keeper," she says. "She claims he stole her inheritance, and he said she gave it freely. And of course you've got the state of Texas sticking its nose into people's business."

The inheritance issue is an especially sore subject with her, since she tried to have an addendum to her mother's will overturned, and was unsuccessful.

When I get up to leave, Jenny says, "I have something to tell you. You remember my colleague, Will Devereaux? I've been out with him a time or two." Her face gets red. She hates more than anyone I've ever known to discuss personal matters.

"That's nice. He seemed like a solid person, and I know he cares about your well-being."

"That's all well and good, but I have a problem."

"What's that?"

"He's taken me out to eat a couple of times and I told him I'd make him a meal one night." She grimaces.

"Uh-oh." Jenny doesn't cook. As far as I know the only time her stove has ever been turned on is when she heats up stew I've brought over. "How can I help?"

"Could you show me how to cook something?"

"Jenny, why don't you go ahead and tell him you can't cook? For all you know, he's a whiz in the kitchen."

"I think it's time I learned to cook at least a couple of things. It doesn't seem right that I can't even boil an egg."

"I'm not exactly the right one to ask. My cooking is as basic as it gets. I know how to make beef stew, steak and potatoes, and red beans and rice. And maybe a couple of other things if I'm really bored with those."

"Beef stew doesn't seem that hard. At least everything's kind of mixed together so it doesn't have to look beautiful. Maybe I could learn to cook that. I don't want him to think I'm a complete idiot."

"Have you ever even shopped at a grocery store?"

"Of course I have. Where do you think I get cheese and crackers?"

We both laugh, and it feels good to laugh with her.

"All right. When do you want to do this? Saturday? You have to go to the store with me. I'll show you what to buy, and then we'll come home and I'll tell you what to do. Have you ever peeled a carrot or a potato?" I take a look at her face and say, "Of course you haven't. I know your mamma was a saint, but she didn't do you any favors by not teaching you a little cooking."

"Yes, she was a saint, but I'll tell you something I've never said to another soul. She couldn't cook for anything. Everything she made was either burned or half raw. So I come by my deficiencies honestly."

CHAPTER 9

"Why do you want to know who Nonie babysat for?" Charlotte asks. She's not as friendly today as she has been. We're sitting in the living room again. From upstairs come sounds of someone pacing and Adelaide's pleading voice.

"I've got some leads I'm following up on."

Charlotte's eyes dart in the direction of the sounds from upstairs. "Mamma is busy right now. I don't know how Nonie's babysitting could be considered a lead anyway."

"Let's see if your mamma can't get away for a few minutes."

Charlotte sighs. She gets up and leaves the room. In a few minutes, Adelaide comes downstairs. Her hair is disheveled, and she's wearing a bathrobe. It's ten o'clock, and she looks like she was just rousted out of bed.

"I'm sorry to disturb you," I say. "Charlotte told you what I was after?"

"I don't know what difference it makes, but Nonie babysat for the Mosley children." She glares at me.

"Did she get along well with the children?"

"She seemed to. Judy Mosley said the kids loved her. And she seemed to like babysitting, although I think for Nonie it was more that she liked the money than that she cared for the kids."

"Charlotte?" A man's voice calls from another room.

"She's upstairs, Billy. I'm in here with Chief Craddock."

In steps a wiry young man who wears his hair in a ponytail and has a belt buckle the size of your fist—one of those buckles that rodeo riders get when they win a major prize. He's taller than Charlotte but looks so much like her they could be twins.

"Don't get up," he says, but I do anyway.

I stick out my hand and introduce myself. He shakes my hand, but his face closes up. I wonder what happened to make him uncomfortable with a lawman.

"Sorry to meet you under such hard circumstances," I say.

"Yep, it's a sorry business." He takes a tin of tobacco out of his shirt pocket and tucks a pinch into his cheek.

Adelaide makes a sound of distress and says, "Oh, Billy, I wish you wouldn't do that. It's such a nasty habit."

"Mamma, we're not having this discussion again." He lifts his eyebrows in her direction.

"So what brings you here?" he says to me, still not friendly.

I should think it would be obvious, but I say, "Trying to figure out what happened to your sister Nonie."

"Maybe you'd be better off asking around town than bothering my family. We're in mourning and we don't need to be hounded by the law."

Adelaide gasps. "Billy, Chief Craddock needed some information. He's not hounding me."

"All I'm doing is telling him he needs to leave us alone."

"Billy, in my home you're to be polite to visitors," Adelaide says.

"He ain't exactly a visitor," Billy says, his eyes challenging me.

"Son," I say, "whatever beef you have with the law has nothing to do with me. I have no intention of bothering your family any more than is absolutely necessary, but I am investigating a murder, which means I will have questions I need answered." I turn to Adelaide. "Thank you for your information. There's one more thing I need to do. I need to talk to John. You or Charlotte can be there, but I need to have a conversation with him. Maybe you can let me know what time of day he'd be most agreeable."

"Now wait a minute," Billy says. "There's not a thing my daddy can tell you. He's not right in the head. Everybody knows that."

"Nevertheless, I need to talk to him. You have any idea when would be a good time?"

"He's at his best first thing in the morning," Adelaide says. "But some mornings are better than others. Would it be all right if I call you on short notice? He's a little riled up right now. He had sort of a meltdown last night and we were all up late."

"Let me know when it's convenient. And I need to talk to you about one other matter, and I'd prefer that I ask you in private."

Adelaide touches her hair as if aware for the first time that she isn't dressed according to her usual standards.

Billy says, "If it's not clear to you, it ought to be: you've come at a bad time. Does it have to be now?"

"It does," I say.

"Do you mind if we talk in the kitchen?" Adelaide says. "I can get myself a cup of coffee."

"That'll be fine."

I follow her into the kitchen. She pours herself a mug of coffee and one for me, too, without asking. Her whole demeanor is distracted. She makes no move to sit down, but she looks me in the eye. "What is it you wanted to ask?"

"This has to do with Nonie trying to hang Charlotte. It was very responsible of your family to call the police afterward. Some families would have covered up the incident, maybe thinking it was a child's game that got out of hand."

She takes a sip of coffee, peering at me over the rim of the cup with watchful eyes but saying nothing.

"What made you decide to call the police?"

She sets her cup down abruptly on the counter with a bang, and I can see that she's swaying on her feet.

"Here," I say. "I know bringing this up is hard, and I wouldn't do it if I didn't have to. Why don't you sit down?"

She slumps onto a chair and closes her eyes, a hand over her mouth. Finally she says, "It was the last straw."

"You mean she had had other problems?"

"Of course she had." She smiles sadly. "But this was the worst. It may have happened a long time ago, but I'll never forget it. Nonie was out of control. Her moods had been up and down for a while anyway, and after Billy stopped her, she went off the deep end. She screamed at him and tried to hit him. John had to wrap his arms around her to get her to calm down. Even though she had had episodes of anger before this, we were shocked. We didn't know what to do."

"You didn't think of calling a doctor?"

"We did. We called Doctor Taggart, but that didn't seem like it was enough. You had to have seen Charlotte. She had rope burns on her neck, and she was so scared that she'd wet herself. That's when we decided we needed help. I knew something was wrong with her, and ever since that day I've wished I had paid attention to it sooner. I think if I'd gotten help for her early on, she might have lived a perfectly normal life instead being in that institution."

"When she was examined by the psychiatrist, do you remember what her diagnosis was?"

"Oh yes. They said she was manic-depressive. I think they call it bipolar these days, though what difference it makes, I don't know."

"There are pretty good medications for bipolar illness," I say. "I'm still surprised that they kept her in Rollingwood for so long."

Adelaide's lips are trembling, and she has grown deathly pale. "We had her kept there. We took out a court order declaring her incompetent so she couldn't get out. Is that so horrible? After what she did?"

Charlotte steps into the room. "Is everything all right, Mamma?"

"It's fine. Has your daddy settled down?"

"He's finally asleep, though goodness knows how long he'll stay that way."

When I leave, Charlotte and Billy follow me out the door. I climb into my truck and look back to see Billy staring at me. When he sees me looking, he steps to the edge of the porch and spits over the side.

It occurred to me when I was having my exchange with Billy that

I need to question him, but I want to find out something about him before I do. I have a feeling he'd lie to me if it suited him, and it would be best if I have knowledge of him in advance.

As soon as I'm back at headquarters I go on the computer to find out what Billy's relationship is with the legal system. Twenty minutes later I'm looking at a record of petty quarrels gone wrong in a dozen towns in Texas. He's been jailed five times for getting into drunken brawls. There are no felony arrests, just misdemeanors. Small stuff, but it makes me think he might share Nonie's poor impulse management.

I call Jim Krueger at the school. "I hate to bother you, but I need Billy Blake's school records as well as Nonie's."

"It's all right. Eileen hasn't gone over to retrieve that file yet, so I'll have her get records for all four of the kids."

While I'm talking, Zeke Dibble wanders in and plops himself down at his desk. Although he only works part-time on our official schedule, he also comes in at random when he pleases. And he usually pleases when his wife has set him a chore that he doesn't much want to do. Today he tells me she's had the bright idea to have him dig up her flower beds so she can start planning her fall planting. "Do you know how hot it is out there? It's over a hundred. She's trying to kill me."

"Did it ever occur to you that she might just want you out of the house?"

He grins. "Might have. She has her bridge club at the house today and I have been known to wander in and give my opinion on somebody's bridge hand. Not always appreciated."

I bring him up to date on the Blake case. He has a lot of experience as a cop, although he has never worked homicide. He was in vice. Sometimes he has a good suggestion, but today he shakes his head. "I don't know how you'll figure out this one. That family is closing ranks. Not that I blame them. One of them likely killed that girl."

We stare at each other for a couple of minutes. I don't like what's running through my head. I usually feel like I have a good chance of getting to the bottom of a problem through my knowledge of the town and its workings; through the past and my relationships with people. But I don't know the Blakes, and they present a smooth exterior with no way for me to pry my way in. Zeke isn't any help. It's like we're running out of steam, too old to be on this kind of job. Maybe it needs a younger brain.

Zeke shakes himself, and I can't help wondering if he's having the same doubts. He points his finger at me. "Here's a question. Have you checked for sure that the older son was actually in Denton, like his sister said? It's not that far away. He could have snuck back here, killed the girl, and then gone back to where he was supposed to be."

"That's a good thought. The kind of thing you'd be good at checking out," I say.

"I'll get right on it," he says.

Judy Mosley died a few years ago of lung cancer, but that doesn't seem to have stopped her husband, Everett, from filling his house with cigarette smoke so thick you could choke on it.

"Sure, I remember Nonie," Everett says. "How could I forget? We left her with our kids—trusted her. And then come to find out what she did to her sister. I don't mind telling you, Judy had half a mind to drive out there and slap the girl in person." He has a raspy cough and I wonder how long it will be before he follows his wife into an early grave. He's a thin, stooped man who looks older than his fifty years, his face wrinkled as a lizard.

"You knew Nonie was back in town?"

"You'd have to be under a rock not to know that," he says. "You know there were some people thought she ought to be banned from the town." He takes a heavy drag off his cigarette and stubs it out. "Nasty habit," he says. "I know I ought to quit. Anyway, I didn't hold with that notion. The girl had something wrong with her, and it's been twenty years. I expect they wouldn't have let her out of that place if they thought she was a danger. Besides, she'd have to know that everybody would be watching her every move, so I can't see her getting away with a lot."

"Did you see her after she got back?"

"Who, me? How would I see her? The way I heard it, they kept her to herself out there at the Blakes' place. Most likely didn't want her to be a spectacle."

"Did she try to contact you?"

He stares at me. "Why would she do that? The kids are grown and gone." He shakes another cigarette out of his pack and lights it.

"Apparently she wanted to contact somebody here in town, and I'm trying to find out who it was."

"You're thinking whoever that was might have killed her? All I can tell you is that it wasn't me. If Judy was still alive, you might look to her, she was that mad, but I say that's a long time ago and no sense in bringing up old problems."

"Did you ever catch Nonie snooping in your business?"

"My business? I own a service station. Why would she be interested in that?"

"You didn't own it at the time. You bought it a few years ago."

He wrinkles his forehead. "You're asking if I, what, cheated Russ out of the station and Nonie somehow got wind of it? You're getting close to insult here, Chief. You can ask Russ Matlock. I bought that business fair and square when he wanted to retire. That's the end of it." His indignation sends him into a coughing fit. "Goddam, I've got to quit this habit." He starts to stub out the half-smoked cigarette but sets it down in the ashtray instead. "You can talk to Russ. He'll tell you. He lives out in a place on the lake. Me and him go fishing together."

"You understand I have to ask. This isn't personal."

"It is to me." He gets up from his seat. "I don't know what else I can tell you, but I'll tell you flat out I had nothing to do with that girl being killed. If I was you, I'd go looking closer to home."

"What do you mean? Did Nonie ever indicate that she had problems with her family?"

"She might have. I don't want to get anybody in trouble, but she might have hinted around that she'd like to get away from her family. And that's all I know about it."

I don't know whether he's attempting to draw attention away from himself or if Nonie really did complain about her family. And if she did, it may have been nothing more than a teenager's normal rant.

It's a relief to be outside. Even if it's twenty degrees hotter outside than in the house, at least I can breathe. On the porch, one more thing occurs to me. "Everett, do you know if Nonie babysat for any other families?"

He shakes his head. "Judy would have known, but I don't think I ever heard her say so."

"Your kids still live around here?"

"Daughter does. She's married and lives in Bobtail. Has a couple of kids."

When I get back, Zeke is pleased with himself. "I talked to an old boy I know in the Rodeo Association. There was a rodeo in Denton a couple weeks ago. Billy Blake won the bronc-riding competition. This guy gave me the name of somebody in Denton who runs the rodeo there. Name of Arlie Cole. Cole told me that Billy marked his home base as New Braunfels."

"So why was he still in Denton after the rodeo? That's where his sister said she located him."

"I asked Cole, and he said if Billy was hanging around, it was probably to do with a woman. He said Billy is quite the man for the ladies, but that he'd try to find out more for me."

CHAPTER 10

Everett Mosley's daughter, Kaylee Tharp, has two youngsters, ages three and one, but she looks like a teenager who has stumbled on a couple of kids to take care of. She's wearing short shorts and a halter top, and she's snapping gum like she's trying to kill it.

"I was as sad as I could be when I heard what happened to Nonie," she says. "Sorry about the mess in here. Both the girls have been up since five-thirty, and I can't wait for naptime so I can straighten up a little bit."

She and her husband live in a small house in a subdivision in Bobtail. She's brought me into the chaos she calls the living room to talk about her old babysitter. As soon as I arrived, she plunked the three-year-old in front of the TV to watch a program that appears to be about penguins who talk gibberish. She's holding the one-year-old on her lap. Her energetic management of the two kids is proof of why it's youngsters who have children.

"You have fond memories of Nonie?"

The baby fusses, and Kaylee bounces her on her knee. "Not so much of Nonie herself, but the fact that Nonie replaced a witch of a babysitter that we hated—she talked to her boyfriend on the phone all the time and yelled at us if we made a peep. Nonie didn't care much what we did as long as we left her alone."

"What did she do while she was there that she wanted to be left alone for?"

"I didn't think much about it at the time, but thinking back, I'm pretty sure she probably snooped around in my parents' business. She'd go in their bedroom. I followed her in there a couple of times and she'd be poking through drawers and stuff."

"Did she get mad at you for following her?"

"No, she'd put my mamma's jewelry and makeup on me and tell me I looked pretty."

"Your brother liked her?"

"My brother only wanted to watch TV. That was it. She let him watch his programs, so he was happy."

The baby is fussing harder. "Hold on a minute while I get her a bottle. She's about ready to go down." She glances over at the TV where her older daughter is giggling at the program. "Stacy Marie, you stay right there while I get Lizzie's bottle. You want anything?"

The girl shakes her head without turning to look at her mother.

While I wait for Kaylee to come back, I try to make sense of what Stacy Marie is watching on the TV. It seems like there's a lot of activity with no point to it, but she seems highly entertained, especially when one of the penguins slides around on the ice.

Kaylee doesn't have anything more to add with regard to what went on in the household while Nonie was there.

"Do you know if Nonie babysat for anyone else?"

"I didn't know it at the time, but when she was killed, my girlfriend Kimberley Havranek called and told me Nonie used to babysit for her, too."

"Havranek. Why do I remember that name?"

"Probably because a few years ago Kimberley's mamma kicked her daddy out of the house and asked for a divorce. There was a big uproar. He sued her for custody of the kids—can you imagine that? Anyway, he lost and moved to Bobtail because he was so embarrassed."

"Did Kimberly ever say what led to the divorce?"

"She said her daddy had a bad temper, although she loved him to pieces. Look at that." She gazes down fondly at the baby, who has fallen asleep with the bottle slipped out of her mouth and a bubble of milk at the corner of her lips. "She's the sweetest thing . . . especially when she's asleep." She laughs quietly. "I'm going to go put her in her crib."

She's back soon and says, "Stacy Marie, you've got five more minutes. Then we'll go in the kitchen and get lunch." She turns to me. "I don't like for her to get in the habit of eating in front of the TV. They say that's a good way for kids to put on weight."

When I leave, I have a good feeling. This girl may be young, but she's got a firm hold on life the way she's living it. I wonder if she ever had a desire to have a job and live a different way, or if she's doing exactly what she wants to do. My nephew Tom's wife, Vicki, told me she knew she wanted kids, but she also knew if she had to stay home all the time, she'd lose her mind. I remember a time when those choices weren't so easy to make, and it seems like it's better for women to have the choice.

Since I'm in Bobtail, I go down to city hall and look up Bruce Havranek's information. He works as a CPA for a trucking company with headquarters in Bobtail. I call him at his work, and the receptionist tells me he's out for lunch. I leave a message for him to call me on my cell. Then I put in a call to Wallace Lyndall, a cop I got to be friends with a while back, and arrange to have lunch with him. Over sandwiches, I ask him if the law in Bobtail has had any dealings with Bruce Havranek, but he doesn't know the name.

By the time we're done, Havranek hasn't returned my call, and when I phone his place of work, they tell me he decided to take the afternoon off. I wonder if he decided this before or after he got my message.

He lives in an apartment complex of four units. He doesn't answer his doorbell, so I leave him my card with a note to contact me as soon as he gets it.

On my way home, I get a call from Nonie's old psychiatrist, Richard Buckley. "My secretary was able to get that report you asked for. How soon do you need it?"

"The sooner the better. How big is it?"

"A lot of pages. I'll have her ship it by FedEx overnight. Do you have an account I can charge?"

I didn't even know there was such a thing. I suppose FedEx does deliver things here, but I've never had occasion to use them. "Tell you what," I say. "Let you me call you back with a number. I expect the sheriff's office has one."

Sure enough, the duty officer in Bobtail tells me they have a Federal Express account, and I can use it for what I'm after.

Buckley says he'll send it right out, and I should have it in the morning. I hang up and marvel at the wonders of the modern world. Not that I was exactly alive during pony express days, but seems like not that long ago when I would have had to wait at least a few days for the report to be delivered in the mail.

CHAPTER 11

Nonie Blake's funeral is Friday, and attending falls under the category of work for me. I sit at the back to be as inconspicuous as possible, since I don't want to draw special attention to the ongoing murder investigation. A lot of people have come to the funeral to gawk at the family. I'm gratified that Loretta has enough character to stay away, although there are plenty of curious attendees who have no business being here who will be able to fill her in on the details later.

Skeeter isn't in attendance, so I assume he has been put in charge of keeping a watch on John back home, which will serve my purposes. Charlotte has brought Trey but turns him over to a young woman, who takes him outside to play. It's a short service, handled by the funeral director, Ernest Landau, since the Blakes have no declared church affiliation.

At the reception afterward, Charlotte and Adelaide keep their heads high and greet everyone as if it's quite natural that they be there. Billy tries to do the same, but he's not as good at hiding his annoyance.

I see Kaylee Tharp talking to someone her age and go over to say hello. She introduces me to her friend, and as I'd hoped, it's Kimberley Havranek.

I hesitate to bring up the subject on the somber occasion of a funeral, but this may be the best chance I have to talk to her without having to track her down, so I plunge in. "I've been trying to contact your daddy and haven't had any luck. You know where I might find him?"

"Daddy? I hardly ever talk to him." Her tone is dismissive, but her eyes give away her concern for him.

An older woman walks up and says, "Kimmie, we'd better get home if you insist on going back to Houston tonight. I want to at least have a little time together before you leave."

I introduce myself to Kimberley's mother and find out her name is Nelda Havranek.

"I don't believe I've seen you around," I say.

"I work over in Bryan-College Station and hardly ever go out here. I probably ought to move over there, but I've lived here so long that it would be a chore to move."

"I understand Nonie Blake babysat for your kids a few times. Would you have time to answer some questions for me about Nonie this afternoon?" I see her hesitate. "After your daughter leaves. I don't want to bother you while she's here."

"Of course."

I give her my cell number so she can call me after Kimberley leaves.

After that I hustle out of the funeral home. I've got some business out at the Blake ranch. Theoretically I should have a search warrant, but no judge in his right mind would grant me a warrant simply because I want to pry. But if I go out there now, I can get Skeeter's and John's verbal okays to look around. And I may have a chance to talk to John, which will be good, since I'm pretty sure Adelaide isn't going to let me at him anytime soon.

Skeeter meets me at the door looking wild-eyed. "Chief Craddock, I don't mind telling you I'm glad to see a familiar face. Maybe you can help me figure out what to do. Daddy's driving me up the wall."

I hear John in the other room yelling.

"Let's go see if we can calm him down," I say.

In the kitchen John has a skillet on the stove and is attempting to turn on the burner. "Goddam contraption never works! I want some eggs. Is that too much to ask? How come nobody ever feeds me? I can feed myself if you'll—" He stops abruptly when he sees me and then says, "Can you turn this stove on?"

"Daddy, you had a whole plateful of eggs an hour ago."

"I did not."

"I made them myself," Skeeter says.

"Prove it."

Skeeter makes an exasperated sound. "Let me show you again." He pulls a trashcan out from under the kitchen sink and points to a handful of eggshells. "That's from the eggs I cooked."

"They weren't very good," John says.

"You want some toast?" I say.

"Toast! I could go for some toast," John says. "Two pieces. With a little jelly. We got any strawberry jelly?"

Skeeter rolls his eyes at me and pulls a loaf of bread out of the refrigerator and pops two slices into the toaster.

"John, while we wait for the toast, will you show me around outside? I need to look at a couple of things."

John's face lights up. "I'll be glad to." He turns to Skeeter. "We've got some important business. I'll see you later."

Skeeter laughs silently, shakes his head, and mouths "Thank you" to me. He might not thank me if he knew my intention wasn't entirely aboveboard.

Outside, I say, "John, can you show me where you keep your garden tools?"

"You mean like a spade? Or the lawnmower?"

The question is startling because his voice sounds perfectly rational and straightforward. "That's what I mean. Both."

"They're in the barn." He points to it. "You know we used to have cows and we used the barn for storing hay and feed and stuff for the cows. But now it's mostly garden stuff." And then he stops abruptly and peers at me. "Are you the new gardener?"

"Something like that," I say. It's unsettling to talk to people with dementia. They check in and out of the conversation, and you never know from one minute to the next what version of the person you'll be talking to.

I'm looking for the weapon used to murder Nonie Blake. Not that I expect to find it—I imagine whoever killed her took it with them, but I want to make sure I cover the bases. Bill Odum did a cursory check around the property the first day we were out here, and I want to look at possible hiding places a little more closely. It's always possible that someone hid something in plain sight after removing traces of blood.

I'm surprised when we open the barn door to see an ancient tractor parked inside, quietly rusting away. It has to have been here for a long, long time. "John, when was the last time this tractor was used?"

"We never used it," he says, back with me again. "It was here when we bought the place, and we never got around to getting rid of it. Want me to start it for you?"

"No, that's all right."

In the heat of the day the interior of the barn is stifling. Light sifts through the dusty, cobwebbed windows in uneven rays that shimmer in the air. The floor of the barn is strewn with remnants of hay and feed from however long ago the Blakes kept livestock. I'll bet the mice that live here are fat and happy.

The interior of the barn looks as if nothing has been disturbed for quite a while, which should make it easy to spot anything out of place. Most of the cavernous barn is empty. But at one end of the structure I find a room with gardening implements. There's a fairly new power mower and a gas can against one wall. A big workbench holds various tools like a hammer, a can of nails, screwdrivers, wrenches, rusted saws, and the like. They aren't put away in any order but lie scattered on the table as if whoever uses them plops them back down at random.

The garden tools are propped against the wall in a haphazard manner. There are several hoes—some that almost look like antiques—spades, two axes, different kinds of brooms, and rakes. I take my time looking them over for any traces of blood or to see if any of them look out of place from being wiped down recently. But they all look as if it's been a long time since they were handled.

John seems taken by the tools, picking them up and putting them down at random as if they are artifacts from another time and he's not quite sure what they're used for.

I walk the length of the barn for anything I might have missed, but I find nothing that could have been used as a weapon to do the kind of damage the coroner described. I steer John outside, and we walk the perimeter of the barn. I spend a little more time scouting around the outside of the house, poking under the back steps, peering into a rotting wooden box, with John walking patiently beside me. It seems that when he's in motion he's calmer.

I'm pushing my time limit, so I take John back inside. Skeeter is nowhere to be seen. Most likely he's retreated to his room, glad to give up John's care to me for a while.

"I'm hungry," John announces as soon as we're inside.

"I imagine that toast is ready," I say.

He follows me into the kitchen. The cold, dry toast is still in the toaster. I open the refrigerator and take out a jar of jelly and put some on the toast. I hand him a piece, which he's content to nibble on. At one end of the kitchen there's a door that leads to a utility room. There's a washer-dryer and laundry items, but nothing in the room that looks like a weapon.

I can't think of anywhere else in the house that might hold what I'm looking for, unless the guilty party hid an implement in a bedroom or attic, but I'm not betting on it. It was a wild chance anyway. Most likely the killer got rid of the murder weapon. The possible ways of doing that are endless.

"Let's sit down at the table," I say. "You want something to drink?"

"Is there any juice?" he says in that eerie way of sounding completely normal.

In the refrigerator I find some orange juice and pour him a glass. We sit down at the table.

"John, you had a visitor last week," I say. "Who was that?"

"They told me it was Nonie," he says.

"Your daughter."

"She's not my daughter," he says. His voice has become suddenly loud, and he is moving his hands restlessly over the tabletop as if he's playing the piano.

"You don't remember Nonie?"

"She's not my daughter," he repeats, louder, looking at me like I'm the one who has dementia and has failed to understand what he said.

"Do you know what happened to her?"

"Of course I do! Somebody killed her. Serves her right, too." He rubs his hands across the tops of his thighs, getting more and more agitated.

"What do you mean by that?"

"She was not a good person. She was a thief."

"A thief? What did she steal?"

Suddenly he becomes still. His eyes narrow, and he gets a crafty look. "I know what you're trying to do. You're trying to find out our secret. You think you'll get me to talk. But you're not getting anything out of me." He makes a lip-zipping gesture.

"When Nonie was here, did anybody have arguments with her?"

"I'm not telling you anything." He makes the lip-zipping gesture again.

"Hey Daddy, how you doing?"

Skeeter has come in so quietly that I didn't hear him.

"We were having a chat," I say.

"Good luck with that," Skeeter says. "Right, Daddy?"

In response, John starts rubbing both hands across the top of his head. "My lips are sealed," he says.

"You can say whatever you want to," Skeeter says.

Suddenly John jumps up. "Where is Adelaide? I need Adelaide. I'm going outside. I've got work to do."

"No, Daddy, you stay right here," Skeeter says. But John pushes past Skeeter, knocking him up against the doorframe.

"Daddy, I'll be right out there." Skeeter turns to me. "What did you say to get him riled up?"

"Asked him about Nonie."

"Oh yeah. He didn't like her. Had it in his mind that she was somebody else. I guess somebody he knew a long time ago and didn't like. Anyway, I should go catch up to him."

On the way home for a late lunch, I stop by headquarters and find that the psychiatrist's report has been delivered. I want to read it now, so instead of going home for lunch I run over to Town Café and get some enchiladas and bring them back to the office. While I eat, I settle in to read. I glance through the physical exams, which indicate that Nonie had nothing physically wrong with her at the age of fourteen. At 5'5" and weighing 120 pounds, she was in the right percentile for her age. She had no broken bones, and her blood tests indicated no physical abnormality. A brain scan was done that also showed no abnormality.

I read the conclusion of the report, which echoes the letter Buckley wrote. And then I tackle the meat of the evaluation. Buckley describes Nonie Blake as "intelligent, coherent, and with well-organized thought processes." She's also "skittish, anxious, and provocative in her speech." After a few sessions, he speculates:

> She exhibits narcissistic thinking, in which she is the hero of her own story. I believe she is enjoying the attention that her actions brought her and seems to have little understanding of the consequences of what she did to her sister. She exhibits no interest in her sister's well-being and still blames her brother for stopping her from doing "what she needed to do." When I suggested to her that she may have to spend some time in a juvenile detention facility, she was quite surprised. She seems not to understand that her actions could seem abhorrent to others.
>
> She is dismissive of her family and describes them as "fools." In one conversation she indicated that there were things about the family that she could tell me that they wouldn't want known, but she refused to elaborate. She insisted, however, that she did not endure any sexual or physical abuse from her family or anyone else.
>
> She also described her teachers and the townspeople as fools,

saying she should not have been "forced" to live in a small town, that her parents had the means to live in a more cosmopolitan environment, which would have suited her better. She describes her classmates and their parents as "simpletons." In particular she said several times that she could "put one over on any of them." When I asked what she meant, she indicated that she had "found out things" that people wouldn't want aired in public. Again, she refused to elaborate, saying that she had ways of "finding out things."

I hesitate to attach the label "sociopath" to a fourteen-year-old, but I admit that this girl has attributes that tend in that direction. But I also wonder from what she described if there is a toxic family situation that has pushed her into a state of disequilibrium. Therefore, I recommend that she be evaluated more thoroughly in a mental facility where she can be observed over time.

It's a frustrating document with its hints of things that Nonie knew. At the time, it must have seemed no more than "tall talk" from a troubled girl. I have to see it differently—as a hint that she knew things that might have gotten her killed. And I'm no closer to finding out what those things are.

And there's another thing about the report that interests me. Adelaide said that the doctor indicated that Nonie was bipolar. There's nothing in his report like that. I wonder if he told Adelaide that because he didn't want to suggest the more chilling possibility that Nonie was truly disturbed; possibly a sociopath.

The last thing I do before I head home is phone Luke Schoppe, the Texas Ranger who theoretically is in charge of investigating the murder. I ask him to arrange to have the Blakes' pond drained.

"That's expensive," he says.

"It's got to be done. I haven't had any luck finding the murder weapon."

"All right. I'll let you know."

"The sooner the better."

"It'll be Monday at least."

CHAPTER 12

B ack home, Loretta is sitting outside on my porch waiting for me.

"It must have been some funeral for it to take all day," she grumbles. "What took you so long?"

I settle into the rocking chair next to her. "I hate to disappoint you, but it was pretty tame as funerals go."

"Who all was at the funeral home?"

I fill her in as best I can, but I'm restless and I don't feel much like indulging her curiosity. I keep thinking about John Blake and his focus on not telling secrets. I don't know if that's some manifestation of his dementia or if there's something he really has in his mind that pertains to Nonie's death. Coupled with Nonie's claims that the family had some kind of secret they wouldn't want known, I can't help thinking there's something to his ravings.

"Getting information out of you is like pulling teeth," Loretta says. "I can tell your mind is somewhere else. I'll be better off talking to my ladies. It beats me how you think you can figure out who killed Nonie Blake when you don't pay attention to the details."

"Different details," I say. But maybe not. Maybe I'm missing a detail that's staring me right in the face. Again I have that uncanny feeling of being past my prime. I'm not used to the feeling and I don't like it.

I'm saved from having to pursue those thoughts any further by my cell phone ringing.

Loretta jumps and puts a hand to her heart. "I'll never get used to having people's phones ring in their pockets."

I see that the call is from Nelda Havranek, and I hold up a finger to tell Loretta to wait. Nelda says that Kimberley has gone back to Houston and I can come over anytime.

"I'm sorry," I say to Loretta. "I have to go. You're probably right. One of your ladies can describe the finer points of the funeral to you."

Nelda Havranek lives only a few blocks away from me. If it weren't so hot, I'd probably walk over there. But it is, and I don't.

When she opens the door, cool air drifts out. I don't normally care much for air-conditioning, but in late August, I'm glad for it. It's still over a hundred degrees outside.

"Let me bring you some iced tea," she says. "You want sugar in it?"

Time was, nobody asked that. All tea was sweetened to a saturation point, but times have changed. I tell her I'll take a little sugar.

She's back in a few minutes and sets the tea down with a plate of cookies that don't stand up to Lottie Raines's cookies, at least visually.

"Now what can I do for you?" She smiles pleasantly. Even her smile seems efficient.

"I've been trying to get in touch with your ex-husband."

The smile shuts off like a faucet. "You've come to the wrong place if you want to know how to get in touch with Bruce. I don't know a thing about him. Don't want to know."

Both mother and daughter have cut off the man of the household, and I wonder what it might have to do with Nonie Blake, if anything. "I hate to press on this. I don't want to open up old wounds, but can you tell me what turned you so completely against your ex-husband?"

"Since you're chief of police, I don't mind telling you, but I have to have your word that you won't tell a soul. It's a secret I've kept for many years, and I don't want to hear it all over town at this late date."

"If it's something illegal, I don't know that I can give you my word.

But if you're referring to some way he wronged you, nobody will hear it from me."

"It's both, but no charges were filed and it's all taken care of, so I suppose it won't hurt to tell you in confidence. Bruce was stealing from the people he worked for here in Jarrett Creek. He's a CPA who worked for Gabe LoPresto. You know Gabe?"

I nod. "We're good friends."

"Gabe came here one day and said he needed to talk to Bruce and me. He sat right here in this living room and said he had found out that Bruce had been stealing from him for a long time. He said if Bruce would confess right then and agree to pay back the money, it would go no further. But if he didn't agree to that, Gabe said he'd call the law and then it would be spread all over town."

"Since I never heard anything about it, I assume Bruce agreed."

She looks down at her hands. "He didn't want to at first. But I had known for a while that something was going on. Bruce had been funny. Kind of jumpy. Our marriage wasn't all it could be, and I thought he was trying to work up the courage to leave me. But as soon as Gabe started talking, I knew that's what had been bothering Bruce. So after Gabe laid out what he'd found in the books, I worked on Bruce and eventually he confessed."

She drops her head with a big sigh that sounds like a half-laugh. "Bruce didn't make a good thief. The amount he took wasn't worth the trouble. He only embezzled a couple thousand dollars a year. I've often wondered if it was the thrill of being a thief that made him do it. I've always worked and we had enough money for our needs plus a little extra to put away, so it wasn't like we needed the money. We paid Gabe back out of our savings account."

"It was good of Gabe to let your husband have a chance to make amends without going to the law."

"I've been forever grateful to the man, although I can still hardly look him in the face. And there's no way I could stay married to Bruce after that. It might have been wrong of me to turn our daughter away from him, but eventually when she got old enough to understand and I could trust her to keep it to herself, I told her what he had done. So now you know why I don't have anything to do with Bruce."

"I do understand. And I have a question to ask you. When did the embezzling start?"

She thinks. "Has to have been over twenty years ago now."

"I understand that Nonie Blake babysat a few times for you."

She looks puzzled. "Yes, she did. But we didn't go out much, so she was only here two or three times. Thank goodness. I was fit to be tied when I found out what she had done, thinking it could have been my daughter she got mad at and tried to kill. But what does this have to do with Bruce?"

"Is there any way Nonie could have found out that Bruce was embezzling money from Gabe's company?"

"I don't see how that's possible."

"That's why I need to talk to your husband."

Understanding dawns. "You mean you think Nonie was blackmailing him and when she came back here he killed her?" She starts to laugh, but it's not a laugh of delight. There's a hard, bitter tinge to it.

"You're laughing. Why is that funny?"

"It never ends, does it? I mean, he was a thief and a cheat, and after all these years I find out he may have done even worse. I keep waiting for the day everybody in town finds out that he embezzled that money. I'm always afraid that Kimberley will let it slip or that Gabe will think enough time has gone by. I keep thinking I ought to move out of here so I can let go of it. And now this."

"Nelda, don't borrow trouble. It's likely that Nonie's death has nothing to do with Bruce. I just have to follow up on it. And I'm going to suggest something else to you, even though you didn't ask for my advice. You ought to tell people what happened. It's a long time ago, and people aren't going to judge you. It's Bruce who was the thief, not you."

She shrugs. "You might be right. But I don't trust people as much as you do, and I'm not ready to test it out."

When I stop in at headquarters, the faxed autopsy report is sitting on my desk. Thankfully it isn't nearly as long or involved as the psychiatric report I had to wade through. Autopsy reports always make me a little queasy. They're intimate and cold at the same time. After death, no one knows the dead person's body more intimately than the doctor who has to cut and poke and weigh and examine. And yet, the doctor may be completely ignorant about the person who lived and breathed in that body.

I read the general information about the head wound that killed Nonie, and the fact that there wasn't water in her lungs, which indicates that she was dead before she was thrown into the water. Then I glance over the physical details. A 5'4" woman who weighed 135 pounds, brown hair and eyes, et cetera. I find one interesting thing. At some point, Nonie had a broken leg. In the psychiatrist's report, it was noted that she had no broken bones, which means she has to have broken her leg sometime in the last twenty years. I wonder how that happened in a mental facility. That will be a good question to start off with when I phone Rollingwood on Monday morning.

CHAPTER 13

Saturday afternoon is the time Jenny and I have fixed for her first lesson in domestication—her words, not mine. She insists on taking her car, so I walk over to her place. On the way to the Quick Mart, the only real grocery store in town, I tell her that a female Hispanic cop has been assigned to Jarrett Creek.

"That ought to shake things up."

"How so?" I don't mean to sound defensive, but I'm pretty sure I do.

"In case you hadn't noticed, I'm a woman. I've had more than a few people tell me they don't think a woman ought to be a lawyer. I can imagine what they'll think of a woman cop. Not to mention that there's a pretty strong thread of prejudice in our neck of the woods."

"Oh, come on," I say. "We have blacks and Hispanics who are friends with everybody in town."

"True. But that doesn't mean a newcomer isn't going to be suspect because of the color of her skin as much as for the fact that she's a stranger."

She asks me how the investigation is going, and I admit I'm revving the engine but not going anywhere.

"I ought to be working on it this weekend, but the manager of Rollingwood isn't in on the weekend, the pond can't be drained until next week, and we're waiting for word on Billy Blake's activities."

"You need a break anyway. It'll be good to hit it fresh."

Although I don't want to admit it, I know she's right.

"I'm as nervous as a kid starting first grade," Jenny says, as she wheels into the parking lot at the Quick Mart. The lot is crowded, this being Saturday. "All right, let's get this over with."

Inside the front door, I walk over and grab a shopping cart and say in a teacherly voice, "We call this a shopping cart. We use it to contain our purchases. For times when you are making only a few purchases, you can use those fine plastic shopping baskets stacked over there." I point.

She laughs. "Don't be a smart aleck."

We stop first at the meat section. I select a package of stew meat and toss it into the cart.

"How do you know how much to buy?" she says.

"For two people, you buy about a pound of meat if you want leftovers, less if you don't."

She looks at the packet of meat as if it might leap up and smack her in the face. "You've got a little bit more than a pound there."

This may be harder than I thought. I explain that it isn't an exact science. "If you have a recipe, you can fudge here and there. The way I make beef stew doesn't need a recipe."

"I might be more comfortable if I had a recipe I could look at and follow precisely."

"Then you've got the wrong chef," I say.

We proceed to buy carrots and potatoes, me having to explain that it's a matter of proportion and you have to use eyeball judgment. I also explain that it helps to be able to imagine what something might taste like. "For example, I like a little green bell pepper in my beef stew. Some people might not like it."

"I like it," she says. "Do you think Will would like it?"

"I have no idea. You're the one dating him."

She looks daggers at me.

We buy an onion and bell pepper and a can of tomatoes. I figure she'll be better off with a can of beef broth than with making broth, so we put that in the cart. "Are you going to have a salad, too?" I ask.

"Do you think I should?" Her forehead is beaded with perspiration, despite the fact that it's cold in the store. I'd laugh if it weren't so pitiful.

"I don't know what kind of eater Will is," I say.

"Neither do I!" she says, flinging her hands up.

"You said you'd been out to eat with him. What did he order?"

She looks at me like I've completely gone off the rails. "I don't know. I'm not interested in what people eat, so I didn't pay any attention." She peers at the contents of the cart. "Maybe I'd better forget this whole thing. I can go buy some enchiladas at Town Café and serve them with cheese and crackers and that will be the end of it."

"Oh, no," I say. "We've gotten this far and we're going to see this project through to the end."

She groans. "Let's get on with it then. And I like salad, so let's get some salad kind of stuff."

By the time we get back to her place, Jenny is quiet and grim. She pulls items out of the sack and puts them on the counter haphazardly. "I'd rather prosecute an axe murderer than do this again," she says.

It usually takes me a short time to throw together a beef stew, but having to explain every step takes most of the afternoon. I take pity on her and peel the vegetables myself, but I have to answer a pack of questions, like "How come you peel the vegetables? How come you peel the carrots and potatoes and not the bell pepper? Does the peel taste bad?" and "How do you know how big to chop up the vegetables and meat?"

But eventually beef stew is bubbling on the stove, and the salad greens have been washed and put in the refrigerator in a bowl covered with plastic wrap, which I've had to fetch from my house. I've also had to go back a few times for herbs and for a bottle of salad dressing, since I forgot that she has absolutely nothing in her kitchen cabinets.

I leave her with strict written instructions on how and when to proceed and with the admonition to call me if she has any questions. As I walk out of her house, I'm chuckling to myself. I picture her running off to the bedroom to call me surreptitiously numerous times and Will wondering what the heck she's up to.

The lesson took longer than I thought it would, and it's late afternoon. I call Ellen Forester and ask her if she'd like to go with me to get some Mexican food for dinner. I know she'll get a kick out of hearing about my session with Jenny, and I'm interested to hear her thoughts on the new cop. Any excuse to spend a little time with her will do.

The restaurant is crowded on a Saturday night, and we have to wait for a while. I turn down the owner's offer to slip us in early, me being chief of police. I don't need to hurry the evening along. I like being with Ellen, and while we wait I describe Jenny's incompetence in the kitchen.

"You shouldn't make fun of her," Ellen says. "I guess if a woman doesn't learn to cook from her mother, she's at a disadvantage."

"Now let me ask you something," I say. "Isn't that a sexist thing to say? What about a man? Is he at a disadvantage if his mother doesn't teach him to cook?"

"Or his father?" she says.

"Oh, right."

She smiles up at me. I'd be hard-pressed to say why, but she looks prettier than usual tonight. She's wearing a dress that I think of as summery, maybe because it's got some kind of abstract flowers on it. And she smells good when she's up close.

"I never heard you use the term 'sexism' before," she says. "What brought that up?"

I tell her about the woman coming to mix things up in the police department, and I'm worried that she won't be favorably impressed with the state of our headquarters.

"Let me ask you this," Ellen says. "Can you imagine a man coming in who likes things organized and tidy, and who wants the place to look nicer?"

I let the question sink in. "I see what you mean."

"Have you ever asked Bill Odum if he'd like to have someone come in and clean the place? Has he ever volunteered to clean up? Will you expect this woman to come in and make the coffee? Or to clean the bathroom?"

"Thank goodness I didn't get that far in my thinking," I say. "Because I suspect I may have gone in that direction before I thought about it."

She nods, her eyes dancing with humor. "Believe me, I've had enough of a man expecting me to do all the 'lady' things, and I'm done with it."

"So you're saying if I start to ask her to do something, I should consider whether I'd ask a man the same thing?"

"Wouldn't hurt."

They finally tell us our table is ready. Once or twice this evening, I've seen a look of concern flit across her face. After we've ordered I ask her if everything is all right.

"Oh, my son in Dallas sounds unhappy," she says. "He's had a summer job and I don't think he likes the idea of going back to school. He's used to bringing in some money and he likes it. I think I need to go up there and have a talk with him. I don't want to pry, but I might have to."

A brilliant idea comes to my mind. "I need to drive up to the Dallas to talk to the people at Rollingwood where Nonie Blake was for the last twenty years. It's near Dallas. We could drive up together. I could leave you with your son and do my business. Maybe we'd stay overnight and go to one of the art museums in Fort Worth." I like the idea of the art museum. The Modern Art Museum in Fort Worth was one of my wife Jeanne's favorite places, and I haven't been back since she died. It occurs to me that I might not want to be there with Ellen and all the memories it will bring up, but it's too late, I've already mentioned it.

She doesn't jump at the idea the way I thought she would, but she says she'll give it some thought.

Sunday I've arranged with Truly Bennett to drive to Navasota to a cattle auction. A man who keeps a big herd of white-faced Herefords is selling off his whole stock, and we're hoping to buy a couple of good yearlings. I keep my herd at twenty head, plus or minus, but it's always good to infuse some new blood into the lines, and I can sell the extras next spring.

Truly knows more about livestock and horses than anyone, and it's fun to go to an auction with him and have him point out little things that I wouldn't pay attention to. We spend some time when we arrive checking out the cattle, and Truly says the rancher has kept them in top condition. "I appreciate that in a man," he says. "Some ranchers when they get ready to fold up their business stop paying attention to the stock, and the cattle fall apart pretty fast."

Normally you can't get Truly to string more than a few words together at a time, but when the subject is cattle, he can get downright chatty.

We're pleasantly surprised to be able to keep up with the bidding on a fine young bull. I've only had the one in my herd for two years, and I usually keep them for three, but Truly says this one looks good and I might as well replace mine now. "It'll take some time to bring this one along so he's ready to breed by next spring."

At the end of the day, we arrange to have two cows and the bull transported early next week. If I were only buying one, I would have brought a trailer along, but at a big sell-off like this one, there are always some young men trying to make a little money who will transport your cattle as cheaply as you can do it yourself.

CHAPTER 14

On Rollingwood's showy website, you'd think they were describing a five-star resort instead of a mental hospital. There's barely any mention of the residents' mental state. Words like "relaxing," "soothing," and "state-of-the-art" are sprinkled liberally throughout. The woman who answers the telephone when I call Monday morning has the voice of an angel. I tell her who I am and what I'm after, and she says she'll be happy to put me through to the director, Mrs. Lannigan.

Mrs. Lannigan is equally delighted to hear from me. "The receptionist said you needed some information. Let me assure you that I'll do everything I can to help you, within legal limits, of course."

"I'm calling to ask some questions about a patient who was recently released from Rollingwood. Nonie Blake."

Silence prevails. It reminds me of the silence that the psychiatrist, Richard Buckley, greeted my questions with. "I'm sorry. Can you give me the name again?"

"Winona Blake. She's called Nonie."

"Can you let me put you on hold for a second?"

The second stretches into several minutes. Just when I think my line might have been dropped, Mrs. Lannigan comes back. "I'm not sure what to tell you," she says.

"What I'd like is the name of the doctor who evaluated Nonie. And why she was kept there for so long. As I understand . . ."

"Wait. That's not what I mean. What I mean is, I had to look up her name. Winona Blake has not been with us for more than ten years."

"You're sure?"

"Of course I'm sure." Her voice is amused. "It would be unusual for us to simply lose a patient. That's why I couldn't figure out who you were asking about. I've only been director here for five years, so I never knew Winona Blake. Give me a moment to read what it says on the computer file about her release." She's silent again. "Apparently at age eighteen her family declared her incompetent to handle her own affairs so she was kept here. At some point, she petitioned to have the declaration overturned. Her doctor determined that she was able to function well enough to be in charge of her own affairs, and the declaration was overturned. She left shortly thereafter."

"Does it say whether the family was informed?"

"There's no reference to that here. She didn't have to inform her family if she didn't want to. I must say I know nothing about the matter, but it's unusual for a family to go to the trouble to have someone declared incompetent after they are of age, and I'd have to refer you to the doctor who signed the order to find out why he agreed."

"Any idea where she went when she left?"

"There's no forwarding address here."

I get the name and contact information of the doctor who signed the order declaring Nonie incompetent and for the doctor who released her. When I hang up, I sit and stare out the window for a few minutes. Where the hell had Nonie been all this time? And how come the family didn't know she had left the facility long ago? How come she told them she had only recently been released? And then I realize that regardless of what Nonie told them, they had to have known she had been out a long time because bills from Rollingwood would have stopped coming. At the very least, Adelaide would have known that Nonie was no longer there.

Since it was Adelaide who told me that the facility called to say that they were releasing Nonie, she's obviously lying. Why? What could be gained by pretending that Nonie was still in the facility all those years? Surely she would have known that in the course of my investigation I would call Rollingwood to check up on Nonie's stay there.

As I'm mulling this over, a car drives up and parks in front, and a stocky Hispanic woman gets out. She pauses and looks the building up and down. All of a sudden I realize who she has to be. I was thinking the new hire would be coming later in the week and that I'd have a chance to talk to Sheriff Hedges and get more details. Why hasn't anybody sent me an official notification?

I glance over at the fax machine and see a yellow light blinking. It's out of paper, which explains that part of it, although not to my satisfaction. Anyway, it's too late. The new officer is at the door, and I don't even know her name.

I get up and put a smile on my face. Lord, what a time for her to show up!

"Morning," I say. "I bet I know who you are."

"Maria Trevino, reporting for duty, sir," she says, which surprises the heck out of me. I'm not used to that kind of formality. Her voice is tight. I can't figure out if her expression is angry or terrified. Her skin is the color of a pecan shell. She wears her black hair cropped short, and the only makeup she appears to be wearing is bright-red lipstick that contrasts with the somber clothing she's wearing—black pants and a gray short-sleeved shirt.

"Welcome Deputy Trevino. And you can dispense with the need to call me sir. 'Chief' will do fine." I follow her glance around the room. She has dark, intense eyes, and they aren't particularly friendly. "Uh, I guess you can see that I wasn't expecting you quite this early in the week."

"Sheriff Hedges said he faxed you the information Friday afternoon." Her eyes pin me like a bug under a microscope.

"That's right. Unfortunately, it looks like the machine was allowed to run out of paper and I didn't notice it."

She looks over at the machine and then cuts her eyes back to me. "What should I do? You want me to come back later?"

"No. We'll just ... if you'll help me, I'll take these boxes off this desk and we can get you set up. But first, let me feed some paper into the fax machine." I don't remember when I've felt so flustered. Not a good way to start off our working relationship.

I get the fax machine set to spew out more paper, and sure enough the letter from Sheriff Hedges is there, the overly formal language obviously put together by the state agency that is funding the minority program. Behind the letter comes a hiring report on Maria Trevino's background and qualifications. Then there are several pages taken directly from the Texas Commission on Law Enforcement regarding minority hiring.

Hedges's letter explains that the state of Texas is paying for the salary and uniforms of the officers hired under the program. It also gives an e-mail address of the person to contact in case of problems. The whole time I'm reading the letter and qualifications, the fresh information I've gotten from Rollingwood is simmering in the back of my mind, and I have to force myself to concentrate.

I look up to find Trevino watching me. "Says here you're from Houston. How's it going to be for you being in such a small town?"

"We didn't have any choice where we were sent. I'll make it work."

"Do you have a place to live?"

"Not yet. I'm staying at a motel in Bobtail for a few days." Every time she responds, it reminds me of when I was in the military. They required snappy replies that gave only the answer to the question. Nothing more.

"Why don't we make that your first order of business? There are a couple of apartments in town. I don't know if they have vacancies. If they don't—"

She puts up her hand to stop me. "I appreciate the help, but I'll take care of that on my off time."

"The thing is . . ." I hesitate because I don't want to tell her I don't really have anything for her to do. It seems inhospitable, not to mention unprofessional. I don't want her to feel like I'm being dismissive. "I'll level with you. Something has come up that I need to deal with right away and I don't have time to sit down with you at the moment. What I'd like you to do is familiarize yourself with the town. Drive around. Go up to the lake and explore the back roads. Familiarize yourself. You can use one of the squad cars."

Her face goes blank. I don't have a clue what she's thinking. "I'll use my own car, if that's okay."

"If that's what you want. Write down your mileage, so you get paid for it. Let's meet back here at, say, two o'clock this afternoon. If you want lunch, Town Café has good food. Tell Lurleen, the waitress, to put it on my tab."

"Do you have a map of town?"

I can't help smiling. "No map. It's a pretty small place. I don't think you'll have any trouble making your way back here. The railroad tracks border us on the east and the lake on the west."

She doesn't smile back.

"Let me make a call." I call Marietta Bryant at the real estate office down the street. She says her office has a hand-drawn map. It's with the greatest relief that I send Maria Trevino on her way. As soon as she's out the door I wonder if I should have had Zeke or Bill Odum come in and show her around.

Before I leave for the Blakes' place I call Loretta and tell her there's something I need to discuss with her. I agree to stop by her house for lunch and she says she'll have a sandwich for me. I need to tell her about Maria Trevino and ask her to make sure Maria gets a welcome from the town.

On the way out to the ranch, questions crowd in on me. Why did Adelaide pretend that Nonie had come straight home from Rollingwood? Did anyone actually call pretending to be from Rollingwood, or did Adelaide make that up? Most pressing of all, where has Nonie been the last ten years, and why did she come back now?

CHAPTER 15

When I tell Adelaide Blake that the director of Rollingwood said Nonie hadn't lived there in ten years and demand to know why she told me that Nonie had just gotten out of the mental institution, she's still as a stone. We're sitting in a room I haven't been in before, a TV room off the kitchen. It's small and a lot more inviting than the formal living room. If I expected her to reply, I was mistaken.

"So you knew she'd been out for several years," I say. "Why did you lie about it?"

She licks her lips, and when she speaks her voice is almost a whisper. "I should have told you, I realize that. I was just trying to make it less complicated."

"Less complicated? Telling me all that stuff about Nonie's medication and her taking a bus here from Rollingwood? Telling Charlotte that? How was that less complicated?"

"I know, I know. I didn't know what to say."

"Why not tell the truth? Suppose you tell me the truth now? What really happened?"

"It happened almost the way I told it. Nonie called here a week or so ago and said she wanted to come home. And she did take a bus. I didn't make that up."

"You knew ten years ago that she was out and you hadn't tried to contact her all those years?"

"No." She lifts her chin in defiance. "I told you why. I didn't want anything to do with her after what she did."

"Then why did you let her come home now?"

Adelaide is wringing her hands. "She said she had some things she wanted to talk to me about. She wouldn't take no for an answer."

"What was it she wanted to talk to you about?"

"I don't know. We never got around to that. I was afraid to ask too many questions." She fixes frightened eyes on me.

"Afraid of what?"

"I left her there for all those years and was afraid she was going to be mad. You don't know what she was like. She had a way of threatening you, even when she was little."

"Did she threaten you?"

Adelaide's face is flushed. "No, I don't mean that. I mean she . . . oh, I don't know what I mean."

"You acted like she was back here to stay. Was that what she intended?"

"She didn't say. But you mentioned that she didn't have many things with her, and I noticed that, too. I assumed she was here for a short time. I just wanted to get her visit over with."

Adelaide baffles me. My own mamma didn't like to face reality, but I don't think even she would have ignored the strange circumstances of Nonie's homecoming that Adelaide seems to have shied away from.

"Adelaide, what were you afraid of? Were you scared she was here to get revenge for you sending her off to Rollingwood? Did you think she would hurt you? Kill you?"

"Oh, no." She waves her hands back and forth. "Nothing like that. It's that I didn't want her to get all worked up. I thought if I kept things calm, she'd get around to telling me what she wanted, and then she'd be on her way."

"And you have no idea what that was?"

"No, I don't."

"She didn't try to blackmail you?"

"No, of course not. How would she know anything to blackmail me about anyway? She's been gone for twenty years."

I don't believe Adelaide. She has told so many lies that I can't imagine how she even keeps the stories straight in her own head. There's something going on here that Adelaide will do anything to keep secret, no matter how many lies she has to tell. The question is, how am I going to uncover the secret if she continues to stonewall me?

I stand up. "I'd like to talk to your son Billy. Is he around?"

She tells me Billy is outside in the barn. "Although I don't know what you think you're going to get out of him."

I find Billy in the barn looking over the old tractor. He's in a scruffy T-shirt and jeans, and sweat is beaded on his brow. He's looking exasperated. "Why the hell did they let this thing sit here all these years?" he asks.

"Going to be hard to get rid of," I say.

He grunts and focuses his glare on me. "Is there something I can do for you?"

"I want to ask you a couple of things. Did you ever go visit your sister in Rollingwood?"

"No. Mamma said I was too young to—"

I interrupt him. "I mean after you were out on your own."

"No, I didn't." His look is guarded. There's something he's not telling me. He folds his arms and leans against the tractor.

"It turns out that she left the facility ten years ago. Were you aware of that?"

His hesitation is so slight I might not have noticed it had I not expected it. "No."

"Have you talked to Nonie in the past ten years? I'd appreciate the truth."

He looks down the empty stretch of the barn, and I can tell he's trying to decide whether to come clean. "Okay, yes, I did talk to Nonie, and I knew she was out."

"That's progress. When was this?"

"It's been a while. Maybe a year after she got out."

"So you would have been what, twenty-one, twenty-two?"

"That's right. So what?"

"How did she know where to get hold of you?"

He cocks an eyebrow. "She saw a poster that had my name on it advertising a rodeo that was coming to town. First time I had made the big time."

"Where was this?"

"Up in Denton."

"That's where she was living?"

"I didn't ask her, because I told her straight out that I wanted nothing to do with her. I didn't want to talk to her at all. She begged to know how Mamma was, and I told her everybody was fine, no thanks to her."

"Did she ask about Charlotte?"

"I didn't give her a chance. I told her she had hurt the family enough, and to stay away."

"Why do you think she called you and not anybody else in the family?"

"You'd have to ask her that."

"Did you tell anybody that you'd talked to her?"

"I did not." He straightens, and his look is poisonous. "What would be the point? It would hurt Mamma and stir up Charlotte. Charlotte was always talking goodie-two-shoes talk, like she wanted to bring Nonie home. It would have been a mess. I figured it was better if I didn't bring it up that she'd gotten out."

"Seems like if you were worried about their safety, you would have let them know she was out."

For the first time he looks troubled. "I guess I didn't see it that way. As it turned out, it didn't matter."

"Something I intended to ask you, do you know anybody by the name of Susan Shelby?"

"No. Who is she?"

"There was a container of pills upstairs with her name on it, and your mamma said you might know who it belonged to."

"Never heard of her."

It occurs to me that maybe Nonie was using another name. Maybe she didn't want anybody to find out about her past.

"Is Charlotte home?" If Nonie got in touch with Billy after she got out of Rollingwood and he brushed her off, it's within the realm of possibility that she also called Charlotte.

"Why do you want to bother Charlotte again? She's told you everything she knows." Billy's stance is aggressive. "We can't drop everything and have a little chit-chat every time the mood strikes you."

"Son, you don't seem to fully appreciate that someone was murdered right here on this property. Somebody that everybody here was acquainted with, saw every day, and had a troubled history with. I can appreciate that your feelings for Nonie were less than cordial, but it's my job to find out who killed her and bring them to justice. I'm sorry if that's an inconvenience, but you're just going to have to put up with it."

Billy's face has gotten redder as he listens to me, and his fists have clenched up tight. "None of us killed her. And I think you ought to leave Charlotte alone. She suffered enough."

"Let me put a hypothetical to you. Suppose when Charlotte called to tell you Nonie was back, you didn't feel that Charlotte was safe with Nonie here. Suppose you sneaked down here, lured Nonie out of the house, hit her over the head, threw her body in the tank, and hightailed it back to Denton."

"I did no such thing. You don't have any evidence of that."

"I don't have any evidence to the contrary either. So let's just agree that it's a working hypothesis along with a lot of others. If you want to provide evidence of your innocence, I'll be happy to listen to you."

Charlotte is so shaken by my revelation that Nonie had been out of the hospital for ten years that I have to believe she knew nothing about it. We're in the living room, but neither of us is sitting down.

"Where had she been all this time? And why did she decide to come home now and lie and tell us she had just gotten out?"

"She didn't. It was your mamma who lied to you. She knew Nonie was out all those years."

Her mouth falls open. "That can't be true."

"Oh yes, it is. And Billy knew. It appears that you're the only one who was kept in the dark. You and Skeeter, of course. Nonie never mentioned anything like that to you? You were with her for an entire week and she never brought it up?"

"Never. Although..." She looks toward the window where the August light is streaming in and waves of dust dance in the air.

"What?"

"I wondered how she seemed to know so much about the world."

"What do you mean?"

"I assumed that someone who had been in a mental institution for twenty years would be like somebody who had been in prison for all that time. That they wouldn't know little things, like ... I don't know, how to dress. Her clothes seemed in style. She seemed comfortable in the world." She walks to the window. Her voice trails away. Suddenly she wheels back toward me. "I know something that seemed odd. I was going to the grocery store and asked her if there was anything she particularly liked. She asked me to bring her a particular brand of cookies—LU raspberry cookies. At the time I thought it was strange that she knew about that kind of cookies. Would they have an expensive brand like that in a mental hospital? But I rationalized it by thinking if someone is in a really costly facility, maybe they were provided with high-quality food items." She shrugs.

"Anything else?"

"I thought it was odd that she could navigate the bus schedule from Dallas to Bobtail and manage to get a ride to the house. I wondered why she had gotten a ride instead of calling us from the bus station. It seemed to me that she would be terrified."

"But you didn't ask her about any of those things?"

"There are several things I wish I had asked her," she mutters.

I tell her about the man who called to tell me he and his wife had given Nonie a ride. "The man told me that Nonie made some hints as if she were going to blackmail someone. She never mentioned anything like that to you?"

She shakes her head. "Why would she tell that to a perfect stranger and not to us?"

"My question exactly. I wondered if maybe she told your mamma more than she told you. Or, if you are being entirely honest with me?"

"What do you mean?"

"I had a talk with Les Moffitt. He told me that the family considered calling a lawyer before you called me after you found Nonie's body. And yet you pretended to me that you didn't realize Nonie had been murdered. How am I supposed to trust anything any of you say?"

She runs her hands over the top of her head. "Look, I admit it. We screwed up. Okay. I didn't know what to do. Les thought we ought to call a lawyer, but I thought if we hadn't done anything, we didn't need that."

"But you thought maybe your father had done it."

"No! I didn't think so. That was . . ."

"Adelaide."

She sighs. "Do you blame her? He's really hard to deal with. She's at her wits' end."

"Then why not put him in a facility?"

"You're going to have to ask her that."

"I have something more to ask you. Did you ever feel afraid of Nonie?"

She struggles to find words "It was awkward at times. But I wasn't afraid of her. Mostly we kept out of each other's way. She didn't want to be around Trey, and . . ." She plays with the string of pearls at her throat. "Quite frankly, after what she did to me, I didn't much want her around him, either."

"Did she ever apologize for what she did?"

"Ha! In that way, she hadn't changed one bit—Nonie was never one to apologize for anything."

I ask Charlotte for permission to go upstairs and get the bottle of pills from the bathroom Nonie used when she was here, and she agrees readily.

On my way back to headquarters I get a call from Zeke Dibble. "Samuel, there's a woman here claiming to be a new officer. I . . ."

My heart sinks. I assumed that since Bill Odum knew about Maria Trevino, Zeke did, too.

"Zeke, I apologize. I got some information about the Blake case that I had to follow up on this morning and completely forgot to call you. Is she there now?"

"Yeah. Said you told her to drive all over town and she did and wants to know what she should do now."

"Tell her I said she can have the afternoon off to go find a place to live. When she comes in tomorrow morning, I'll have a plan worked out."

CHAPTER 16

"I'm glad you called. I've got some things to talk to you about," Loretta says. She has a determined gleam in her eye that makes me uneasy.

"Okay. Shoot." She has a place set for me in her kitchen and has made me a chicken salad sandwich. She makes the best chicken salad in the world, so I'm eager to get to it.

"No, you go first," she says. "You called me."

I tell her about Maria Trevino showing up and me not being ready for it.

She chuckles and gives me a knowing look.

"What are you so smug about?" I say.

"I wonder what she's going to report back. That she walked into that office and it looks like cavemen live there?"

"It's not that bad. Just a little messy."

"Samuel, have you ever taken one look around what you so grandly call headquarters? When is the last time you had somebody come in and clean?"

Uh-oh. We're on that one again. A few months back, Loretta announced that I needed a cleaning lady. I gave in and hired the woman. Two weeks later she quit, telling Loretta she couldn't work for a single man because I couldn't give her any instructions about the way I wanted things done. Loretta was pretty sure I had treated the woman badly, but I swore I hadn't. "I'd have to say it's been a while," I say.

She snorts. "Never is more like it. And I'll bet before you know it, all three of you men will expect her to be tidying up around there. That poor woman is going to wonder whether she was hired to be a police officer or to be a maid."

She's echoing what Ellen Forester said. "Since when did you get to be such a feminist?"

Her chin juts out. "I'm not one of those feminists. But I know how men act."

"What should I do?"

"You could get Zeke Dibble to clean up. I'll bet he's handy with a broom. I imagine his wife sees to that." She gives a gleeful chuckle.

"All right. I'll figure something out, but the woman officer is one of the things I wanted to talk to you about. She doesn't seem all that friendly, and I want to be sure the town ladies don't take against her."

Her look is hard. "You mean because she's Mexican? We have plenty of Mexicans in town and nobody thinks much of it."

"I mean because she's a lady cop."

"You do get some ideas. If you watched a little more TV, you'd find out that half the programs are about lady police officers, so we're all used to it."

"You may be used to it on TV, but I don't know whether you're ready for it in Jarrett Creek."

"You want somebody to ask her to tea?"

"I don't know that tea is what I have in mind. But at least I'd like everybody to be friendly."

"The same way we were supposed to welcome Nonie Blake?"

With these words, I know we're down to the meat of what Loretta wants to talk about. "That was different."

"It sure was. People are getting riled up because you haven't caught the person that killed her. Folks are wondering if there's somebody dangerous on the loose that we ought to be careful of, and what the police department is doing about it."

I would dismiss her notion out of hand, but the truth is I don't know who it is they should be worried about. "Listen, has there been speculation that you think I ought to hear?"

"Of course everybody thinks it was probably Charlotte. She has that little boy and she has to have worried with Nonie around him. If I was her, I'd be terrified that Nonie would strike again. It would only take one slip. . . ."

"If she was worried that Nonie would hurt her boy, don't you think it would make more sense to send her on her way than to kill her?"

Loretta ponders the question. "You're right. But where would Nonie go? She's been in an institution for twenty years. They may have thought she couldn't make it on her own."

I hesitate, wondering whether to tell Loretta that Nonie wasn't actually in the institution for the past ten years. But I can't help thinking that if I don't know whether I should say something, it's probably better not to say it. I can always tell her later, but once I tell her I can't untell her. Better to change the subject.

"Let me ask you this. Have you heard anybody suggest that Nonie might have tried to blackmail anybody?"

"Blackmail them? What could she blackmail somebody about?"

"That's what I'm trying to find out. She hinted that she had information that somebody would pay her not to tell. That's blackmail, even if she didn't use that exact term."

"Hinted to who?"

"I'm not going to go into the particulars. Take my word for it. And if you hear anything like that, I'd appreciate your passing it on to me."

She finally takes a bite of her sandwich. Loretta loves to feed everyone else but has little interest in food herself. I've practically wolfed down my lunch, and she's barely touched hers. When she's finished with her nibbles, she dabs at her lips with a handkerchief. "The kids who knew her and are all grown up now say she was a sneak. That she was always snooping around trying to find out things about them. Cathy Langlois said Nonie was creepy. Is that what you mean?"

"Exactly what I mean." I get up to leave. "But I better get on back."

"Wait a minute. I had something to talk to you about, too."

I sit back down. "What is it?"

"You remember somebody cut some of my roses?" Her expression is grim.

I nod.

"They took flowers from two more people. Jess Lowden and Mary Alice Murray."

"Neither of them has any idea who did it?"

"How would they know? It happened in the night."

"Loretta, you're in luck. This sounds like a job for Deputy Trevino to take care of."

"Wait a minute. She doesn't know anybody here in town and won't know what to look for."

"That's right. Never hurts to have fresh eyes."

I still haven't heard back from Bruce Havranek, but this time I call him at work, and they put me right through to him.

"I didn't know you had called," he says. "I've been busy and haven't listened to my messages. It's always somebody wanting me to buy something." He's got a querulous voice that sounds like he uses it mostly for whining, like in his mind he's always the wronged party.

He grudgingly agrees that I can come by his place after he gets off work at 5 o'clock.

I phone the pharmacy in Tyler that issued the pills to Susan Shelby. They tell me she has a standing prescription and give me an address for her in Jacksonville, near Tyler, and a phone number. I call the number and get an answering machine. I don't leave a message. When I go to Rollingwood, I might go through Jacksonville and stop to find out more about her, like if she and Nonie Blake are one and the same person.

Bruce Havranek lets me into his place, which is shabby and cheaply furnished. He's a thin, hunched man who looks old, although he's probably not much past fifty. His hair is thin, and it's been a while since it was cut. Before I even get seated, he starts complaining. "I know this isn't a very nice place, but my ex-wife bleeds me dry. I barely have enough left over to pay my bills."

He motions me to sit on a red-, blue-, and silver-checkered sofa that would put your eyes out if you had to stare at it too long. "What is it you want from me?"

"This goes back a ways, to a babysitter your family had. Nonie Blake."

"The Blake girl? The crazy one?"

I had wondered if his wife might have called to warn him that I'd be asking questions, but he appears to be genuinely surprised.

"I don't know if she was crazy," I say, "but she had some issues."

"What about her? Last I heard she tried to kill her sister and got sent away." It seems that he hasn't kept up with the gossip in Jarrett Creek.

"She came home a couple of weeks ago and last week was found murdered."

He rakes his fingers across the top of his hair. "Oh, my goodness. But I don't know what that has to do with me. I haven't seen her since she was packed off to the crazy-house."

His words are so grating that I toss niceties aside.

"I want to know if, when Nonie Blake was your babysitter, she found out anything that she tried to use to blackmail you."

Right in front of my eyes his face sharpens until he looks like a weasel. "I don't know what the hell you're talking about."

"Don't play dumb. I have it on good authority that you were embezzling money from Gabe LoPresto. I'm wondering if Nonie found out what you were up to and tried to blackmail you."

"Ho!" The sound comes out as a growl. "Did my wife tell you that lie? Or was it LoPresto? Both of them made up all kinds of stuff. That was put to rest a long time ago. They were probably sneaking out together and cooked up this story. Why my wife goes on and on about it frosts me. If anybody belongs in the crazy-house, it's her."

"All I want to know is if Nonie Blake found out what you were up to and tried to get you to pay her off to keep quiet."

"How would she find out something like that, even if it was true, which it's not, no matter what my bitch of a wife says."

"According to people who knew Nonie, she was a snoop."

He's still got that sly look. "So you're going to try to claim that I was scared she'd come back here and tell on me and that I killed her to keep that from happening? That's ridiculous. I didn't even know she was back."

"Even if you didn't kill her, I want to know if she tried to blackmail you. I figure if she blackmailed you, she might have blackmailed somebody else, too."

"She did no such thing." The springs creak as he settles back in his chair.

"Maybe Nonie didn't know about the money you took. Maybe she found out something else. Did you have another secret she snuck around and found out about?"

He licks his lips. "No siree, she did not. At least if she did, she never told me. Way I look at it, the world's better off without her, so I don't know why the law would want to make such a fuss to find out who killed her anyway."

"Nonie never suggested that she knew something about you that you might want to pay to have kept quiet?"

It isn't as if I expect him to suddenly confess. My aim is to shake him up. A nervous suspect will sometimes blurt out something he hadn't intended to pass along. But if I read him right, there's nothing to tell. He's a weasel, but not a murderer.

CHAPTER 17

I'm glum as a lame dog the next morning when I slump into my chair at headquarters. I have to admit to myself that I'm almost at a dead end. I've found not a clue, not a person of interest, nothing to follow up on except going to Rollingwood, and I can't imagine what that's going to do to help me find out who killed Nonie. Even if it turns out she was using an assumed name, what difference would that make? She was killed here. Nonie's family has acted strange, and I have some general suspicion about them, but as for anything specific, I'm stuck. I'm not used to being in this position, and it makes me feel worthless. I've always managed to put together some kind of theory out of the information I come up with, but not this time.

When a car drives up outside and a woman steps out in uniform, I groan. I've completely forgotten about Maria Trevino again. Is my mind going? I've got to find something for her to do. She marches in before I've completed the thought.

"Good morning," I say. "Did you have any success finding a place to live?"

"I think I've found something." I don't know if she's glaring at me because the question is too personal, or if she just doesn't like small talk.

"Good," I say. And suddenly I have an idea.

"Let's move the rest of these things off your desk and then I have something I'd like you to tackle."

Now she does brighten up, her whole demeanor hopeful. "Not filing, is it?"

"There'll be some of that. But right now I have something else in mind."

We get all the boxes moved and stored in the corner. "You see there's got to be some filing done. And in case you think I'm responsible for this mess, I want you to know that the last chief got sick and wasn't able to keep up the way he should have. In other words, I inherited it."

She eyes the boxes with an expression that can only be described as leery.

"There're two things I want you to do. First, make a list of things you need for your desk, and before you come to work next time, go to the Walmart in Bobtail and get your supplies. Pens, paper, and whatnot."

"You don't have that here?"

"We'll pay for it, but no, we don't have much. I don't know what they told you, but this town went bankrupt several months ago and we're still clawing our way out from under. It means there's not a lot of money for extra supplies."

"You mean frivolous things like pens and paper." Do I detect a hint of teasing? I hope so.

"But here's what I want you to do now." We sit down, and I tell her about Nonie Blake's murder. "I don't mind admitting to you I'm fishing for answers. I need another brain on this case." I bring over the original file on Nonie and the psychiatric evaluation. "I want you to read over all this and see if you find anything that doesn't strike you right."

"Like what?" Her voice sounds cautious, as if she's not quite sure of her abilities, but her eyes have a spark in them that wasn't there before. She's got the drive to do the work, even if she's shy on experience.

I smile. "This isn't a test. I need another opinion. If you don't come up with anything, you're not doing any worse than I am. I'm grabbing for air here. The way it looks now, I'm worried that somebody's going to get away with murder." Something had been bothering me about the report, and I took another quick look at it earlier, but I couldn't find whatever it was. Maybe Trevino will come up with the answer.

"We shouldn't be handling this anyway. It ought to be up to the highway patrol or the Rangers."

I sit down, turning my chair to face her. "That may be true, in theory, but in the real world it doesn't always work that way. The Rangers can't get around to it right away, and when they do I don't see that they'll have much more to go on than we do. And I have one advantage. I know the people in this town and I know who to question and what to look out for." That isn't entirely true with the Blakes, but she doesn't have to know I'm fudging.

I realize she's laughing at me.

"What?"

"I don't want to make you mad, but they told us in training that you people in small towns are like that."

"Like what?"

"Thinking because you know everybody you ought to be able to solve cases by doing nothing but talking to people. They call it the 'good old boy' syndrome."

"Maybe they're right." I have to admit her words sting. "But until the Rangers come in and take over, we might as well try to figure it out." I nod toward the files I've handed her. "Maybe you can find a discrepancy there that I've missed."

"You're the boss." She says it like she doesn't really believe it.

While she reads, I get on the Internet and start trying to find out where Nonie Blake has been for the last ten years. Mostly I have to wade through articles and photos of the actress Winona Ryder. How the search engine can confuse Ryder and Blake, I don't know, but I suspect there's a publicist at work somewhere nudging computers to notice their actress.

Putting in her middle name, Lee, narrows it down a bit, but I still get a lot of false hits. But one entry does catch my eye. According to an east Texas name search website, there is a Winona Lee Blake living in a rental property in Jacksonville, Texas. I start searching to find out who owns the place, and suddenly things get odder. The home is owned by Susan Shelby—the name on the container of thyroid pills in the bathroom. Maybe I was right and Nonie really was using an alias.

"Did you notice this?" Maria interrupts my thoughts.

I get up and go to her desk. "What's that?"

"There's a discrepancy here between her height when she was examined by the psychiatric office and when she was autopsied. It's a whole inch."

Bingo. It slots right into the nagging in the back of my brain. At the time I'd read it, I'd thought of a possible explanation for it and meant to check it out. "I thought maybe it had something to do with the difference in her lying down and standing up."

She frowns. "I doubt it. Shall I call the coroner and ask?"

I have to rein myself in from saying I'll do it myself. "Sure. His number is on the autopsy report."

"I know it. I'll call him right now."

"I'll be back in a bit. I have somebody I need to talk to," I say.

She barely looks up as I leave. I head over to talk to Ellen Forester at her gallery. When I first thought up the idea of driving to Rollingwood, it was a random thought. Now it's clear that I need to go up to that neck of the woods. I want to talk to Nonie's psychiatrist at Rollingwood and go to Jacksonville to the address where Nonie Blake lived.

For once, when I stop by the gallery, Ellen isn't giving a class. I never guessed when she moved here and opened an art gallery and workshop that there were so many potential artists waiting for someone to unleash their hidden talent. She has a lively business in workshops, although how much art she sells, I don't know.

I catch her working on a watercolor. She drops her brush and gets up hastily to greet me, a flush rising in her cheeks. I don't take that personally. She blushes easily. "What brings you here?" she says.

"Remember when I said I might have to go to north Texas to find out more about Nonie Blake?"

"Yes."

"Turns out I do have to go, and I'd like you to go with me. We'll take the time to go by a couple of art museums in Fort Worth."

She grimaces. "I considered it. I really did. I wish I could, but I've got my classes to think of."

"Couldn't you cancel them for a day?"

Annoyance flashes in her eyes. "Men. Always think that the things women do isn't important enough to commit to. Suppose I asked you to shut down the police department for a day so we could take a little trip to Galveston?" She brings her hands to her mouth. "That sounds stupid. Of course giving art lessons isn't as important as policing. But why do men always assume women can drop what they're doing?"

"I'm sorry if I offended you." What I'm really thinking is, "men"? She probably means her ex-husband. But what does that have to do with me? What did I do to bring this on?

Now her face is bright red, and she looks like she could cry. "I didn't mean to jump on you. I guess I'm sensitive because Seth always used to dismiss anything I did as drivel. If he had something—anything—to do, it was more important than what I was doing."

I know better than to push this. I know how raw her feelings still are with regard to her ex-husband. "Look, it was an impulsive idea," I say. "I should probably go up and come back in one day anyway, and forget going to an art museum."

"It's not your fault. I'm trying to take myself as seriously as I want other people to."

"Let's don't worry about it. It's short notice, I know. We'll make a long-term plan sometime."

With that, I flee, leaving her looking bewildered, like I just asked her whether she'd rather die from drowning or being hit by a train.

If that weren't enough, I walk back into headquarters to find Truly Bennett, hat in hand, and Maria Trevino pacing the floor. They both speak at once.

"Wait." I hold up my hand. "Truly, what can I do for you?"

He glances at Maria out of the corner of his eye, and I wonder if they've had some kind of altercation, but I'm not going to ask. "Those cows they brought today?" he says.

"Yes." I had asked Truly to take care of the delivery of the cattle we bought at auction Sunday.

"They sent the wrong ones."

"What? How can that be? Are you sure?" Of course he's sure. There's no need to ask.

"I believe I know my cattle," he says without rancor.

"I know you do. Are all of them wrong?"

"Yes sir. For one thing, we bought a bull and there's no bull in the trailer."

I'm aware that Maria is looking at us like we're speaking in tongues. "Maria, I know you were trained in Houston, but where are you from originally?" I ask.

"I grew up in San Antonio. In the city," she adds in a dry tone.

"So you're not up on cattle," I say.

"That would be correct."

I grin and turn back to Truly. "Is the trailer that brought the cows gone?"

"No sir, I told the man driving it that it was the wrong lot and told him to go over to Town Café and get a meal, and I'd come and get you to sort it out."

"Give me a few minutes, and I'll come back to the house and take a look at the cows."

"Yes, sir." With one more furtive look at Maria, he scoots out the door.

"Now," I say to Maria, "what's up with you?"

"I'm mad at myself for doubting you. The coroner says you're right, that the one-inch difference could have to do with the position of the body when the measurement was taken." Her face is ferocious.

Good Lord, I've had to deal with two women in the last half hour with a bee in their bonnet. At least I have some knowledge of Ellen's background. "Maria, what led you to become a law enforcement officer?"

"What? Oh, that. I always wanted to be a cop. And I don't think of 'cop' as a bad word, either," she adds fiercely. "I can't tell you why, but it always appealed to me."

"Good. I expect there are all kinds of reasons for people wanting to be lawmen . . . and women," I add hastily. "We'll try to get you broken in right." I realize that she doesn't know who "we" are, so I fill her in on Bill Odum and Zeke Dibble, since she hasn't had a chance to meet them yet.

She nods when I describe Zeke. "I'm familiar with Officer Dibble's career. When they told me I'd be coming here, I looked up the people I'd be working with, and I checked out his law enforcement career in Houston and thought I could learn something from him."

I'm beginning to feel the slightest bit defensive around Maria Trevino. I'm a little jealous that she thinks she can learn something from Zeke and not me. I suspect she won't admire what I'm about to do. "You okay here for a little bit? I need to go take care of the situation with those cows."

"And leave me here, as new as I am?"

"Maria, this is a small town. I'd be real surprised if anything comes up that you can't handle. But if it does, call me on my cell phone. It'll take me three minutes to get here. And it's nearly noon anyway. Bill Odum will be in soon and you can rely on him."

I feel like a scalded cat and get out of there as fast as I can. As I drive away I remember that I still haven't hired anybody to come to headquarters to clean the place up.

Not only are the cows I've been sent the wrong ones, but they are a motley trio of heifers.

"I have to get on back," the driver says in an aggrieved voice. "I went and got some lunch like your man told me to, but I don't have time to hang around here all day. I'll come back to pick these cows up when it gets sorted out."

I know better than that. Once he leaves here, I'm stuck with the wrong cows, so I have to deal with it now. "You need to stick around while I call the seller."

As I listen to the phone ring, I say, "By the way, Truly Bennett here is not 'my man.' He's an independent contractor." Because Truly is black, I know he gets talked down to by some people, like this temporary driver, and it irritates me.

The phone number of the seller on the bill of sale has been disconnected, so I call the auction house. It takes a while, but eventually I track down the agent for the auction house who arranged the sales. At first he doesn't want to admit there was an error.

"Let me remind you," I say, "that discrepancies in cattle sales have roots in cattle-rustling laws. I know the laws don't involve hanging like they once did, but they still carry some pretty heavy penalties. The descriptions of the cows on this bill of sale don't match. But even more important, I bought a bull, and if my eyes serve me, none of these three has the equipment you expect in a bull."

Truly is trying to get my attention. "Hold on a minute," I say. "What is it, Truly?"

He holds up his cell phone. "Chief, you might tell him I got pictures of the cows we bought."

I do tell him, and that changes the conversation. "I hate to tell you this," he says, "but we've had a few other complaints arising from this sale. Why don't you go ahead and load up those three cows . . ."

I look over at the cows. Their heads are hanging down like they're pretty sure things are not going to go their way. I feel bad that they'll have to be loaded back into the trailer and hauled back to Navasota.

"Wait," I say. "Any chance I can buy these three cows in addition to the ones I bought at auction?"

Hearing my words, Truly rolls his eyes at me, then turns his back and walks a few feet away.

"I'm going to make a couple of phone calls and get right back to you."

"I don't mind telling you, I don't have time to while away with this," I say. "I need to hear from you now. I'm chief of police here and I've got a big situation I'm trying to handle."

"Chief of police?" he says, his tone flat. "I wasn't aware of that. I'll tell you what. I'll get back to you fast."

As soon as I'm off the phone Truly says, "Mind if I have a word with you?" He glances in the direction of the driver.

"No need. I know what you're going to say. These cows aren't worth a dime. But I can't load them back up. They need some recovery time." The cows are looking at me, and I swear they understood what I said and they've begun to look hopeful.

"All right. I might have known you'd have a soft spot. I'll put them out into the back corral." That's the small enclosure where we put a cow if it needs to be quarantined. It'll be close quarters, but they'll only be there a day or two while Truly makes sure they aren't carrying any contagious diseases.

The auction agent calls me back a lot faster than I thought he would. "The owner said he mixed up a couple of orders and if you'll throw in a little money for the three you've already got, he'll send the two cows and the bull right away." He mentions a figure I can live with.

"I'll send this man here who has the trailer to pick them up this afternoon, if he's willing."

"I expect that will work fine. The seller was eager to make amends."

Back at headquarters I explain to Maria Trevino that I'm off to Dallas tomorrow and tell her I'd like her to take on the case of the missing flowers.

"Is that really important?" she says with her perpetual scowl.

"Is it as important as murder? No, but sometimes things that wouldn't seem important to somebody in Houston is a big deal in a small town. Besides, it will give you a chance to meet a few people. Pay attention to Loretta. She knows everybody and she's the source of a lot of information that can help you from time to time. And she's a good person."

Trevino rolls her eyes. "You mean she's like a small-town CI?"

It takes me a second to realize that she means an informer. "Something like that."

CHAPTER 18

I spend the afternoon securing a warrant from a judge in Bobtail to see the records Rollingwood has on Nonie Blake. "You understand," he says, "up in Dallas they may tell you that I don't have any jurisdiction. If that happens, call me and I'll see if I can locate a judge to fix you up."

I keep hoping that Ellen will call to say she's changed her mind, but by the end of the day, I realize that's not going to happen.

Before I leave work, I consider whether I ought to call the Blakes to tell them I'm going to Rollingwood to get to the bottom of things there, in case they have anything else they want to tell me. But I decide I don't want them to know I'm going.

The next morning when I get on the road before eight o'clock, I realize that it's probably best that I'm alone. I don't know Ellen well enough to know how punctual she is, but I wouldn't have wanted to wait around. The psychiatrist I arranged to meet with said he'd have time at one o'clock. I want to be on time.

The drive to Dallas is only a few hours long, but it's boring. Mile after mile of scrubby land punctuated with a small town every now and then and a lot of billboards. I stop in Waco for coffee and a cinnamon roll that doesn't come close to the ones Loretta makes and am in the Dallas suburbs by noon. Rollingwood is on the west side of the city. Doctor Delphine said he'd meet me there.

The long gravel drive is lined with a boxwood hedge overhung with graceful trees. It's so elegant, you wouldn't know this is an institution. The front entrance is colonial style, with a white porch and impressive columns. Only the bars on the windows indicate this is anything other than a stately old building.

Inside, it's cheerful—the walls a soft yellow, hung with bright art.

As soon as I walk into the spacious entry, I see a central garden court-yard that has places for patients to sit outdoors with visitors. I go to the front desk and am ushered into the administration office. Mrs. Lannigan, the director, whom I talked to on the phone, greets me. She's a large, imposing black woman with a cordial smile. "Dr. Delphine said he might be a few minutes late and asked me to make you comfortable."

I ask her if she'll show me around, and she does so with the eagerness of someone trying to close a real estate deal. You'd think she personally knows every patient; an attitude I'll bet serves her well. This place can't be cheap, and I expect most of the people who pay to have their loved ones here won't stand for anything but the most attentive service. An exception being the Blakes, who don't seem to have cared one way or another.

"Did you ever find out what the mix-up was with Winona Blake?" she asks. "Why everyone thought she was still here?"

"Apparently back when she got out, she only let one family member know, and he didn't want to talk to her."

"That's a shame. I didn't know her, but it's always a disappointment when the family of a patient shuns them for being institutionalized. It isn't as if anyone wants to have a mental illness. And yet some people seem unable to get past the notion that a person with mental problems should know better."

A wiry man with a head of bushy hair bustles up, carrying a brief-case. "You must be Mr. Craddock. I'm Doctor Delphine. Maureen, is there a room where Craddock and I can talk?"

She says we can use her office; that she needs to make rounds of the facility. Delphine rushes ahead of me almost at a sprint. As soon as Maureen Lannigan closes the door behind her, he hoists his brief-case onto her desk, opens it, and takes out a file folder. He doesn't waste time on small talk.

"I looked over this last night after we talked. I didn't work with Ms. Blake myself, but the doctor who did, Dr. McBride, is retired, so I had to bring myself up to speed. What is it you want to know?"

He doesn't mention a court order to look at the files, so I don't either. "I told you that Nonie Blake was murdered and that I'm chief of police in Jarrett Creek, so I'm trying to find out what happened. I discovered that she might have been blackmailing somebody. I wondered if she ever mentioned anything like that in her talks with the doctor."

He's nodding. "According to the notes, she had a narcissistic personality with paranoia."

"Can you explain that to me?"

"It means that she had a pretty grand idea of herself. People like that think others are out to get them and that they are able to see through people's schemes—that's where the paranoia comes in—and that they have the right to be judge and jury."

He shuffles through the paper some more, reading here and there. "She talked a lot about people not being who everyone thought they were . . . you know, people pretending to be good people and finding out they have wicked secrets. That isn't unusual for her type of illness. And it may not mean she actually had information about anybody—it's a paranoid fantasy. I also see that her doctor said she showed signs of being a pathological liar."

"Signs?"

"It's not a very secure diagnosis. Very few patients are full-out pathological liars. Most of them lie when it's convenient, and some find it comes more easily than others. I gather that Winona was able to lie when it suited her and make it convincing."

"What kind of diagnosis did he give? There was some mention of her exhibiting signs of being a sociopath."

"That's a label that gets attached a little too freely, in my opinion. It's a harsh diagnosis, and I guess Dr. McBride didn't see any reason to go that far. He said she was somewhat disassociated, but his diagnosis was more in line with a borderline personality trait."

"What does that mean?"

"It can have a variety of manifestations. Like I said, Ms. Blake had a narcissistic streak and a bit of paranoia, and she was a liar. But what set her apart from the full-blown sociopath is that she did have a conscience."

"Did she ever seem sorry about what she did to her sister?"

"Not exactly. Dr. McBride indicated that Winona Blake thought she was doing the family a favor. I don't mind saying that's a little far-fetched, but it isn't the mindset of a sociopath."

"Any idea where she might have gone when she left here?"

"Dr. McBride noted that the Blake girl had made friends with someone who was here at Rollingwood the same time she was. Woman by the name of Susan Shelby."

Not an alias, then. A different person altogether. "Can you tell me anything about the Shelby woman?"

He shakes his head. "I've stretched the limits of legality by telling you what's in the Blake file, but even if I knew anything about Susan Shelby, I couldn't break that patient confidentiality. I can tell you she left here a few months before Winona Blake did."

I haven't been back to the Modern Art Museum in Fort Worth since before Jeanne died. We used to come up here together every couple of months when Jeanne's mother was still alive, and then a couple of times a year afterward. As soon as I walk in, I'm glad Ellen Forester isn't with me. The memories that come rushing back are so strong that I have to take a deep breath before I can go up to get my ticket.

I've never let our membership lapse, so when the young woman who takes my card sees the membership level, she jumps off her stool and says, "Sir, let me get the curator. He's going to want to welcome you."

"That's not necessary. I was in the area and thought I'd stop by. I can't stay long."

She's already around the desk and she comes up close and says,

"He'd have a fit if he knew you'd come and he hadn't had a chance to talk to you."

"I understand." What she means is he wants to find out if I've got any more money so he can move me up to a higher donor level.

To my surprise, I recognize the man who hurries up, hand extended. "You remember me?" he says. "Cole Hamilton."

"I certainly do. Cole, you've come up in the world."

"Yes, and I love this job." When Jeanne and I knew him, he worked at a big gallery in Fort Worth. "I went back to school and got a master's in museum curation and went to work at one of the smaller museums. Then I moved over here. I got this promotion last year. How's your lovely wife?"

I tell him she's been gone a while and that I haven't had the heart to come back since then.

"I am so sorry to hear that. She was a wonderful woman . . . and her mother, of course. They both had an intuitive eye."

And a big wallet. Jeanne's mother, as I recall, spent a lot of money at the gallery where Hamilton worked.

"You're going to have to let me buy you lunch and then show you a couple of things I know you haven't seen."

I had planned to sneak in, look around, and sneak out, but I find myself really glad to spend some time with Cole Hamilton. He's a natural for the job, remembering that Jeanne and I were partial to the California School artists. So we spend a little time in that section, which I realize now has been superseded by more contemporary work. But there's a Motherwell that I still think is one of his finest. And they have a Diebenkorn I've always liked. Then he takes me to the newest wing. Most of it doesn't appeal, but there's a piece by a man named Hodgkin that I'm not familiar with that I like very much.

Before I know it, it's late afternoon and I'm running behind. Before I head for Jacksonville, I call Truly Bennett, and he tells me this time the cattle that arrived were the right ones. "So that's one bunch he can't sell twice," he says. He hates a cattle cheat.

CHAPTER 19

I arrive at dusk and spend the night at a motel outside of Jacksonville, an unsatisfactory place that seems to be a rendezvous for various rowdies who keep me awake until the early hours. So I'm grumpy and badly in need of coffee when I pack up and leave the place at 7 o'clock. If I were so inclined, I'd crank up my radio and blast everybody out of bed before I wheel out of the parking lot, but my radio hasn't worked in years, so I have to make do with slamming the door of the truck, which doesn't yield me the same satisfaction.

The morning is redeemed by a diner that serves a loaded cup of coffee and a good plate of eggs. Then I'm off to find out what Nonie Blake and Susan Shelby have to do with each other.

Jacksonville is an old town in a beautiful setting among pine trees and surrounded by rolling hills. There's a big lake here that Jeanne and I visited a long time ago, but I won't have time to get out to see it.

I'm pulling up to the address I got from my Internet search for Susan Shelby when my cell phone rings. It's Maria Trevino. "Chief Craddock, I have something I need to tell you." I hadn't noticed in person, but Maria has a slight accent.

"What's up?"

"You might not like this, but I saw Doctor Roland Taggart's name in Winona Blake's file and I decided to go ask his opinion about the autopsy report."

"What do you mean, his opinion?"

"I mean he's a doctor and I thought he might read something into the autopsy report that you and I as laypeople wouldn't read into it."

How can I possibly explain to her that Taggart isn't likely to take the autopsy seriously, and that, as a doctor, he's fine for everyday things, but he scarcely counts as a forensics expert. "I think that's fine," I say. "I don't know that it will come to much."

"It did actually. That's why I'm calling."

That stops me in my tracks. "What do you mean?"

"He found something odd. You remember the coroner found evidence of a broken leg in the past?"

"Yes, I remember."

A woman walking her dog stops right next to the car and makes no secret of the fact that she wants to know what a man is doing sitting in his pickup in her neighborhood. She's pretty sure I'm up to no good.

"Doctor Taggart said he didn't remember anything like her breaking her leg when she was a girl. So I said maybe she broke it recently. He called the coroner's office and they went back over the notes and the coroner said it was obvious from the way it healed that she was a young girl when it happened."

I've been sort of dogged by the notion that Maria Trevino has a little more initiative than I feel comfortable with, but now that egotistical problem flies out the window. "Good work, Trevino. Any estimate of how old she was when it happened?"

"They said probably no more than ten years old. They can tell because there's a certain way the plates in the leg grow as a child ages."

"What do you make of that?" I say. Since she's the one who has found a little nugget, she should get a chance to run with it.

"It occurred to me that maybe the family didn't want people in town to know that she had a broken leg, and they took her somewhere else to have it set."

"No," I say slowly, my mind working furiously. "That's a good stab, but it makes no sense. They wouldn't have been able to hide the fact that she was in a cast. But the bigger problem is that the physical they did for the initial psychiatric report cited no evidence of past broken bones."

"Oh, you're right. But . . ."

"But what does that mean? I'm not sure yet."

"Yes, sir. You want me to go out and ask the Blake family if they can explain it?"

"No, I don't. Wait until I get back and we'll decide the best way to approach them."

The neighborhood I drove through getting here is middle class, with nice lawns and houses that are kept up, but the address I'm sitting in front of is a borderline block. The house is a duplex on a double lot, the two sides separated by garages. The place is painted the ugliest color of yellow I've ever seen, with brown trim that looks like mud smeared around the window and doorsills. The yard is fifty blades of grass shy of bare dirt, and a shade tree in the front yard has been allowed to shrivel. It's a big building. Probably each side of the duplex is a three-bedroom apartment.

I walk up to the "A" side of the duplex and ring the bell in vain. Then I knock, in case the doorbell doesn't work. Still no answer. When I knock on the "B" side, the door opens a few inches, and a wisp of a woman of about sixty peeks out at me.

I introduce myself. "Ma'am, are you by chance Susan Shelby?"

"No, sir."

"Does she live next door?"

The woman opens the door a little wider so I can see her. She cranes her head to look in the direction of the other duplex as if it might tell her who lives there. "I don't know the people who live there. Two women. I don't see much of them. I don't like to get too friendly with neighbors. You never know when they'll take advantage."

"Do you mind telling me who owns this place—who you pay rent to?"

She frowns and hesitates, leery to be too quick to answer, even though I told her I was a lawman. "I pay my check to a real estate office. It's called Ledford and Baker Realty. Their office is downtown." She frowns. "What's this about?"

"I was hoping your neighbor would be able to help with a matter I'm looking into."

"You said you're a police chief. Are they involved with criminals or something?"

"Not that I know of. Any reason you think they might be?"

"No, but like I said, I keep to myself. I don't think it does anybody any good to be poking in somebody else's business."

In a town that looks like it struggles for economic survival, Ledford and Baker Realty might be the most prosperous business in town, with a big new brick building that stands out from its meager surroundings. A marquee sign outside proclaims that it has been in business since 1959.

A man jumps up to greet me when I walk in. He's decked out in a black Western-style suit with wide lapels, a nipped-in waist, and white stitching outlining the edges. He's wearing pearl-gray cowboy boots and has his hair slicked back in a style that would have been appropriate for a movie set in the 1930s. "Glen Webb at your service," he says. He's from Tyler, I can tell. Natives of this area have a deep twang you don't hear anywhere else, like they're talking through their nose.

I tell him who I am and where I'm from. "I'm looking for somebody and my search has led me here."

"I hope I can help you," he says, the world "help" sounding like "hnnelp."

"I'm looking for two women, one by the name of Winona Blake and the other Susan Shelby."

"I don't know the Blake woman, but Ms. Shelby owns a couple of duplexes in town that we manage for her."

"She lives here?"

"Yes, she lives in one of the two duplexes." He goes over to a file cabinet and comes back with a folder that he puts on his desk. "Here's the address."

"I went by there this morning, and the woman who lived next door says she hasn't seen Ms. Shelby in a while. Have you talked to her?"

He shrugs. "No need to. I collect the rent and put it in her bank account. If the tenants need something, I take care of it and send her the bill."

"Seems funny that she'd get a manager if she only has a couple of properties."

"Some people don't like to mess with having to ask for rent and taking care of maintenance. That's where we come in."

"So you don't know anything about the Blake woman who supposedly lives with her?"

"No, I know most of the tenants. I get the contracts. But . . ." He frowns and starts flipping through the papers in the file. He shakes his head. "I thought maybe I'd forgotten the name on the contract, but I haven't. The place belongs to Ms. Shelby, so she can have anybody she wants living there without a contract."

"Do you have a work number for Ms. Shelby?"

"I do. She's an assistant manager out at the Walmart on the edge of town."

CHAPTER 20

The Walmart looks like every other big-box store: a big sprawling building with a huge parking lot that's only half full. Inside, I go straight to the office and ask to speak to the manager. "That's Mr. Sweet," the young girl at the window says. "I'll get him for you."

Mr. Sweet turns out to be a man who looks around twenty-five years old. "Barry Sweet," he says, sticking out a smooth young hand. "How can I help you?"

I tell him who I am. "I'm looking for one of your employees, Susan Shelby."

"Oh, that's a shame. Susan's out on vacation."

"Really? How long has she been gone?"

He blinks. "Let me look." He darts away from the window and disappears into an inner office. He comes back in a minute. "The master time sheet says she's been off for a couple of weeks. She'll be back next Monday. Anything I can help you with?"

"You know where she went?"

"I'm sorry, I don't know that."

I'm aware of the growing line behind me, but he doesn't seem inclined to take our business off to the side. "She got any friends here that I can talk to?"

He gets a funny look on his face. "Uh, I'll tell you what, let me take you back to the employee break room. Maybe somebody there can help you."

He comes out of the office area and leads me to the back of the store, through metal swinging doors and into a room with a couple of chrome-legged tables with folding chairs and a Mr. Coffee setup.

There's a vintage refrigerator at least fifty years old and a row of vending machines. A couple of older women in powder-blue uniforms come to attention with a wary eye at Sweet.

"I'm going to turn you over to these two ladies," he says. His eyes drop to the nametag of the nearest one. "Uh, Mrs. Barstow, this is . . ." he turns to look at me, and I realize he's completely forgotten my name.

"Samuel Craddock, chief of police down in Jarrett Creek."

Mrs. Barstow licks her lips. "What can I do for you?" She casts a fidgety eye to her boss.

"If you don't mind, I'll leave you," he says. "I've got a lot to take care of today."

When he's out the door Mrs. Barstow's companion says in a low voice, "Yeah, a lot to do. Playing those computer games. They say that's what he does all day."

"I'm wondering if either of you can tell me who might be friendly with a woman by the name of Susan Shelby."

It's like a door slams shut on both women's faces. Mrs. Barstow smooths her uniform. "I don't really know who might be a close friend," she says. The two women cut their eyes at each other.

"I take it she's not well liked here?"

Mrs. Barstow looks me up and down. "You could say that."

"Happens that way sometimes," I say. "Mr. Sweet said she's on vacation and I need to get in touch with her. I'm looking for somebody who can tell me where she might have gone."

They both look at me blankly.

"Anybody you can think of she might have told?"

"I suppose you could ask Nonie Blake," Mrs. Barstow says. "I believe they're friendly."

I try not to show how startled I am. "How might I get in touch with this woman, Nonie Blake?" I say cautiously.

Mrs. Barstow screws up her face. "I believe I saw her over in menswear today. Or was it the boys' department?"

"You saw her today?"

"This morning."

When I leave the two women I walk slowly toward the big sign that says "Boys/Men," my brain in turmoil. If Nonie Blake is here in Jacksonville, who is lying in her grave? I'm getting a very bad feeling that I know who.

I have no trouble recognizing Nonie Blake. She's a little heavier than her sister, Charlotte, and a little shorter, but they look so much alike, with their almond-colored eyes and light hair, that I would have known they were sisters. Approaching her, I feel like I'm walking up to a ghost.

"You're Nonie Blake?" I say.

Her eyes meet mine boldly. "Yes. Who are you?" A firm voice, bordering on aggressive.

"My name is Samuel Craddock and I'm the police chief of Jarrett Creek, Texas." I wait for her reaction.

"Jarrett Creek." She takes a step back, her face clouding over. She was holding a stack of neatly folded boys' shirts, and she sets them down so haphazardly that they topple over. "What do you want?"

"I need to talk to you in private."

"Has something happened to my mother or father?" I notice the formal words she uses for her parents.

"No. It's something else."

"I'm working. I can't walk away from my station without good cause. Even then, I'd have to talk to my manager. He's not going to like it. He doesn't like employees to take care of personal business during work hours." She has lowered her voice, and there's an urgent note to it.

"I can speak with Mr. Sweet if that would help."

"Not a great idea. I don't want to lose my job."

"This is pretty important."

Her eyes hold mine steadily. "Tell me right here. If a customer comes up, I'll have to take care of them, but as long as you're quick, it'll be okay."

"When was the last time you were in Jarrett Creek?"

She picks the shirts back up, hardly glancing at them. "I assume you know my story." She slots the shirts into an empty space on the table.

I nod.

"I haven't been back since I left when I was fourteen."

"I see. Well, someone claiming to be you came to Jarrett Creek and stayed with your family."

"Really?" She cocks her head like a little bird, but her eyes look more like a hawk's. "She claimed to be me? Why would somebody do that?"

"I hoped maybe you would have some idea."

"Me? How would I know? Why don't you ask her?"

"She was murdered after she'd been there a week."

"You're kidding!" She crosses her hands over her heart. Color rushes to her cheeks. "What happened? I mean, who killed her? And why?"

"That's what I'm trying to find out. Until five minutes ago, I thought it was you who had been killed. Everybody did."

She frowns. "You mean my mother didn't recognize that whoever it was, it wasn't me?"

"As I understand it, it's been a while since she saw you." Even to me, this sounds like a thin reply. The more I think about it, the more I realize that ever since the woman who called herself Nonie Blake was murdered, the Blakes have told me one lie after another.

"But still. You'd think she'd recognize her own daughter."

"Do you know a woman by the name of Susan Shelby?"

"Susan? Of course I do. We share a house. I mean, it's her place and I rent a room, but we're friends."

"How did you meet her?"

She raises her eyebrows. "I met her in Rollingwood, the place where my parents parked me after . . . you know."

"Why was she in Rollingwood?"

"She tried to kill herself, and her parents had her committed." She says it in an offhand way, as if it was an everyday occurrence.

"Miss?" A big woman with thick arms and legs and a look of permanent grievance, dragging a disheveled three-year-old boy, interrupts. "If you're not too busy, could you help me?" She glares at Nonie and at me, as if I'm guilty by association.

"Of course. What are you looking for?" Nonie is no mouse. Her voice is polite, but there's hint of steel in it.

The woman says she's looking for pants for her son. Nonie leads her to a nearby table. The woman takes her time, asking pointless questions and fingering one garment after another. Once or twice Nonie glances at me, her expression unreadable.

Eventually the woman is satisfied and drags the three-year-old off, carrying a stack of jeans and T-shirts. I'm wondering why she didn't get a cart for her purchases when Nonie says, "She comes in here for entertainment. She's here at least twice a week and never buys anything. Drags that kid around like a rag doll, lets him play in the toy department, and makes work for everybody."

"Doesn't seem all that entertaining."

"Tell her that."

We watch the woman toss the stack of goods a few tables away and keep walking. Nonie lifts an eyebrow. "Where were we?"

"We were talking about Susan Shelby."

"Why do you want to know about her?"

"I have reason to believe she's the woman who was killed."

"Susan?" She jerks her head in what I take to be a nervous tic. "No way. Why would she claim to be me?"

"That's what I need to find out. She didn't tell you she was headed down around Jarrett Creek?"

She shakes her head, her cheeks flaming. "She's supposed to be on vacation in Corpus. You know, Padre Island."

"Did she have a reservation somewhere?"

"I don't know. I assume so, but she didn't tell me the details of her trip."

"Would you mind if I take a look at her belongings in your house?"

She hesitates. "Just hers?"

Strange question. "Yes, of course. I can get a warrant if you prefer."

"Can I be there to watch you? I mean, what if it isn't her? Why do you think it's her?"

"I found something at your folks' house with her name on it." And now that I'm thinking about it, I wonder why she got her prescription filled at a pharmacy in Tyler if she worked at Walmart.

"What was it you found?"

"Let's talk about that when I come over later. What time do you get off work?"

"This is a short day. I get off at four. Tomorrow I have to work until nine."

"I'll meet you out front at four."

"No, there's a back employee entrance. My car is parked back there. I'll meet you there and then I can lead you to the house."

I go into town and find a coffee shop where I can have some lunch. I'm still unsettled from finding out that Nonie Blake is alive. And I'm increasingly angry about the lies the Blakes have told me. I don't believe that Adelaide Blake could have thought that Susan Shelby was her daughter. They've been playing me for a sucker.

As I'm eating my lunch, I realize there's something else that has to be done. The medical examiner has to be notified that the wrong person is buried in Nonie Blake's grave. As soon as I finish lunch, I call the medical examiner's office. When T. J., the coroner, comes on the line, I say, "We've got a problem."

"Those are words to chill the heart. What kind of problem?"

"The woman we buried as Nonie Blake? She's not Nonie."

"What? How do you know?"

"I just talked to Nonie Blake."

"Who the hell did we bury? And how come the family identified her?"

"That's what I'd like to know. I'm in Jacksonville right now, but tomorrow I'll be talking to them. Let me ask you something. By law do you have to dig up the remains?"

He's quiet for several minutes. "That's going to depend on who we buried and what her relatives have to say."

"First I have to find them."

CHAPTER 21

Following Nonie's old Toyota Celica to her house, I try to imagine why Adelaide and Charlotte misidentified Nonie. I remember John's confused insistence that "she's not my daughter." If he knew it, they must have known it, too. Why pretend otherwise? Why has Adelaide told me one lie after another?

The front door of Nonie's place opens directly into the living room, a room cluttered with mismatched furniture that focuses on a giant TV perched on a sturdy table flush against the wall. Every surface is crammed with magazines and knick-knacks. A bowl containing a few pieces of popcorn and a glass with a few inches of clear liquid sit on the coffee table in front of one of the chairs. The house smells stale, as if the windows haven't been opened for a long time. The air-conditioning is set so it's cold, but it also feels damp. There's something discouraging about the room. I imagine the two women sitting here night after night fighting over which TV show to watch. They're young, but the place feels old.

Nonie has me wait in the living room while she changes clothes. I take a look at the numerous photos in the room, recognizing Susan Shelby as the woman I only saw when she was dead. But I also notice that Nonie and Susan look a good bit alike. Nonie's face is a little narrower, but they both have dark, round eyes set slightly close together. They both wear their hair chin length in a cut so similar that I wouldn't be surprised if they got their hair cut by the same person. Most striking, and for some reason it gives me a shiver, both of them have their mouths quirked in a smirk that makes them look like they're up to something.

I pick up one photo in which the two of them are standing side by side at a lakefront. They're both wearing jeans and T-shirts and grinning. The casual observer could mistake them for sisters—or at least cousins. It makes me reconsider whether Adelaide could have mistaken Susan Shelby for her daughter.

"That picture was taken out at the lake last spring." Nonie has snuck up on me, and I'm startled.

"Lake Jacksonville?"

"Yes. We rented a cabin there for Easter weekend."

"Looks like you were having a good time. You were pretty good friends?"

"We got along okay." She plucks the picture from my hand and sets it back on the table.

"How long have you lived together?"

"Since I left Rollingwood. It was convenient. Cheaper and safer."

"You ever get on each other's nerves?" I'm wondering why she doesn't seem particularly cut up at news of her friend's death.

"I guess everybody does sometimes." She shrugs.

"She owned this place and you paid rent?"

Annoyance flashes in her eyes. "You ask a lot of questions, don't you?"

"It comes with my job."

She sighs and rolls her shoulders like she's trying to relax. "Yes, I paid her rent, but she didn't charge me much. She was fair. More than fair."

"How did you happen to get together with Susan after you got out of Rollingwood?"

"She helped me get out. When we were inside, I told her that my parents had me declared incompetent so I had to stay there. Several weeks after she was released, she came back to visit and told me she had looked into it, and I was old enough to apply to have my parents' declaration nullified if my doctor would certify me as fit. I knew he would. I wasn't crazy—I made a mistake, that's all. Susan told me that when I got out, she'd get me a job and I could split the rent here with her."

"You've been working at Walmart all this time?"

"No, Susan's folks had a stationery store in town and we both worked there until a couple of years ago when they died." While we talk, her fingers play over the photos on the table, and she stops here and there to look at one.

"What happened to the store after they died?"

"She inherited the store, but she didn't want to run it, so she sold it. She thought it would sell for more than it did. She was hoping not to have to work." Nonie has a nervous tic that makes her jerk her head occasionally, like now. "That's why she went to work for Walmart. She worried about money."

"Do you know who inherits this place with her gone?"

Anger flashes in her eyes. "Why do you want to know that?"

"I'm wondering what will happen to you, if you'll have to move."

"That's not it. You're asking who inherits because you think that's a motive for killing her, don't you? You think somebody would kill her for a couple of measly rental houses? That's stupid. Anyway, I don't know who inherits. All I know is it won't be me."

"Are you sure?"

"I'm not her blood relative, so why would she put me in her will? I hope whoever inherits will let me buy this place so I don't have to move."

"You know how to contact any of Susan's kin?"

"No." She has turned surly. "I mean, I know she has some relatives, but I don't know how to find them."

"They'll want to be notified of her death."

"I doubt if any of them will care much that she's gone. She was like me, the black sheep of the family. I can't say we had a lot in common, but we did have that. But of course if they find out she died, they'll fall all over themselves to get hold of her property."

I get the feeling that Nonie thinks that if no one knows Susan is gone, she can go on living here, paying rent, and everything will be fine.

"Maybe we could take a look at Susan's room now."

Unlike the living room, Susan's bedroom is light and airy and hyper-feminine. The carpet is a light blue, and the bedspread is a riot of blue and pink flowers. The bed is piled with extra pillows all in pink and blue, and with a fluffy blue teddy bear in the center. There's a powerful smell of potpourri, which makes me feel claustrophobic.

"Frou frou," Nonie says in a flat tone. "She was into girly stuff." She wanders over to an ornate white dressing table set with bottles of cologne and all kinds of makeup, and picks up one of the perfume bottles and sniffs it.

I walk over to the chest of drawers and pull out the top one. Lingerie. I open a couple of the dresser drawers, but they're full of cosmetics—more than seems necessary for one person. I found hardly any cosmetics in her room at the Blakes' house.

I look around for anything that might contain business effects, but this is all personal. "Does she have a desk somewhere?"

"Yes, it's in the guest room."

"I'd like to take a look at it."

For a second I think she's going to balk, but then she shrugs. "I suppose that's okay. It's not like she's going to care."

A computer sits in the middle of the desk. I open the lid and hit the "on" button. It stays off, and I see that it isn't plugged in. I find the cord and plug it in, aware of Nonie's vigilance.

"You have a computer?" I ask.

She shakes her head.

"I thought all young people these days had computers."

"Too risky. I don't like having all my business on the Internet. If you get hacked, you're screwed."

While I look through the history of Susan's computer use, Nonie sits in a chair at the side of the desk watching my every move. I find that Susan did a lot of online window-shopping. She was particularly interested in jewelry. Her e-mail is full of ads, although she does have a correspondence with someone named Betty Corcoran. "You know who Betty Corcoran is?" I ask Nonie.

She sniffs. "Some lady Susan knew from when she was in high school."

"Where did she go to high school?"

"She grew up in Tyler. But Betty moved back East. I don't know why she talks to her all the time. They haven't seen each other in I don't know when." I detect a bit of resentment in Nonie's voice. Jealousy maybe.

I open one after the other of the e-mails and find that they consist mostly of gossip about people they knew in high school. But one of the last ones Susan sent to her friend says, "I'm going to come out to see you before too long, if you really mean it." The next one says, "I can't wait. I've never been anywhere. Virginia sounds so pretty."

"Did you know Susan was planning to go visit Betty?" I turn to look at her when I ask the question and am surprised to see that her expression is enraged. She's biting her knuckles. When she sees me looking, she yanks her hand away and immediately shuts down her expression.

"Why shouldn't she?" she says. She gives a ghost of a smile. "Of course now that won't happen. I guess I ought to write to Betty and tell her what happened, but I never met her, so I don't exactly know what to say."

"She'd probably appreciate knowing."

"Yeah, you're right. I'm going to do that." The look that accompanies this declaration is cold. I'd be very surprised if she has any intention of following through.

I go through the desk drawers and find an accordion file that contains memorabilia from when Susan was in high school—report cards and a few photos of classmates. In the same drawer there's a picture of her with two people Nonie identifies as Susan's parents. In another photo there are other people posing with the parents. "I wonder if these are aunts and uncles?" I say, passing the photo to Nonie.

"I don't know." She barely glances at it and hands it back.

Someone has written out the names of everyone in the picture on the back of it. I jot down the names. "Mind if I take this photo for now?"

She hesitates for several seconds. "I guess it's okay."

The rest of the desk yields nothing that would tell me why Susan was in Jarrett Creek and, more particularly, why she went to see Nonie's family.

I get up. "Did you and Susan ever have any discussions about your family?"

"Why would we do that? She knew I didn't have anything to do with them. And she knew why." Her arms are folded, and she's rubbing her hands along them briskly, as if she's cold.

"Did she ever suggest that you get in touch with them?"

"No. She knew I wouldn't."

"I spoke to your brother Billy. He told me you called him when you first left Rollingwood."

"Yeah, I called him. He told me that I wasn't welcome back there." Her voice is neutral, but I'm beginning not to trust that neutrality.

"When Susan showed up and claimed to be you, though, they welcomed her."

The smirk again. "Really? Someone killed her. I wouldn't call that a welcome."

"Your sister told me she tried to get your folks to let you come back. That's at least one person on your side."

She snorts. "Why would she do that, after what I tried to do to her? Wouldn't she be scared I'd hurt her kid?"

"She said you were so young that you couldn't have meant to kill her."

She stares at me. I'd love to know what is going on behind her facade. I read people pretty well, but Nonie has an uncanny ability to hide her emotions. "She doesn't know anything about me."

"I expect you got a lot of therapy while you were in Rollingwood. Did you ever get a clear idea of what you had in mind when you tried to hurt your sister?"

Nonie's lip curls as if she is disdainful of this whole line of questioning. "I didn't need any therapy to figure it out."

"I'm surprised to hear that. You were pretty young to do something so drastic. Do you mind sharing your thinking with me?" I don't expect her to, but it doesn't hurt to ask.

She stands up abruptly, as if she's at the end of her patience with me. "She bugged me."

"She bugged you? That's all? You tried to kill your little sister because she bugged you?"

She glares at me. "She wouldn't keep her nose out of my business. That's all I have to say about it. I've spent enough time with you, so you might as well be on your way."

"Wait." I say it softly, not wanting to butt up against her so that she shuts down. "There's something else I need to ask you."

Hands on her hips, she looks like she's ready to kick me out, but then she drops her hands to her sides and straightens her shoulders. "What?"

"The question came up of whether a man might have interfered with you in some way. Did that happen?"

She begins to snicker. "What in the world made you think so?"

"Did one of your teachers bother you? One of the men in the families you babysat for? Your brother? Your daddy?"

Her eyes have softened with amusement, but they turn hard again. "Didn't happen. I don't know where you got that idea, but it's plain wrong."

"There was another suggestion . . ."

"No! I don't know where you're getting these ideas, but they're stupid."

"I'll tell you where I got the ideas. From things that Susan Shelby said to people. She was pretending to be you and she indicated that she was plotting to blackmail someone. Where would she get a notion like that unless it was from you?"

She's shaking her head, and then she puts her right hand up, scout's honor style. "I swear to you I have no idea where she got anything like that."

"Nothing from when you two were in the hospital together?"

She looks at me with what I swear is pity. "I don't even know for sure that it's Susan who was there with my family. You say the woman looked like Susan, but my family said she looked like me. I think you all ought to get your stories straight. Now I'm sorry, but I'm done here." This time she doesn't wait for me to stop her but leaves the room. I follow her into the living room.

"I appreciate your time," I say. "Think over what I said about getting in touch with your family."

She shrugs.

"One last thing. I mentioned that I found a prescription that belonged to Susan Shelby—for thyroid medication. Do you know why she would have gone to Tyler to have it filled rather than filling it at Walmart, where she works?"

"Susan didn't like people to know her business. That's another way we were alike."

I leave feeling as if I've been in a rabbit hole. Nonie thinks that she was generous to me with her time, and I suppose she was. So why do I feel as if I've come away empty? From the photo I found in Susan's desk, I have names of people who may be her relatives, but as for Nonie's relationship with Susan, I'm none the wiser.

CHAPTER 22

It's too late to go to the courthouse to track down the people in the photo I found in Susan's desk, so I go to the police department. Headquarters is away from downtown in a building that looks like it was built using leftover money. It's a motley collection of dun-colored rectangles that look more like a storage warehouse than a police department. It takes me a minute to find the front door, which is hidden around the side. I wonder what would happen if somebody was being chased and hoped to find help in the police department. I walk up to what looks like a temporary ramp into the front area, which is not only deserted but is completely bare. I call out, and a portly officer dressed in khaki and chewing on a toothpick wanders out from wherever he was hiding.

"Help you?"

I tell him who I am, and he says his name is Bart Cleveland.

"I'm trying to find some folks. Wonder if you know any of these people." I show him the photo I found in Susan's desk and turn it over to the back where the names are written.

He squints at the photo and the names and shakes his head. "Don't know any of them. They don't look like criminals." He smiles.

"No, they're relatives of a woman who lives in Jacksonville." I remind myself that Jacksonville is ten times bigger than Jarrett Creek. "Would you happen to have a computer I could use to try to locate any of them?"

"Come on back." He leads me down a hallway to a large room crowded with desks. The walls are covered with notices and crime-scene photos and white boards scribbled with information. "You can use my computer." He clicks to a site that has names and addresses of residents.

To my surprise I find out that all three of the couples from the photo have addresses right here in Jacksonville: Henry and Nancy Shelby; Alice and Robert Johnson; and Louise and Frederick Kellen.

I thank Bart Cleveland and go on my way. Seems funny to me that he doesn't ask me why I want to find these people. Come to think of it, when I told him who I was he didn't even ask to see my badge.

It's after seven, and I don't want to disturb people in the evening, but I also don't want to be here all day tomorrow questioning the relatives. I'll call now to find out if any of them will agree to talk to me tonight.

I start with the Shelbys since they have the same last name as Susan. Henry Shelby sounds guarded when I mention Susan's name. "We haven't seen Susan in a long time. I don't know that I'd be able to give you much information that would help you." I don't want to break the news that Susan is dead over the phone, but it may come to that if I can't persuade him to see me.

"Are you her uncle?"

"Yes, her daddy's brother."

"And you had a couple of sisters?"

He pauses. "How do you know that?"

I'm beginning to think people in this part of the country have a natural tendency to caution if not downright paranoia. It doesn't seem that threatening for me to know that he has sisters, and yet he's suspicious. "I'm investigating a matter, and I ran across a photo that showed three couples." I read off the names.

"You know, you say you're a chief of police, but I believe before I say anything more, I need to see some identification and find out what you've got in mind here."

He suggests that I come by after eight o'clock that evening. "We're fixing to sit down to supper, and we should be done by then."

I realize that I don't have a place to stay tonight, since I'd planned to go back this afternoon. That was before I discovered Nonie Blake alive and kicking. I stop at a service station and find there's an express motel not too far from where I'll be, so I call and make a reservation for tonight. Then I call Truly Bennett and ask him to look in on the cows tomorrow morning.

Henry Shelby is bald and has a face as stern as a Baptist preacher. After I've shown him my badge and ID, he allows me into his home. His wife, Nancy, a tiny, pinch-faced woman with a helmet of gray hair, is sitting in the living room in front of a television set, tuned to a quiz show, with the sound muted.

They offer a cup of coffee, which I decline, and a chair that looks to be the least comfortable in the room, a wooden chair that doesn't go with the rest of the matching upholstered furniture. I suspect they dragged it in here specifically for my visit, so I wouldn't linger. I wonder if they are always inhospitable, or if they are feeling that way because of the subject matter.

"Now what's this all about?" Shelby says, settling onto the sofa next to his wife.

"I hate to break the news to you, but it looks like Susan Shelby has been killed."

"Oh, no. That's a shame. What happened? Was she in an accident?" More curious than distressed.

"No, she was visiting the town where I'm chief of police and somebody killed her."

"She was murdered?" Nancy reaches for her husband's hand. "That's awful. Did you find out who did it?"

"Not yet. I only figured out her identity a few hours ago. One of the reasons I wanted to talk to you is to try to get some background on Susan."

"I don't see how we can be of any help to you," Shelby says.

"Why is that?"

"We didn't have any kind of relationship with her," he says.

"When was the last time you saw her?"

He turns to his wife. "What do you think, Mother, five years?" I've always thought it was odd for a man to call his wife "Mother."

"Oh, longer than that. Celia's been gone that long. That's Susan's mother," she explains to me.

"Thereabouts anyway," Henry says.

"I have a photo here and I'd like to see if you can identify her from it." Nancy Shelby clutches her neck. "You mean a picture of her dead?"

"I'm afraid so."

"Oh my."

I pull the photo out of the envelope I've brought and hold it out to them. Nancy clutches her husband's hand and peers at it. "What do you think, Henry?"

"It looks something like her. Like I said, we haven't seen her in quite a while." They thrust the picture back at me.

"You had more contact with her when her folks were alive?"

"Yes, when she was a youngster we knew her better."

"Can you tell me if she broke her leg when she was young?"

Henry looks surprised at the question, but he nods. "Fell out of a tree. I guess she was around six. Why is that important?"

"The autopsy mentioned it."

"Autopsy? Who ordered an autopsy?"

"In a suspicious death, the state is required to do one."

"I see. This is all very strange. I don't know how we can help you. What else do you need from us?"

"Susan lived close by. Was there a particular reason you weren't friendly?"

"I wouldn't say we weren't friendly," Henry says. The couple exchanges uncomfortable glances. "We don't have anything in common with her, though, the kind of life she leads."

"What kind of life do you mean?"

"We're good Christian people, and Susan chose a different path," Nancy says. "It like to have done her mother in."

"I don't know quite what you mean."

"She didn't live a regular life."

"I see." There's code here, and maybe it will become clearer as we talk.

"I have a question of my own," Henry says. "What was she doing in the town you live in? Jarrett Creek, you say? Who was she visiting?"

"Yes, Jarrett Creek. She was visiting the family of the woman she shared a house with, Nonie Blake."

"What was she doing with them?" Henry says.

This is where it gets a little dicey. "She was posing as her roommate."

Nancy gives a little laugh. "That makes no sense," she says, her tone sharp. "Was the roommate there, too?"

"No. Do you know the roommate?"

"We didn't want to meet her. We don't hold with that kind of life."

It suddenly comes clear what the problem is. "You think they were a couple?"

"We can't say for sure," Henry says. "We didn't pry. But we thought the whole setup was strange. I mean that she decided to let that woman live with her. We didn't think it was a good idea. The woman had been in a mental hospital for trying to kill her sister."

"I sure wouldn't want to live with somebody like that," Nancy says.

"How did you find that out?"

"Susan's mother told me, that's how." Henry speaks sharply. "Celia was scared to death that Susan would be killed in her sleep."

"As I understand it, Susan had spent time in the mental institution, too."

Henry shifts uncomfortably. "It wasn't the same thing," he says firmly.

"I understand Susan was sent to Rollingwood because she tried to kill herself, is that right?"

Henry rears back in his chair. "Who told you that? She was there because she attacked somebody in school. She claimed the girl hit her first, but witnesses said Susan did all the attacking." Interesting. Was Nonie lying when she told me Susan had tried to kill herself—or did Susan lie to Nonie?

Nancy chimes in, "If one of our kids had done something like that, they wouldn't have been able to sit down for a week. They would have had to deal with Henry." She nods at her husband.

"That's right," he says. "And they would have had to come straight home from school for the rest of the year. We didn't put up with any shenanigans. Not like Celia. Instead of punishing Susan, Celia decided to send her to that Rollingwood place where they'd fuss over her and ask her about her feelings." His face is getting red, and his voice has risen.

"Daddy, there's no need for you to get all riled up." Nancy leans over and pats her husband's knee. "Say what you want," she says to me. "But Henry's right. Our kids knew better than to cause trouble."

Despite Henry's assessment of Rollingwood, I suspect Celia didn't send her there to be coddled but to avoid having her sent to a juvenile detainment center.

"Do you know if she ever had problems with anybody after she got out of school?"

Again a look passes between the Shelbys. "Different kind of a problem," Henry says. "Celia told me that there was somebody stalking Susan for a while."

"Stalking her? You mean following her?"

"All I know is what her mamma told me. She said this woman claimed that Susan borrowed money from her and never paid it back and that she was bound and determined to get Susan to pay up."

"What finally happened?"

"Celia paid her off. Said she didn't think for one minute that the woman was telling the truth, but she was afraid the woman would hurt Susan."

"You don't happen to know the name of this woman, do you?"

Henry shakes his head. "Wouldn't remember it even if she'd told me. But I'll tell you one thing—the same thing I told Celia. I didn't doubt for one minute that Susan borrowed that money. She was always careless with money and seemed to think the world owed her a living."

I get a tingling echo of Skeeter's assessment that Nonie, or rather Susan, seemed to think she was "owed."

"She did all right for herself, though," I say. "I understand she owned a couple of properties."

"That came from Celia and Dusty, her folks. They were hard-working people. They put money away for their old age. Shame neither one of them lived long enough to enjoy it."

"Susan was the only child?"

"Yes. Celia wanted more kids but couldn't have any and that's why she spoiled Susan."

"Do you know if Susan has stayed in touch with any of her other relatives?"

"If she kept up with anyone, it would be my sister Louise," he says. "She and Susan got along better because her ways are a little more free-thinking than mine."

Now I have to approach the delicate part of the conversation. "There is a matter that her relatives are going to have to deal with."

"What's that?"

No matter how many times I've rehearsed this in my head, I haven't figured out a good way to say it. I explain that the body was misidentified and subsequently buried in the cemetery in Jarrett Creek.

"What do you mean, misidentified?"

"Nonie Blake's family identified the body as Nonie."

Both of them speak at once. "Who are these people? What's wrong with them? How could they not know if it was their own relative?"

"They hadn't seen Nonie in twenty years, and the two women looked something alike."

The next morning I go to see Louise Kellen, Susan's aunt. She lives in a small house on a tree-lined street with several older, eccentric residences. This one looks like it could be a gnome's house, with little stone sculptures in the front yard surrounded by a wild overgrowth of greenery.

The room Louise shows me into couldn't be any more different from her brother's house. The walls are painted in bright colors and covered with art posters and quirky paintings and family photos. The furniture is a comfortable mish-mash of wicker and cushions.

"She was an unsettled child," Louise says. She's dressed in a long colorful skirt and a kind of lacy black blouse and big hoop earrings that make her look like a gypsy or a throwback to the '60s. Her hair is long and liberally sprinkled with gray, but her eyes are lively and her wrinkles are smile wrinkles rather than the kind you get from pouting. "I always thought it would have been better if I had been Susan's mother. Celia didn't seem to know what to do with her, although goodness knows she tried. She and Dusty."

"Henry said she got in trouble in school—attacked someone—and that's why she was sent to Rollingwood."

"That's right. I wasn't living here at the time. My husband and I lived out near San Francisco, and when he passed away I moved back."

"Did Celia ever talk to you about the attack?"

"I didn't ask, because it didn't matter what really happened, she always stuck up for Susan. She would have told me it was the other person's fault, no matter what."

"It must have been a pretty violent attack for her to have been sent away to a mental institution."

She looks sad. "Even though I didn't talk to Celia, I do know what happened—at least what the newspaper said. Henry gave me the clipping. It said a girl had been teasing her and she went after her with a baseball bat. The girl ended up with brain damage."

"Did you ever visit Susan in Rollingwood or correspond with her?"

"I feel so guilty that I didn't reach out to her. I apologized when I moved back, but by then she had grown a thick skin and she wasn't all that easy to talk to."

"You have children?"

"Two, grown now of course. One of them in Los Angeles—he's an actor—and my daughter lives in Chicago. She married a lawyer and moved there. She's got a couple of little ones that I see as often as I can."

When I phoned Louise this morning, I found that Henry had already alerted her to the fact that I'd be calling, and he had told her what had happened to Susan. When I first came in and showed her the photo of Susan for identification, she cried a little and has held onto it since then.

"Did your kids get along with Susan?"

She sighs. "My kids only met her a few times, and I'll be frank with you, they didn't like her much." She picks at her skirt, eyes averted.

"Any particular reason?" I wouldn't normally ask that, but I have a feeling she's holding something back that she'd actually like to divulge.

"They said she didn't talk nice. I asked them what they meant because I'd never heard them say anything like that, and they said she cursed a lot and . . . that she talked dirty sex talk."

"Do you know if she ever had trouble with boys?"

Her smile is rueful. "I'm not sure she was into boys. I don't know how to describe it; I think she wasn't inclined that way. You know what I mean?"

"Of course. Is that part of what bothered your kids?"

She sighs. "I don't think so. I think it was more the language she used. I figured she was trying to shock them, but some of the things she said . . ."

"Did you tell her mother?"

By now her face is bright red. "No, and I probably should have. But how do you tell somebody something like that about their own child?" She pushes the photo back across the coffee table to me.

"Did Celia ever tell you what Susan's psychiatrist diagnosed?"

"No, and with her and Dusty both gone I expect all those papers were thrown out."

"Did you see Susan at your sister-in-law's funeral?"

Louise goes still. "I didn't go to the funeral. None of us did. Susan didn't tell us Celia died until after the burial. I have to admit it was the only time I was ever really mad at her. She said Celia didn't want a funeral, that she wanted to be buried in a quiet graveside ceremony. I know that was just plain nonsense."

"Susan's folks died young."

"Yes. Both died in their fifties. Dusty went fishing with a friend and had a heart attack. They were so far out on the lake that by the time the friend got the boat back, it was too late. I think when Dusty died, Celia gave up. She died a year later. They said it was ovarian cancer, but I think she died because she didn't want to live anymore."

I approach the matter of the wrongful burial, and, unlike her brother, Louise is distressed. "We've got to bring her home. I feel like we all failed her. There was something wrong with her, and we should have figured out how to get her help. The least I can do is make sure she gets buried among her own people."

I've never been so glad to get back to Jarrett Creek, even though I've got a lot to tackle. All the way home, I plotted how I'm going to approach the Blakes. Although Susan and Nonie looked alike, I still can't help thinking Adelaide would have known that Susan Shelby was not her daughter, even after all these years.

The bigger question is what Susan Shelby intended when she came here. Were she and Nonie up to something together? And if so, exactly what was it?

Finding that Nonie Blake is still alive and that the dead woman is someone else entirely is something of a break in the case, but I still feel skittish about whether I'm going to be able to gather enough facts to figure out who actually killed Susan Shelby. There are no physical clues to speak of, so I have to rely on a prod here, a push there, a hunch, and hard listening. Is that enough? If one of the Blakes did the killing, all they have to do is continue to stonewall. But I've found that isn't always easy for people who commit crimes. Many of them seem to need to push their luck. Is it guilt that drives them to blab a little more than they should? Is it overconfidence?

I think that deep down most of us are pack animals, like dogs and wolves, uncomfortable with being outcast. Murder sets the perpetrator out of kilter with his community. That's what I have to play for—finding out how this crime put somebody at odds with others. Investigating a crime isn't about leaning on one person right away. It's a matter of getting a few facts from one person, then another, and building a picture of what happened and hoping to drive the criminal to make a slip, because at heart he wants back into the pack.

CHAPTER 23

I'm up at dawn and, after brewing a cup of coffee, I head down to the pasture to visit my cows. When I left, the three "extra" cows that were trucked in by mistake were in my two holding pens. Now I see that Truly has rearranged everything. He cobbled together a temporary enclosure for the scruffy cows and put the two cows I originally bought in one of the permanent pens. In the other pen is the fine-looking bull. I'm not one to give human traits to cattle, but if I were, I'd say this bull looks like he's mad at the world.

My communion with the bull is short. I don't have time to sweet talk him for long, just say a few words so he gets used to the sound of my voice while he recovers from the trauma of being trucked over here. You wouldn't think as sturdy looking as bulls are that they would be delicate, but they are. If you rush things with a new bull, you could end up with a sick or insecure animal that can't or won't perform his job.

I get back as Loretta is coming up my front walk bearing a pan of sweet rolls. "I've brought some extras for you to take down to headquarters to that new girl." She says she can't come in for long, but she wants to hear how my trip to Dallas went.

I've thought long and hard about how to introduce people to the idea that Nonie Blake is still alive and well, and that another woman is the victim of murder. As much as I'd like to fill in Loretta, I need to talk to the Blakes before anyone else hears the news. "It was a strange trip," I say.

"Strange how?"

"I want to tell you the details, but there are some people I need to talk to first," I say.

"You were gone longer than you thought you were going to be."
I see by the look on her face that she's calculating how to weasel more
information out of me. I know this trick of hers—easing around the
back of a subject to get a wedge in.

"And glad to be home," I say. "Did you know I bought a new bull?
It got delivered while I was gone."

"I wondered what Truly was up to back there. I saw the truck and
all that activity. I'm surprised whatever happened up in Tyler was so
interesting that you couldn't come back to help Truly." Another foray
into getting information out of me.

"Actually, I was in Jacksonville. Anything happen while I was gone?"

"The new girl is making herself right at home."

"You mean the new police officer?"

"You know that's what I mean."

"Making herself at home?"

"I can be as secretive as you. All I'm saying is that you might be surprised when you get to work today."

"Loretta, did anything ever come of that business with your roses?
I asked Deputy Trevino to look into it while I was gone."

"Since you're too busy."

"Yes, that's right. What happened?"

"She questioned all of us like we had done it ourselves, and as far as
I know she gave up after that. Not important enough, I guess."

With that, she flounces out. I'm beginning to think I'm going to
have to give up on pleasing any of the women in my life.

I'm at headquarters before eight, but I still don't beat Maria Trevino. As
soon as I walk in, I see what Loretta was talking about. The place has
been scrubbed until it squeaks. I figured our linoleum tile floors were

a permanent shade of gray and grayer, and that the walls were another shade of gray. It turns out the tiles are black and white, and the walls are kind of a nice shade of white. All the desktops and file cabinets have been scrubbed. There's a plant on Maria's desk and new wastebaskets beside each desk. Maria is sitting at her desk looking pleased with herself in a fierce kind of way.

"I'll be damned," I say. "You did all this?"

"Yes, I did. I have pride in where I work even if nobody else does. But don't expect me to make coffee."

"I wouldn't want you to. That's my job." I open the door into the jail part of the building and am assailed with the smell of pine cleaner rather than the usual smell of unwashed drunks. "You even did the back room?"

Her eyes narrow. "Not me. When Bill Odum came in and saw what I was up to, I guess he was embarrassed into doing some cleaning, too."

I sit down at my desk and survey the room. "It's like a new place," I say. "I figured we had to paint it if we wanted it to look good."

She grimaces and shakes her head. "Men."

"If I didn't say so, thank you." I straighten a couple of piles of paper, aware that Trevino had the good sense not to touch my desk. "How did things go with the business of the flowers disappearing?"

"I don't know how I can figure out who's doing it," she says. "I realize this is a big deal with these elderly people, but you have to admit it's pretty funny."

It was one thing for me to tease Loretta about it, but I'm annoyed that this green recruit has come swaggering into town laughing at people I've known my whole life. "It won't do for you to take this lightly," I say. "Like I told you, in a small town little things can take on more importance than you might think. If you want to make a place for yourself, you need to understand that."

Resentment flares in her eyes. Her mouth turns down in a pout. "I don't know that I'm planning to make a place for myself here, as you say. I'm here to help out."

"I take it you didn't find anything useful about who's cutting the flowers."

"I guess I didn't." By her surly tone, I can tell she doesn't like having to make this admission.

"All right, we'll wait and see. I've got something else to discuss with you. Something big."

"About the Blake case?"

"Yep. The woman who was killed out at the Blake ranch?"

"Uh-huh."

"That wasn't Nonie Blake."

She's suddenly eager. "So it wasn't the position of the body that made the difference in her height. How did you find out?"

I describe the way things happened in Jacksonville. "We need to go out to the Blake ranch and talk to the family."

"We?"

"You earned it. You took the initiative to call Doc Taggart and uncover that information about the broken leg. You've read the reports and I've brought you up to date. Who better to go out there with me?"

"I don't want to step on anybody's toes. I don't want Officer Odum or Officer Dibble to get mad."

"You've got a point, but you're here and they aren't. It's only Bill who might want a piece of this. Zeke is a good man, but he doesn't have a lot of fire in his belly, if you know what I mean."

She nods but looks serious. "Still, he has a good record. That counts for a lot."

"And not too much ego," I say. "Now if you don't want to go, you don't have to. And basically I want you to observe rather than get into it with anybody. You all right with that?"

"What if I think of something that you haven't covered?"

"If you have something to say, go ahead and say it."

Before we leave, I call the medical examiner, T. J. Sutter, and tell him that I've visually confirmed the identity of the woman we buried as Nonie Blake. "Her name is Susan Shelby. I brought a hairbrush and a cup from her bathroom that might have some DNA for testing. And a couple of photos." I'm aware of Trevino listening to everything I say.

CHAPTER 24

On the way out to the Blake ranch, Trevino plies me with one question after another about the Blakes—why they live way out here, their position in the community, what their personalities are like, and how long they've been here. Good questions. She'll be a good cop.

"You said the father isn't able to work," she says. "How do they make a living?"

"I know they have made some investments, because I interviewed their financial advisor. But I don't know where their money came from."

"Financial advisor?" She snickers. "What are they doing with a financial advisor living out here in the country?"

"You've got some wrong ideas about small towns," I say. "When you were familiarizing yourself with the town, did you drive out to the lake? Did you see some of those homes out there? People move in here from the city and they bring some of their city ways with them."

"All right, don't get all bent out of shape. I'm sure this town is nothing but modern." Trevino is a hard combination of eager beaver and snapping turtle.

Billy Blake's truck is still parked outside, which surprises me. I figured he'd be out of here first chance he got, since I hadn't cautioned him to stick around.

When I open the car door I hear the roar of a machine from behind the house.

"What is that?" Trevino says.

"I expect they're draining the pond," I say. "Looking for the murder weapon." We walk back to the pond, and sure enough there's a big truck there with a generator working a suction pump. A big pipe leads several yards back away from the house to a sloping section of the property that can handle the runoff.

Billy opens the door, his face livid. "What the hell do you have to say for yourself? Nobody told us a thing about draining the pond, and these guys showed up here this morning with an order. You can't disrupt people's lives that way."

"I apologize. I was hoping to tell you before they set it up, but I was out of town."

"A little vacation?" His voice drips with sarcasm. I sense Trevino tensing beside me.

"Mind if we come in? You're letting the air conditioning out."

He stomps away from the front door, leaving us to follow and close the door behind us. At the door to the living room he confronts us again, hands on his hips. "Well? You going to tell me what you hope to gain by that?" He gestures widely toward where the pond operation is taking place.

"We're looking for the murder weapon."

"You really think somebody is stupid enough to throw it in the pond?"

"I'm sorry it's an inconvenience. It shouldn't take them too long. But I'm here about something else."

"More hassle."

"There has been a development and I need to talk to your family. By the way, let me introduce Deputy Trevino. She recently joined the department."

"It'll be interesting to have a girl cop around here," Billy says.

I flinch and wonder how Trevino is going to handle being called a girl cop.

"I'm looking forward to serving the community," Trevino says, with a little bite to her tone, which I approve of.

"I need to talk to your mamma and daddy, and then the three kids," I say.

He starts to protest and then shakes his head as if to say he's given up. "I'll go get them."

"We'll wait in the living room," I say. I normally wouldn't be that forward, but I always feel like I have to establish my territory with Billy.

Charlotte comes downstairs right away, but it takes time for Adelaide and John to make an appearance. When they do, John's got a big grin on his face. "Hey, Samuel," he says, "I haven't seen you in a good long time. How've you been?"

He apparently doesn't remember that I was here only a few days ago, and we were in the barn together. Maybe I can jog his memory.

I ask Billy and Charlotte to give us some time to talk.

"One of us should be here," Billy says. "Mamma may need someone to help handle Daddy."

"I'll be fine, son," Adelaide says. "Now go on and leave us alone."

Charlotte goes back upstairs, and Billy heads out the front door, slamming it behind him. Adelaide looks nervous, but John looks at me eagerly, as if he's happy to be engaged in some activity, even if he doesn't understand what it's about.

I introduce Maria Trevino, and although Adelaide is polite, she's too nervous to take much notice that we have a new cop on our small force.

"Adelaide, I need to tell you something, but first I want to ask John a question."

John blinks at me and shuffles his feet back and forth as if he thinks he's going to have to get up and walk around.

"Stay right here," I say. "John, I was here a few days ago. Do you remember that? We went out to the barn?"

"You what?" Adelaide says.

"I came over while you all were at the cemetery."

"You mean you snuck over here to get at John." Her voice is bitter.

"That's an interesting way to put it," I say. "Almost like you think he had something to hide. John, do you remember when I was here?"

John looks to Adelaide for help, and when she doesn't say anything he shakes his head and mumbles that he doesn't remember.

"At the time, you told me you didn't think the woman who came here to visit was really your daughter. What made you say that?"

His face darkens. "She wasn't. She didn't look right and she didn't smell right."

"John, stop that," Adelaide says. "You're being silly."

A sly grin tilts the corners of his mouth. "All right, I made up the part about the smelling." He giggles, but then his faces twists and he brings a fist down hard on his knee. "But I'm telling you she didn't look right."

"And you?" I say to Adelaide. "Did she look right to you?"

Adelaide is wringing her hands. "What are you asking me? I don't understand."

"I think you understand perfectly. Did you recognize the woman who came here as your daughter?"

Adelaide brings a fist to her mouth and presses it hard against her lips. Tears well in her eyes. "It's true then? She wasn't Nonie?"

"She wasn't Nonie. How did you not see that?"

"I admit I had my doubts."

"You had doubts?" I don't even try to hide my skepticism.

"You don't understand. I didn't think it was Nonie, but she knew all kinds of things that I thought only Nonie would know. At first I thought maybe my memory was at fault and I didn't remember her right." She opens her hands out in appeal. "I didn't know what to do!"

"Did you tell her you didn't recognize her?"

"No, I didn't. To tell you the truth, I was a little afraid of her. What kind of person comes here pretending to be somebody else? Who was she?"

"Did Charlotte know?"

"What are we talking about?" John says, looking from Adelaide to me. "Why don't we have some lunch?"

Adelaide gets up. "If you don't mind, I'm going to get Charlotte to take John in to the kitchen. He doesn't need to be upset by this."

She goes out to the entry and calls up the stairs to Charlotte, who comes rushing down. "What's wrong?"

Adelaide says, "I believe your daddy could use some lunch."

"But it's . . ." It's barely ten o'clock, but when Charlotte looks at Adelaide, a look of understanding comes across her face. She goes to John's side. "Daddy, I'll get you a sandwich. Come on in the kitchen."

Trevino gets up and says, "I believe I'll go outside and take a look at the pond, see how they're getting on."

"That sounds like a good idea." I give her a nod.

As soon as we're alone, I say, "Adelaide, let's start from the beginning. Why don't you tell me how things went from the time this woman claiming to be Nonie showed up. And I want you to tell me the truth for once."

Adelaide looks down at her hands in her lap. Her face is flushed. "Like I said, I knew Nonie was coming, I just didn't know exactly when she'd get here, and as it happened Charlotte answered the door. I wish I had been there so it wasn't such a shock to Charlotte. I realize now I should have told her in advance."

"Why didn't you?"

Adelaide's face is sagging like she's aged ten years. "I don't know why. I guess I was hoping she wouldn't show up. Anyway she did, and Charlotte answered the door. Charlotte called me downstairs. She looked like she'd seen a ghost. She told me Nonie was here. I told her to go upstairs and stay with her daddy, and I'd explain later. When I walked into the living room, Nonie had her back to me. When she turned around, right away I thought she didn't look right. She didn't look like any of the other kids. I thought maybe I was imagining things, and that I hadn't seen her in so long that I'd forgotten what she looked like. You can't imagine how rattled I was."

"You say she knew things that Nonie would know?"

"Yes, when I took her up to her old room, she recognized it. Or said she did." Adelaide's eyes are distant. "I wonder what would have happened if I'd taken her into another room and told her it was her old room . . ." Her eyes widen. "This woman who came here . . . did she know Nonie?"

"Yes, she did."

"Do you suppose Nonie described the house—where things were and all that?"

"I expect that's the way it happened."

Adelaide swallows. "You talked to Nonie?"

"Yes, I did."

"How was she? Does she have a job? Does she look all right?"

"She seems fine. She has a regular life, a decent job. But let's get back to this imposter. You showed her to her room, and then what?"

"When I took her to her room, Charlotte came in for a minute and hugged her and said she was glad Nonie was back."

"So you all had dinner together. How did you introduce her to Skeeter?"

"I told him his sister Nonie had come back, that's all."

"What happened when John saw her?"

"Oh, I didn't have him meet her that night. He's more confused at night, and I thought it was best for them to meet the next morning."

"When he met her the next day, did he say right away that he didn't think it was Nonie?"

"Yes, but you have to understand, John doesn't always make a lot of sense. He could have said the same thing even if it was Nonie."

"So you didn't pay any attention to him? Even though you had your doubts?"

"I didn't say that. The next morning when she finally came downstairs in the middle of the morning, I took one look at her and said to myself, something isn't right here. That woman is not kin."

"You didn't wonder what she was up to?"

"Of course I did, but I didn't know how to ask. It's so strange having somebody in your house that seems to know you and everything about you, but you don't know them at all."

"Adelaide, you're not making any sense. Why would you let this woman stay in your house if you suspected she wasn't your daughter, and then after she got killed, why go to the expense and pomp and circumstance of having her buried?"

She looks plain miserable. "I don't have an answer for you. I didn't know what to do. I wanted it over with, that's all."

"You could have called me."

"I didn't think of it. It seemed like a family problem."

"Or like you wanted to get her buried so nobody would know that she wasn't Nonie. Is that what happened?"

"No, it wasn't like that. After she died, I thought it would be easier if we pretended she was who she said she was."

At that moment, Skeeter stumbles into the room bare-chested, wearing pajama bottoms. "What's going on? Where's everybody at?"

"I'm talking to your mamma right now. Charlotte and your daddy are in the kitchen. Maybe you want to go in there."

He yawns. "That's right. I got to get me some coffee."

Adelaide jumps to her feet. "I wonder how John's doing?" She heads for the kitchen, and I hear her say in an overly cheerful voice, "What's going on in here?"

I follow her into the kitchen. I have plenty more to get straight with Adelaide, but right now I want to get her kids' reaction to my news.

"Charlotte, now I need to talk to you, Billy, and Skeeter," I say.

Charlotte is staring at her mother "What's happened?" she says.

"I'll tell all of you at the same time," I say.

Adelaide meets my eyes. She looks defeated. "I'll take John upstairs," she says. "Maybe he'll take a nap."

"I don't want a nap. Let's go somewhere."

"All right, let's go upstairs and get ready to go out," Adelaide says.

He smiles in anticipation and follows her.

"What's going on?" Skeeter says.

"I'll tell you in a minute," I say. "I need to get Billy in here." I go out front and find Billy and Maria Trevino talking on the front steps, looking comfortable with each other.

When we're settled around the kitchen table, I say, "I went looking for information about what your sister was up to before she came here, and it turns out the woman who was here was not your sister. Nonie is alive and living in Jacksonville."

Charlotte's mouth falls open. "Nonie's alive? Are you sure?"

"I talked to her myself."

"What the heck? Who's the woman who came here then?" Skeeter says.

"I'll be damned," Billy says. He looks at Charlotte. "You mean you didn't have any idea?"

"You're sure the woman you talked to was Nonie?" she says.

I nod. "Charlotte, your mamma told me she had suspicions about this woman . . ."

Charlotte stops me. "Does this woman have a name? Who was she?"

"Let me ask the questions for now. Did your mamma tell you she didn't think the woman was Nonie?"

Charlotte darts a quick look at Billy. "I had no reason to think she wasn't exactly who she said she was. I was young when she left and my memory of her was hazy."

"That's not what I asked. Did your mamma tell you she thought it wasn't Nonie?"

"She might have mentioned it. And Daddy . . . all I can say is that he was not happy about her being here."

"Did you call Billy and tell him your mamma thought she was an imposter?"

"Hell, no, she didn't tell me that," Billy says. "If she had, I'd have come back here in a flash, rodeo be damned. As it was, I was planning to come back here the minute I could. I didn't want Nonie in our house." Some of this is bluster. From what Zeke Dibble dug up, I know that Billy didn't come back the minute he could, the most likely explanation being that he was shacked up with some woman.

"What about you, Skeeter? Did you have any suspicion that the woman was not who she said she was?" I don't expect Skeeter to have been astute enough to catch on, but he startles all of us.

"I might have."

"Goddammit, Skeeter, you did not," Billy says. "You're trying to get attention."

"You don't know me, Billy. Don't tell me what I saw and what I didn't see."

Trevino raises her eyebrows at me.

"What did you see?" I ask him.

He looks trapped. "Nothing."

"See what I mean?" Billy says, with an eyebrow cocked at me.

"But I heard something," Skeeter says, glaring at his brother. "Something weird."

"What did you hear?" I say.

"I heard her talking to herself. Everybody said she wasn't crazy anymore, but it made me wonder if she was really okay."

"Where and when was this?" I ask.

His eyes dart from his sister to his brother. They're both staring at him. "I wasn't listening on purpose. I happened to be outside one day under her window and I heard her talking."

"What did she say?" Charlotte says. Her teeth are clenched, and she's staring at him.

"Nothing important, but I thought it was weird that she was talking to herself out loud."

Billy and Charlotte start talking at once. "Why didn't you say something?" Charlotte says.

"Wait," I say. "This is important. What was she saying?"

"She kept saying the name Nonie, like she was trying to talk sense to herself. Mostly it was mumbling, but she said, 'Nonie, you wait and see if I don't.' They may not be her exact words, but something like that."

CHAPTER 25

On the way back to headquarters, I ask Maria what she and Billy talked about when they were together on the porch.

"I asked him questions about being in the rodeo. He's had a good run. Never had any major accidents, so I guess he's lucky."

"Did you have a chance to look around out there?"

"Just around the pond. I found Billy watching them drain it, and then we walked around the house to the front porch. I asked him to tell me if he knew where the body was found, but he said he wasn't around at the time, so he didn't know. I asked him where he was when they notified him that Nonie had been killed, and that's when he told me he was a rodeo rider. He said he had recently finished up a rodeo in Denton and was hanging around there when his sister called him and told him what happened. That's when we got on the subject of the rodeo. You think he might have snuck back here and killed that woman?"

"You want to know the truth? I don't have a clue. There's something going on with that family, but I don't know what. But I'll tell you this, I'm going to find out one way or another."

I look over to see her with a doubtful expression.

Before we left the Blakes, we found out that the dredging operation would take the rest of the day. As we get out of the car, Trevino says, "If you want me to, I'll go back out there and keep an eye on it."

"That sounds like a good idea."

We walk into headquarters and find Zeke there. We also find a dog there that looks familiar. "Frazier?" Sure enough, he comes wriggling over to me.

"I'm glad you're here," Zeke says. "That dog has been a nervous wreck."

Frazier is looking at me expectantly. He is some kind of terrier mixed with a more substantial dog, so he has a sturdy build with a terrier's personality—or so Ellen told me. I'm not sure what she meant.

"What is he doing here? Where's Ellen?"

"Ellen came by an hour ago," Dibble says. "She said she had an emergency and had to go to Houston and asked if I'd prevail upon you to take care of the dog. She said she'd call you later." I don't care for the speculative look in Zeke's eyes. He's wondering why Ellen feels close enough to me to ask me to keep her dog.

Trevino crouches down and starts making cooing noises to the dog, who is so thrilled that he's practically crawling on his stomach as he makes his way to the deputy. "Who's a sweet doggie? You are!"

Zeke and I roll our eyes at each other. "What am I going to do with this dog?" I say. "My cat will have a fit if I bring a dog in the house."

"Cat? You have a cat?" Trevino says, looking up at me. "I hate cats. They're so sneaky."

"You want to keep this dog with you?" I say.

"I can't. They won't let me have a pet in the apartment."

"You have room for a dog?" I say to Zeke.

"No siree, we already have two dogs, and my wife is ready to send the three of us packing. She says between the dogs and me we create enough dirt for ten people."

I've met Zeke's wife, and she isn't nearly as fussy as he makes her out to be. She's a thin whippet of a woman with a sharp sense of humor.

"I guess it's up to me, then." Although it occurs to me that Loretta could maybe help me out. But Loretta is not home any more than I am.

"How long did Ellen say she'd be gone?"

"She didn't say. Said her daughter needed her."

And what about those precious classes of hers, I think. She couldn't cancel them for me, but she could cancel them for her daughter. I'm glad nobody can know those thoughts because I instantly regret being so self-centered. Ellen must have her reasons.

I'm looking at the dog and thinking that Loretta doesn't have any pets, and that leads me to the Blakes. They live on a big property meant to be a farm or a ranch, and I didn't see a sign of any animals. What in the world led them to become so inward? I get the sense that they are hovering on the edge of fear of the future, as if something holds them together and keeps everyone else out. Everyone except Les Moffitt, the financial advisor. Maybe it's time I had another talk with him. There's got to be some way in with this family, and I intend to find it.

The dog settles down at Trevino's feet. Zeke asks us what we've been up to. I tell Trevino to fill Zeke in, thinking if I hear if from her mouth, something might come to me.

She gives a thorough accounting. And while she talks I think about Susan Shelby coming here—not driving here, but taking the bus—and pretending to be Nonie. Why? It sounds like she might have intended to blackmail somebody. But if Nonie told Susan something she could use to blackmail somebody, why didn't Nonie come here and handle it herself? And who was the blackmail victim?

I had assumed that Nonie found out something about someone in the community that she could use as blackmail. But suppose it was her own family she knew something about? Suppose she found it out when she was fourteen? Nonie said she had tried to kill Charlotte because she stuck her nose in where it didn't belong. Maybe Charlotte found it out, too, and Nonie thought she wouldn't keep her mouth shut.

When I talked to Nonie, she acted like she was surprised that Susan Shelby had come to her family's house, but that can't be true. She knew! I think back to the conversation Skeeter overheard her having. When she said, "Nonie," Skeeter thought she was talking to herself, because he thought she was Nonie. Now I know that Susan wasn't talking to herself—she was talking to Nonie. Nonie lied to me. Without a doubt, she did know Susan was here. From the psychiatric report I read, it seems to have been Nonie's way of doing things— lying and sneaking. And it means something else, too. If Susan Shelby was talking to Nonie, she must have had a telephone with her. So where is it?

I come back to the conversation to hear Zeke telling Maria, "I don't know what to say. I wasn't in homicide in Houston, but I do know the murders they got were pretty straightforward. It usually involved a guy who killed somebody for looking at him wrong, or drug deals gone bad, or domestic quarrels that got out of hand. This small-town stuff . . . these people can be pretty close-mouthed."

"Funny," Trevino says, "I always used to think of small towns as full of gossip so it would be hard to hide anything."

Gossip. It's time I talked to Loretta and let her know what's going on and find out if she has any memory of something that might help me find out what the Blakes are up to that almost got Charlotte killed and may have been responsible for Susan Shelby's death.

I can see that Maria is itching to get back to the Blake ranch. "Maria," I say, "why don't you take this dog with you when you go back out to the Blakes?"

The dog seems to understand that Trevino is his best chance of having a good day and trots after her readily. It could be that he likes women better than men, having been mistreated by Seth Forester.

As soon as they're gone I call Loretta. She's not home, so I leave a message for her to call me as soon as she can. I go home to see how the cows are doing and to give myself a little time to plan my strategy. I'm halfway home when Loretta calls, sounding out of breath.

"I came by my house for a minute and found your message," she says. "What do you need?"

"I need to talk to you. Are you home now?"

"I was on my way over to the church to put things away from the women's auxiliary meeting this morning. It can wait. Why don't you come on by and I'll make us some lunch."

When I walk in Loretta's door, she's got grilled cheese sandwiches cooking and has opened a can of tomato soup. Over lunch I tell her that the woman who was staying at the Blakes was not Nonie Blake; that I talked to Nonie Blake in person.

"I never heard anything so crazy," she says. "Who is the woman who was killed?"

I tell her about Susan Shelby. "And I have no idea what she wanted."

"You say Nonie knew her? Did she know why the Shelby woman came here?"

"Loretta, I didn't completely trust what Nonie had to say. Don't tell anybody I said so."

Loretta loves to gossip, but I know that if I ask her to keep quiet, she will.

"I need you to tell me everything you know about the Blakes. There's something off with that family and I don't know what to make of it. You hear things, and I'd like to know what people are saying."

"There's been a lot of talk, but most of it is nonsense." She takes a sip of her soup. "People telling wild tales about Nonie Blake that can't possibly have been true."

"Like what?"

"Oh, like she was sneaking off with one of her teachers, and her sister found out and that's why she tried to kill her."

"That doesn't sound so wild to me. Nobody has explained to my satisfaction why she did try to kill her sister."

"Did you talk to the psychiatrist who examined Nonie? Did he know why she did it?"

I shake my head, chewing the last bite of the sandwich. "Only that Nonie insisted that she had her reasons."

Loretta sees me eyeing the other half of her sandwich, so she passes it onto my plate. I don't hesitate. I know she's not sacrificing. She'd throw it out if I didn't eat it. Although she's frugal, she doesn't like to eat leftovers.

"Have you asked Charlotte?" she says.

"No, she was eight years old when it happened and I don't know that she would have much memory about it."

"It couldn't hurt to ask," she says. "I'm always surprised what my kids remember from when they were little."

"Is there anything you've heard about the family that would explain why they keep to themselves so much?"

"Of course everybody says it's because of what Nonie did. But I remember that family before it happened, and they were always standoffish."

"Did you know Adelaide's mother?"

"Not well. She was several years older than me. She came to town when Adelaide was a little girl. She was a pretty woman. Lilah, her name was. She said her husband had been killed in the war and . . ."

"In what war?"

"Korean War. She said he was drafted."

"Loretta, how do you remember that?"

"I don't know. I just do. I think because I was relieved that my husband didn't get drafted to Vietnam."

"What was Lilah's last name?"

Loretta has to think for a minute. "Cousins. Lilah Cousins."

"And her husband's first name?"

"I don't remember."

"It sounds like she didn't keep to herself like the Blakes do."

Loretta ponders my question and eventually says, "She lived in town, which means she had more of a chance to run into people. I expect she was lonesome, just her and Adelaide. Maybe it's John Blake who decided they need to stay to themselves."

"Maybe." But I remember John Blake as a kid, a few years younger than me. He was always running around, wild and popular enough. What drove that family to circle the wagons?

CHAPTER 26

When I get in my pickup, I sit contemplating what kind of secret would make a family turn inward. Shame might do it, but it seems they were like that before Nonie's dreadful act. I'm trying to think what I might not want people to know about me. I don't have any peculiar sex habits, but if I did, I suspect I wouldn't want anybody to know. Beyond that, my family history isn't all that savory, but there'd be no point in my hiding out because of it—and John and Adelaide don't have any notorious relatives that I know of. I don't see signs that any of them are addicted to drugs or alcohol. The one thing that might make me want to be discreet with others is money matters. I don't mind if people know that my wife and I inherited money from her family and that it left me comfortable—better than comfortable. But I wouldn't want people knowing the particulars.

I remember that I intended to talk to Les Moffitt again to find out if there's something about the Blakes' financial situation that they don't want known. Moffitt is the only outsider I know who seems to be on good terms with the family—as well as being their financial guru. I call him and tell him I'm on my way to see him. Before I can put the key in the ignition, my phone rings.

"Samuel, did you go by the office and get Frazier?" Ellen's voice is high with tension.

"Yes, I've been by there. The dog isn't with me at the moment. He took a liking to the new deputy I told you about, Maria Trevino. Frazier is riding around with her this afternoon."

"He'll like that. He loves to ride in the car."

"Zeke said you told him your daughter needed you. Is she all right?"

"She called me from the hospital this morning. She was walking into work, and somebody had spilled something that made the tiles slippery. She fell and broke her leg in two places."

"Oh, my." I feel guilty because I was a little jealous of her daughter.

"When I got here, they had her in surgery. She's out now and they said she'll be fine. I'm sorry I left the dog with you without asking. I was so flustered I didn't know what to do."

"It's not a problem. Take your time."

"So much for not canceling my classes. I feel foolish, since I made a fuss about not wanting to do that when you asked me to go to Tyler with you."

"Your daughter has to be more important to you. And as it turns out, it was better for you not to come along anyway. The trip took longer than I thought it would. You would have been stuck with nothing to do while I worked on some things."

"Did you find out what you needed to know about the Blake girl?"

"I did. You're not going to believe this. The woman who was killed was not Nonie Blake."

"That's bizarre. Who was she?" I can tell she's tired and distracted and making an effort to sound interested.

"We'll talk about it when you come back. Don't worry about the dog. We'll get along fine. What about his food?"

"I must be losing my mind. I didn't even think about that."

"You have a spare key somewhere? I can go in and get it."

"It's so stupid. I haven't given anybody a spare key. It's only been a short time since I moved in, and I haven't thought about it."

I ask her what kind of dog food he eats and tell her I'll go buy the food. I don't tell her my worst fear, that my cat Zelda will terrorize the dog.

Les Moffitt doesn't act like he has any problem with me questioning him again. In fact, he seems happy to see me until I break the news that Nonie Blake was not the murder victim.

"Then who was it?" he says. I'm always interested in how long it takes somebody to ask that question. He cuts right to the chase.

"A woman by the name of Susan Shelby."

He frowns and shakes his head slowly. "I don't believe I know who that is. Is she from around here?"

"No, she's from east Texas."

"Have you talked to the Blakes? Didn't they realize it wasn't Nonie? Why did they let the woman stay there?" His voice trails away, and his jowls sink as he realizes how much it all doesn't make sense.

"That's the question, isn't it? Adelaide says she didn't know her, but that she thought it wasn't Nonie. And still she didn't call the law. I'm trying to pin down why that's so. You have any ideas?"

"Me? How would I know? Like I said, I only met her briefly, and I've never met Nonie, so I wouldn't have any idea that it wasn't her."

"What I mean is, do you have any ideas why they let the woman stay if they realized she wasn't Nonie?"

He has an odd expression on his face. Not exactly calculating but headed in that direction. He straightens up a couple of pens on his desk before he speaks. "You said Adelaide knew. Did Charlotte know, too?"

"I'm having trouble figuring out exactly who knew what. John is the one who seems to have instinctively known right away that the woman wasn't his daughter."

"John." He sighs. "Whatever he knew, you can't count on it."

"I'll tell you what I think, and you can chime in. I suspect that this woman had some dirt on the family that they don't want known. You have any idea what it could be?"

Moffitt looks decidedly uneasy. "I don't understand why you'd think I'd know. I'm their financial advisor, not their confessor."

"I'm wondering if whatever this woman knew about them had to do with their finances. Any idea?"

Moffitt raises his eyebrows. "Like I said before, I can't go into the details, but I can say they were better off before the economy went all to hell." He pauses. "You're not suggesting that I've been up to something funny with regard to their finances, are you? Because I'm telling you, I'm on the up-and-up. I'll open my business to scrutiny by any auditor or federal overseer."

"Calm down. I'm not accusing you of anything. I'm curious to know where they got money to begin with, though. I've been acquainted with the Blake family for a long time, and as far as I know there wasn't any money in the background. And Adelaide's mother was a single parent whose husband died in Korea."

Moffitt's eyes suddenly shift. The comment hit some kind of nerve, but in what way?

"Did Adelaide's mother inherit money and leave it to her?" I ask.

He starts to speak, considers, and then says, "All I know is that the initial money they started with came from her side of the family. I assumed she inherited it. I didn't feel like I needed to pry."

"I thought a financial advisor was obliged to make a good-faith effort to make sure money they were investing for people came from legitimate sources."

"Come on." He spreads his hands wide. "I mean, Adelaide didn't strike me as somebody who made a bundle selling drugs. I didn't feel like I had to dig into her background."

"How much money are we talking about?"

"I can't really disclose that. I'll tell you it wasn't millions, but it was enough to keep them comfortable if they invested it properly—which I saw to it that they did."

"How long ago was this?"

He flips to the back of the folder on his desk. "Like I said, they came to me around twenty years ago."

The first time I met Ellen Forester's dog, Frazier, he was a trembling mess, traumatized by Ellen's ex-husband, who had come to her house and caused a big ruckus. Now the dog is positively serene, perched up on the seat next to me in my pickup, looking around outside as if he's never known a care in the world. Wait until he meets Zelda.

"You behave yourself," I say, as we walk up the steps to my house. I have him on a leash, and he's prancing at my side.

Zelda always comes to greet me when I get home. I presume she hears the truck drive up and knows that I bring the possibility of food. Today when she walks from the direction of the kitchen into the front room, she stops cold and ponders Frazier. He lets out a muffled whine.

"It's probably best if you keep quiet," I say. He sits.

Zelda lofts her tail high in the air and walks right up to Frazier and looks at him. He quivers but keeps quiet. She puts her nose up to his for a quick sniff and then turns around and strolls out of the room. The dog looks up at me and I look at him and we both relax. "You better stay here while I feed her," I say. "You challenge her food dish, and I'll be returning a dead dog to Ellen."

Frazier settles to the floor. He can't possibly know what I said, but he sure acts like he does.

I put food down for Zelda and then try to figure out where to feed the dog. I decide it's best to put him on the front porch, tied up. He seems to think there's no problem with that as long as he gets food and water. When he's done eating he whines, and when I let him in he keeps a wary eye out for Zelda.

I've got work to do on my computer, so after I have a bite to eat, I settle down at my desk. Zelda jumps up onto her usual spot crowding the computer, and Frazier eases himself down next to my chair. At least for now, we've got peace.

These days when I need to find out background on somebody, I usually have success on the Internet. But when I enter Lilah Cousins's name, I come up with nothing but her date of death and the name of her husband, Aaron.

It's when I start researching Aaron that things get interesting. He is listed as a veteran of the Korean War, but unlike what Lilah claimed, he wasn't killed in the war.

In old police records, I find that when Cousins was a teenager, he was a rowdy who got into all kinds of petty trouble. He was arrested for stealing a car and joyriding, and for stealing a carton of cigarettes. He was also arrested for assault, a charge that was later dropped. When he was twenty years old he upped the ante and took part in a fraud scheme. Apparently he and two other young men went door to door in small towns, getting down payments on nonexistent sets of classic books. Shortly after he was arrested for this, he went into the army. My guess is that a judge gave him a choice of going to jail or enlisting in the army.

His date of death is almost two years after the end of the war. Finally I find out the information that Lilah kept quiet so the citizens of Jarrett Creek wouldn't know. Aaron was killed during the attempted robbery of a bank in Kilgore. I remember when I said to Les Moffitt that Adelaide's daddy was killed in the war, he got funny look on his face. Did he know the truth? Does he know more than he's saying?

I don't know why Lilah chose Jarrett Creek in particular to settle down with her young daughter, but she probably knew that in a small town many miles from her home, no one would question her if she said her husband was killed in action.

I settle back to think. Frazier sits up, and I idly stroke his head. It's an interesting coincidence that Nonie Blake settled in east Texas, not that far from where her granddaddy was killed in a robbery. I don't believe in coincidence. Did Adelaide tell Nonie that's where her folks were from? Why would she do that after Lilah was so careful to keep it secret? Nonie was only fourteen and liked to tell tales at school.

Wouldn't Adelaide be afraid that Nonie would tell enough to pique somebody's interest in the family's background?

But maybe Adelaide didn't tell Nonie at all. People said that Nonie was a sneak. "Maybe she poked around in her mother's papers and discovered the background for herself," I say to Frazier. He looks puzzled, but his tail wiggles.

CHAPTER 27

After spending last night and this morning researching Aaron Cousins, I've got a much clearer idea of what I'm after.

I find Charlotte outside looking at the drained pond. She turns when I call out to her. When I get to her side, she looks back at the muddy silt. "This is going to be a mosquito haven. I'm thinking we ought to have it filled in with dirt."

"I wouldn't. It's nice having water on a property."

"I suppose. But after what happened here . . ."

"Charlotte, where did the incident with Nonie take place?"

"Right here at the pond." She points to the old stump next to the sycamore. "It was that tree. Daddy cut it down within the week."

"Why did he do that?"

"I suppose he didn't want me to have a reminder of what happened. As it was, Mamma said I had nightmares for a while."

"I wonder if you would take a walk with me around the property?"

She looks surprised. "Sure. Let me change shoes."

I feel as if talking to her away from the house I might be able to get more out of her. We head out into the fallow pastureland to the grove of post oaks beyond, where we'll be out of the sun. Charlotte is no chatterbox. We walk along quietly until we slip into the grove of trees. It has been so hot that many of the leaves are turning brown and dropping off, so that we walk on a carpet of leaves and brush. I think briefly of snakes and keep an eye out for the copperheads that are so plentiful around here. A copperhead bite won't kill you unless you're very unlucky, but it will make you plenty sick.

Charlotte knows as well as I do that snakes abound out here, and that's why she changed into heavy walking shoes. She's got on jeans and a white T-shirt. I notice that she has lost weight in the last couple of weeks.

"Charlotte, what I'm going to ask you will be hard for you to answer, I know. Do your best." I glance over at her. A dew of perspiration shines on her top lip, and her cheeks are pink.

She notices me looking at her and meets my eyes. "I know you might find this hard to believe, but I don't have anything to hide."

"I want you to think back, when the incident happened with Nonie."

"Okay."

"Before Nonie got you to climb up onto the chair with the rope around your neck."

"Ugh! I haven't thought about that in . . . that's not true. I thought about it several times when Nonie—or rather the woman we thought was Nonie—was here."

"Then maybe you can tell me. What did Nonie say to you to get you to put a noose around your neck?"

She stops walking and turns toward me. "You know, that's one thing nobody ever asked me. I guess they assumed I was too young to remember."

"Do you remember?"

She takes a deep breath and lets it out slowly. "A little. I remember she came to my room and said I'd been bad and I had to come with her."

"Did you know what she meant?"

Her eyes search mine, then they focus somewhere beyond me. "I must have. I remember feeling sick to my stomach, as if I'd been found out."

"What kind of relationship did you have with Nonie? She was six years older. Was she nice to you? Did you play together?"

"Billy was the nice one. He always had time for me. Was always patient." She cocks her head. "Nonie . . . what I remember is that Nonie was always off somewhere. Always busy."

"Off somewhere like . . . ?"

"Off in town. She would ride her bike into town. It made her seem a lot older to me. I always wished I could go with her, but when I asked she'd tell me I was too little."

"If she was here at home, where would you likely find her?"

She grimaces and shakes her head. "I don't remember that."

"Okay, so the day she came and got you and said you had been bad, you don't remember what she meant?"

"I remember that I was scared—I don't know why. I had never been afraid of her before. When I saw that she was taking me outside, I was so scared I peed in my pants." A smile hovers around her lips. "That wasn't unusual. I was easily scared and I was always peeing my pants."

"Something she said scared you? Or the way she was acting?"

Charlotte stops walking and puts her hands on her hips and looks off into the trees. Gradually she shakes her head. "I don't know."

"Did she have the rope with her?"

She looks surprised. "No. We stopped by the barn and she got it. I asked her what it was for and she said something smart aleck like, 'that's for me to know and you to find out.'"

"And she took you to the tree . . . and then what?"

"I can see the rope in her hands. It was big, heavy." She opens her palm out as if the ghost of the rope is there. "I don't know what kind of knot it had in it. I don't see how she could have tied a knot in a rope that heavy." She stops and frowns. "I don't have any recollection of her putting it on me. The next thing I recall is her telling me to climb up onto a chair." Awareness floods her face. "I remember asking her what a chair was doing there, and she said she put it there. I must have been afraid of her because I normally would have stood on the chair gladly. I loved to climb onto everything in sight. Mamma was always fussing at me, telling me I was going to fall off and bust my head. But I started crying and told Nonie I didn't want to climb up there. She said I had to. I asked why, but I don't remember what she said."

"Let's take it slow. Did you holler for anybody to come? Did you try to run?"

She shakes her head. Her eyes are full of the horror of what she's telling me. "I remember I was upset because my shorts were wet. And then Nonie said, 'You have to do this because I know you won't keep your mouth shut.'"

"Keep your mouth shut about what?"

Charlotte's eyes widen. "I have no idea. This is the first time I've ever even remembered that. My family tried to get me to forget what happened so it wouldn't traumatize me. Maybe she thought I was going to tattle about something I knew about her, but I don't have any idea what that was."

"But eventually you went ahead and climbed up there anyway."

She nods her head and hugs her arms to herself. "Then she threw one end of the rope over the branch and drew it tight around the trunk of the tree. After that she told me to put my head through the loop in the rope." She shakes her head vigorously as if to clear out the image. "Hard to grasp that this really happened. Seems like something I imagined."

"What's strange to me is that you actually did it. Were you used to obeying your sister?"

"Always. She was older and I thought she was the most sophisticated girl I could ever imagine."

I find Adelaide in her kitchen making a big pot of chili. She tells me that John is in the barn and Skeeter is keeping an eye on him so she can have a few minutes to cook.

I lean against a wall near her. "Did you ever meet any of your mother's relatives?"

"Mamma told me everybody in her family was gone," she says. "Her mamma and daddy died when I was little."

I clear my throat. "That's not entirely true," I say.

Last night I woke up in the wee hours and realized that I needed to look farther into Lilah and Aaron Cousins's past. This morning I located the marriage records and found out that Lilah Cousins's maiden name was Gitlen. Turns out that Aaron Cousins was an only child, but Lilah Gitlen had two brothers, one older, one younger. Her younger brother is still alive.

"Yeah, alive and kicking," his daughter had said when I located her in Tyler. "He lives in a retirement community an hour away from here. Plays golf morning, noon, and night."

Now I tell Adelaide that I found that she has an uncle and some cousins living in east Texas.

"It can't be the same people," she says.

"Did you ever look for relatives?"

She turns off the stove, lays down the knife she was cutting onions with, and faces me. For a minute she stands there without speaking. "Why would I? I believed Mamma. Why would she lie to me?"

I'm beginning to suspect that lying runs in the family. Because I think Adelaide knows more than she's telling. "Could be she had a falling-out with them and wanted to put it all behind her," I say.

"That makes sense. She didn't like to talk about her family. You know how little kids are. They want to know everything and it was the one thing she refused to go into." She goes over to the kitchen table and sits down heavily. I sit down across from her.

"You didn't find anything in her belongings pertaining to her family after she died?"

"No. She wasn't one to keep things."

Adelaide has told me so many lies that I don't believe her. "Are you sure?"

She's looking at me as if I'm holding a hammer over her head. "You say there's an uncle?"

"Yes, and he has a daughter. That would be your first cousin. I talked to her this morning."

She draws a sharp breath. "You talked to her? What did she say?"

"She told me she knew her daddy had a sister—that would be your mother—but he wouldn't talk about her or why they were estranged."

"I see." Her shoulders sag a little, as if she'd expected a blow and had dodged it. "I guess that's why my mother never mentioned him. Like you said, there must have been a falling-out."

"There's more," I say.

She closes her eyes, hand to her mouth. When she opens them again, for the first time she looks really scared. "What is it?"

"Your daddy didn't die in the war."

She nods, but again I get the sense that she was expecting something different—something worse. "I did know that. I pestered my mamma to tell me about him, and she admitted that she told people that he died in the war because it was easier. She said he got in trouble with the law and was killed. I've lived with that since I was a young girl."

"Have you ever told the rest of your family?"

She shakes her head. "Just John. What would be the point of telling the kids? It has nothing to do with them. They never met him or knew anything about him. He was just some stranger from the past, and you know how kids are. If it doesn't have to do with them, they don't have much interest in it."

I'm only half-listening, aware that she is babbling on. And I suspect that she's trying to lead me away from some point that she wants me to miss. But what?

"One more question. You've been investing for quite a long time with Les Moffitt. Where did the original money come from for that?"

She sits up taller, looking outraged. "I don't think I have to tell you that, do I?"

"No, you don't have to. Is there some particular reason you don't want to?"

"It's private. It's none of your business."

"It is if it has something to do with why Susan Shelby was killed."

"That's ridiculous. We invested that money a long time ago. I told you it was money my mamma squirreled away for me. She was very frugal and was a good money manager. I was always grateful that she left me a little nest egg."

"Yes, that is what you told me. But I think you're not telling the truth. I had a talk with Charlotte this afternoon and she told me that when Nonie was persuading her to put that noose around her neck, she said she had to do it to keep Charlotte from blabbing something she knew. And I think you know what it was Nonie was talking about."

"I don't believe Charlotte remembers that at all. It's nonsense. She was eight years old. What could she have known that would make any difference to anybody?"

I get up from the table, tired of going around and around with Adelaide. "Adelaide, I'd like to go back and take another look at the room Susan Shelby stayed in while she was here."

"What for?"

"I'm looking for something. You mind if look? I can get a warrant if you'd prefer."

She snorts. "Go ahead. Won't do you any good. Billy has been sleeping there. He took everything out that belonged to that woman."

"What did he do with it?"

"Threw everything into a box out in the barn."

"Then I'll start there. Is Billy around?"

"No, he went off to buy groceries. Then he was going to pick up Trey after school."

When I walk into the barn, Skeeter is watching John walk around with a saw in his hand.

"What do you need?" Skeeter says to me.

"I want to take a look at Susan Shelby's belongings," I say. "Your mamma said Billy brought them out here."

Skeeter shrugs. "I don't know where they are. Daddy, put that saw down." John wanders back into the room where the tools are kept, and Skeeter follows him.

Over in the corner I find a large cardboard box that wasn't here the first time I was in the barn. I open it and find all the belongings that I saw in Susan Shelby's room. There's a purse that I don't remember seeing the first time. There's hardly anything in it—a wallet with eight dollars, a lipstick and comb, a bus ticket receipt, and a package of chewing gum. But no identification at all. Susan thought ahead. If anybody went through her things they wouldn't have found anything that gave away that she was an imposter. And that's why she told Charlotte she didn't drive, because she couldn't produce a driver's license without giving away the truth. I carefully go through the pockets of the clothing.

Finally satisfied that what I'm looking for isn't here, I straighten up. John is back in the room with the saw, and Skeeter is starting to lose patience with him. "Daddy, let's go back in the house now. There's nothing here for you."

"There is. I know I saw a drill. And I need it."

Skeeter rolls his eyes at me.

"What do you need with a drill, John?" I ask.

He breaks into a grin. "What are you doing here? I haven't seen you in a dog's age."

"We'll have to sit down and talk," I say. "But right this minute I need to ask Skeeter something. Do you mind if we go back to the house?"

"Sure, I need to get something to eat anyway."

Once John is inside, I stop Skeeter and say, "Skeeter, I need to ask you about something you told me."

"Okay, what's that?"

"Remember you said you overheard Susan Shelby talking to herself?"

"Yeah."

"You remember exactly what she said?"

"Sure. She sounded like she was having an argument with herself out loud. It creeped me out hearing her talk to herself that way."

"She was calling herself Nonie?"

"Yeah, she . . ." He stops as he realizes the same thing that I figured out. "Oh man, if she'd been talking to herself she would have said, 'Susan.'"

"She was talking on the phone to Nonie."

"I guess she wasn't as crazy as I thought she was."

"The question is, where's the phone she was using?"

He stares at me blankly. "I never saw her with one. Is that what you were looking for in her stuff?"

"Yep. It's got to be in that room somewhere. Billy never said anything about finding it?"

"No, but he wouldn't tell me anyway."

He trails me back upstairs, intrigued at the mystery of where the phone is. It's possible that Susan had it with her the night she was killed and that her killer took it away with the murder weapon. But the clothes she was wearing had no pockets, and it seems likely that she didn't have it with her.

I'll say this for Billy Blake. He keeps a tidy room. The bed is a little rumpled, but at least he's made the effort to straighten up. His suitcase is set in a corner, and there are no clothes strewn around. The only thing out of place is a pair of boots thrown into the corner. Hands on my hips, I survey the room. Where could Susan Shelby have hidden a cell phone?

Even though I've already looked once, I look through every drawer in the chest and the bedside stand and find nothing.

I'm ready to give up, when Skeeter says, "Did you look under the bed? Maybe it fell under there." He crouches down, picks up the skirt of the bedspread, and looks on the floor under the bed. I can tell him there's nothing there, since I already looked once.

"Or the mattress," he says. He jumps to his feet, dusting off his hands. Again, I already looked, but he says, "Here, I'll hoist it up and you look."

As soon as he lifts the mattress I see a clear plastic bag lying on the box springs near the head of the bed. Inside is a cell phone and charger. I couldn't have missed the cell phone the first time I looked. So how did it get here?

"Whoa!" Skeeter says. He reaches for it.

"No. Leave it alone," I say. I look around and see a box of tissues. I pull one out and use it to pluck the plastic bag from its hiding place. "You can put the mattress down now."

He lowers it. "Why did she hide the phone?" he says.

"She didn't."

He sits down heavily on the bed. "I don't understand what's going on here."

"Skeeter, do you know why your family keeps so much to themselves?"

He looks at his thumb and brings it to his mouth to chew at the corner of a nail. "Because of what Nonie did."

He's wrong, but his answer is so plaintive that I believe that's what he thinks, and it lets him off the hook.

"What the hell is going on here? Why are you in my bedroom?"

Billy is standing at the door, an angry expression on his face. When he sees the cell phone, he blanches. "I was going to give you that," he says.

"Skeeter, I'd like for you to leave us alone," I say.

Skeeter looks at his brother uncertainly.

"Go on," Billy says, his voice not unkind.

"When were you going to give the cell phone to me?" I ask when we're alone.

"I hadn't decided."

"How did you get a hold of it?"

"It was in that woman's purse."

I didn't find a purse when I looked through her belongings the first time. "Where was the purse?"

Billy walks to the window and looks out. "I don't want to tell you."

"Your daddy had it?"

He nods his head, his back still to me. "I can't imagine that he killed her. Mamma keeps an eye on him all the time. How would he have slipped outside and followed her and done anything like that?"

"You're sure it was him and not your mamma who had it?"

He wheels around. "Yes." He looks immeasurably sad. "I was with him one day and he showed it to me like it was a treasure." His voice wobbles and he swallows. "I asked him where he got it and he said he found it. I asked him where and he said it was downstairs in the kitchen. When I looked inside the purse and saw that cell phone, I knew it was Nonie's. I asked Daddy if he took it from her—this was when we still thought she was Nonie—and he said he had found it. But I knew he took it."

"You didn't give it to me right away because you figured it implicated your dad."

He nods.

"I admit it doesn't look good. Your daddy could have been awake and heard Susan leave and slipped out and followed her. We can't know what happened, but he could have gotten mad and hit her—he might not have even known that he killed her."

"But listen," he says. "If he did that, what did he do with whatever he killed her with? He doesn't have the mental capacity to have known to hide it."

"I know, son. But somebody might have seen what he did and they got rid of the weapon."

I know that whoever might have done that is not going to simply confess. I'm going to have to come at the answer in a different way.

Back at headquarters, I plug Susan Shelby's phone in and wait until it has enough juice so I can get the list of recent calls from it. I'm hoping that Susan called someone, pretending to be Nonie, telling him she had something on him that he'll most likely want to pay to have suppressed. I know there will be a phone call to Nonie herself. It's pretty clear from what Skeeter overheard that the two women were in on the scheme together.

I'm antsy with waiting, but eventually the phone gives a soft burr and indicates that there's enough charge in it to use it. I smile to myself as I turn it on, thinking that only a few months ago I didn't know anything about cell phones, and now this one might be the key to finding out who killed Susan Shelby.

I scroll down to find the last few calls Susan made and find that there are no local calls. So much for Susan calling someone outside the family to blackmail them. The last three calls are to the same number—a number in the Tyler/Jacksonville area. It's got to be Nonie's number. I dial it and wait. I'm almost ready to hang up when a message comes on. It's one of those electronic voices that says the caller is unavailable and repeats the number but doesn't give the name of the cell phone owner.

I go to the law enforcement reverse directory and there find that the phone Susan Shelby called belongs to Nonie Blake.

CHAPTER 28

Pine trees that east Texas is famous for surround the retirement community with the unimaginative name of North Tyler Retirement Community. The trees are droopy with the drought and heat, and they give off a strong scent of pine. I drive up the long driveway to the front entrance. The complex is made up of a couple of big structures that look like apartments, each with a small balcony, and several duplexes arranged in a half-circle facing a central park.

I meet Lilah Cousins's brother, Ken Gitlen, for lunch at the golf clubhouse café. Gitlen is a tall, dapper man with a full head of gray-white hair and a mustache to match. He tells me he's retired from the oil business. I spent a number of years as a land man, so we have a subject to kick around before we get down to business. He's vigorous and expansive—obviously popular, as people keep stopping by our table to say a few words to him.

When I tentatively bring up Lilah, though, he clams up. "I'm afraid that's a very sad part of my life, and I don't like to dwell on it."

Keeping the matter as vague as I can, I tell him I'm investigating a family tragedy, and it led me to Adelaide's family tree. "It would be helpful to me if you would put your feelings aside and tell me what you remember about Lilah."

"I'm surprised that Lilah's daughter knows anything about the family. Lilah cut us off without a word."

"The daughter didn't tell me anything. I dug up the information myself. Do you know why her mother cut off the family that way?"

"I was a teenager when this happened, but it made an impression on me. Here's the way it went." He looks around the room furtively, as if what happened all that time ago could reflect back on him if his friends found out. "My mamma and daddy never liked Lilah's husband, Aaron, and she resented it. I was a kid, and Aaron was nice to me, so I didn't understand why my folks were against him. He made me feel included, made me feel like I was important. When I was older I realized that he wasn't all he was cracked up to be."

"What do you mean?"

He shifts in his chair and hunches forward, voice lowered. "He was charming, but he was a criminal, pure and simple. He got into some trouble before the war and was forced to enlist. Later my daddy told me that he thought being in the service would be good for Aaron. But when Aaron returned home from the war, he went right back to his old ways."

"And what was that, exactly?"

"Trying to get something for nothing. First off, he tried to get some Ponzi scheme going—finagling money from widows and old couples. You know how those scams work. He gave the first few people a good return so they'd tell their friends, and they would send him more so-called investors."

"How did he get caught?"

"I don't know that, but my daddy was friends with the sheriff, and he came to my daddy and told him what was going on. Next thing I know, Daddy and Aaron were having it out. Lilah took Aaron's side and said she was never going to talk to my folks again."

"And after that Aaron took to robbing banks."

He shakes his head with a grim set to his mouth. "I don't know why he couldn't settle into making a living by working the way the rest of us did. My daddy said Aaron grew up poor and it did something to him. Made him want to get money any way he could—and the faster, the better."

"I know he was killed in a bank robbery. Do you know if he had a partner?"

"Partner? I couldn't tell you. All I know is that he was killed and Lilah moved away after that. She had a little girl. I guess that would be Adelaide. It about killed Mamma not to get to know her grand-daughter, but she was real religious and she said it was easier for her to pretend Lilah was dead."

His coffee has got to be cold by now, but he stirs it, and I can see he's struggling with a thought. "This Adelaide. How's she doing? You said there was a tragedy? What happened?"

I explain the situation to him.

"You suppose one of Adelaide's family killed the woman?"

"I'm trying to figure that out."

"You know, Aaron was a criminal, and my brother always said the apple doesn't fall far from the tree."

There are deep shadows under Nonie's eyes. Her expression hardens when she sees me on her doorstep. "Have you found out who killed Susan?"

"I think I'm getting closer. I need to ask you to fill in a couple of details for me."

"I've told you everything I know."

"Not quite everything. You mind if I come in?"

She hesitates but then opens the door wider, and I step inside. She stands her ground inside the door. "What is it you want to know?"

"I want to be sure I've got things straight. Susan gave you no indi-cation that she was planning to go to Jarrett Creek?"

"I told you she didn't." She reminds me of Adelaide when she says that—a little defensive.

"Did you and Susan ever discuss where your family's money came from?"

"What money? You've lost me." The answer is quick in coming, and vehement. Every time I circle around the question of money, I hit a nerve with somebody.

"Were you afraid of Susan?"

She jerks her head back. "Afraid? No, why would I be afraid of her?"

"I talked to Susan's family. Sounds like she had something of a temper."

"Oh, what did they know? They wrote her off because they didn't like that she was independent and did things her own way." She's revved up now, and her face is flaming. "They thought because we're two women living together we must have a sex thing going. You probably think the same thing."

"Your intimate life with Susan isn't in question. What I want to know is if Susan ever lost her temper with you."

She shrugs. "Once or twice. But I don't take anything off of anybody, so we got that straight pretty fast."

"Nonie, I know that you were aware that Susan was at your folks' house because someone overheard the two of you having a conversation when she was there. What was the conversation about?"

"I didn't know she was at their house. She just called me to make sure everything was okay here. She didn't tell me where she was."

"Someone overheard her arguing with you. What was the argument about?"

She shrugs. "I don't know. What difference does it make? I can't remember having an argument with her. It couldn't have been anything important, or I would remember."

"One more question. It concerns the incident with Charlotte that landed you in the hospital."

Her eyes go cold. "I told you I'm not going to talk about that."

"Charlotte said when you were trying to get her to put the noose around her neck you said you had to make sure she wouldn't tattle. What were you afraid she was going to tell?"

She claps her hands over her ears. "I can't hear this. I'm not going to think about it." She shuts her eyes tight. "And you can't make me talk about it. The doctor said I didn't have to answer to anyone, that it was the past and I should move on." She opens the door and makes a shooing gesture toward me. "I want you to get out of here. Now!"

"You're going to have to answer these questions, if not with me, then with the Texas Rangers, and you may find they aren't as reasonable as I am."

She takes a deep breath. Her face has done that eerie thing of becoming neutral, as if seconds ago she wasn't raving. She says, "Charlotte doesn't remember what I was afraid she'd tell?"

"Not yet," I say. "But she's working on it."

"Let me know when she figures it out," she says. "I'd love to know what she comes up with."

It's not a good idea to take an instant dislike to somebody who you're going to ask for help, but sometimes it happens that way.

"Duke Rogers," the cop says, not bothering to take his hands out of his back pockets to shake mine. He also doesn't give me his title. Furthermore he's slovenly, with his shirt-straining belly hanging over his pants like he's due to give birth at any moment. If I'm not mistaken, he didn't shave this morning and maybe didn't comb his gray-streaked longish hair in the past week. The duty officer called back to ask Rogers to come to the front desk and talk to me; it took ten minutes for him to shamble out here.

I introduce myself, and there's no appreciable change in his attitude when he finds out I'm chief of police in another town.

"What do you need?" His voice sounds like crushed gravel.

"I'm looking into something that happened a long time ago in this part of the state. A couple of bank robberies."

"You'll have to get that information out of state archives," he says.

"What I'm hoping for is to talk to someone who was around back then who might remember what happened."

He blinks at me and then wheels on the duty officer. "You called me out for this? What made you think I'd know anything about what this man wants?"

I have to keep my anger in check. "This man," he said, as if I'm some bored citizen off the street who has no business asking for his valuable time.

"I asked to talk to somebody who'd been around a while," I say. "Thought maybe I might get a line on a cop who might have handled the case back then."

"How long ago are we talking?"

"Fifty years, give or take."

He puts his little finger in his ear and digs around. "Anybody who was around back then . . . got to be in his late seventies, early eighties. That's pushing it."

An hour later I'm knocking on the door of a modest little house a couple of blocks away from Jacksonville Lake. There's an old pickup and a boat in the oyster-shell driveway.

"You Craddock?" The retired cop is near eighty years old but bright-eyed and easy in his skin.

"That's right. I guess I've found the right place."

"Hubert Styron." We shake hands, and he invites me into the living room.

Although the place is tidy, like mine it's slipping around the edges, and I suspect he's a widower like me. He confirms it, and we commiserate lightly. He brings out coffee and apologizes for not having any sweets on hand. "I've got a little diabetes and if I keep sweets around, I'll eat them."

"The coffee is perfect," I say.

"Now what is it you want to ask about?"

"Like I told Officer Rogers, this goes back a long way. I want to know if you remember a bank robber by the name of Aaron Cousins?"

He frowns. "Name does sound familiar, but . . ."

"He was shot and killed while committing a bank robbery."

Memory flashes bright in Styron's eyes, and he snaps his fingers. "Hell yes, I remember that. Not that I was involved in the shootout or anything, but it brought quite a bit of attention."

"Do you remember how it went down?"

He takes a sip of coffee and wipes his mouth with the back of his hand. "As I recall, somebody—a citizen—saw Cousins's car parked at the side of the bank. Cousins had left it running, and the guy thought it looked suspicious. We'd had a string of bank robberies in the area and I guess he was on the alert. I saw the car later. It was all shot up with bullets. It was an old jalopy—a Ford, I think it was."

"You've got a heck of a memory."

"Not always. I was new to the force, so it made quite an impression on me."

"You said string of bank robberies? I didn't read anything about more than one robbery in the report about his death."

"At the time, there was nothing to tie him to the other robberies. But they stopped after he was killed. I remember the officer responsible got grief for killing him instead of wounding him. The feds wanted to question him."

"Did Cousins have a partner?"

Styron raises his eyebrows. "Now you're asking too much. I know he was the only one killed, but whether anybody else was involved, I don't know."

"I expect his widow went through a lot?"

"Poor woman. She was a pretty little thing. She moved away after a while. Couldn't take the gossip. I remember Cousins was a war veteran who had been in trouble before he enlisted. She swore she thought he'd turned things around."

"These other robberies. How much money are we talking, total?"

"Pretty fair amount. There were five of them and he got anywhere from twenty thousand to fifty thousand dollars in each one."

CHAPTER 29

I t's past midnight when I get home, and Frazier greets me as if he was pretty sure he'd never see me again. There's a note from Loretta. I had asked her to stop in and feed the animals for me.

"That's a cute little dog. I stayed with him until my bedtime. He seemed so sad to be left alone. Zelda was fine. P.S. I'm busy early tomorrow, so I don't know if I'll get to the baking." That brings me up short. Not that I mind if Loretta doesn't bring baked goods, but it's unusual for her not to bake. I wonder what she's up to.

In spite of being so tired from my long day, traveling to and from Tyler and squeezing as much into the day as I could, I can't fall asleep. I play the interview with Hubert Styron over in my head. He said there was no evidence that Aaron Cousins carried out the string of other robberies that ended with his death, but it makes sense that he did. And if so, I suspect that he managed to stash away the stolen money and only told his wife Lilah where it was. In fact, I wonder if it's possible that Lilah Cousins was his accomplice. Not that I'd ever have a way of finding out.

If she did know where the money was, Lilah did the smart thing. Instead of making use of it right away, she moved to Jarrett Creek and established herself in a quiet life. Was it the smart thing, or was she terrified that someone would find out? Did she ever use any of it, or was she too afraid to, and she kept it to pass on to Adelaide?

Whether she was clever or scared, eventually Lilah must have told Adelaide about the money. And more time passed before Adelaide's family felt safe enough to spend it. But why did they wait so long? At some point the statute of limitations would have kicked in. None of them could have been prosecuted for the robbery. I suspect I know the answer: I think the banks could have sued them to get the money back. But I have to look up the legal details to be sure.

Whatever way it happened, they kept quiet because they wanted that money. They didn't want to have to pay any of it back. It was pure greed that kept them quiet. What nags at me is how it affected them. In their fear of being discovered, the whole family closed inward. They may have plenty of money, but they've never really enjoyed it.

If I'm right, and Aaron Cousins was responsible for those bank robberies, and the Blake family has been living on the money knowing it was illegally obtained, they would have done most anything to keep it secret. Would that include murder? Nonie Blake denied that she knew anything about the money. But once again I'm reminded that the doctor at Rollingwood warned me that Nonie was an accomplished liar. And she's not the only one in the Blake family you could say that about.

The next morning I'm cranky and creaky until I get to the pasture for my morning session with my cows. Yesterday I left so early I didn't get down to the pasture, and I arranged for Truly Bennett to look in on the cattle. It's amazing what a few days of good food and lack of stress will do for an animal. The three straggler cows I took in look like different beasts. They are alert and already putting a little meat on their bones. One of them pushes past the others to greet me, and it's clear to me that he's ready to join the herd. Truly found no evidence of any medical problems, so I open the gate and let her out, shooing the other two back in the pen. If I'm not mistaken they look outraged at being held back, but another day of separation won't hurt them.

Even the bull looks more interested in his surroundings. He bellows once when he sees me. The whole visit cheers me up considerably.

When I get back to the house, the phone is ringing. It's Ellen. "How's your daughter?" I ask.

"She's much better, but still a little shaky. We've had a chance to talk—really talk, about Seth and some other things on her mind. I don't want to leave her quite yet. Can you stand Frazier one more day?"

"You know, if you stay gone too long, you may not get him back."

"I knew you'd like him if you got to know him."

"It wasn't me I was worried about." I tell her that Zelda unexpectedly accepted the dog, and she laughs. I'm glad to hear her laugh. Last time I talked to her, she sounded distressed.

As Loretta warned, she didn't make it by this morning, so I take a couple of cinnamon rolls out of the freezer and stick them in my toaster oven on low.

Frazier has been giving me a baleful look ever since I walked out to the pasture without him this morning. I'm not quite ready to trust him not to bark at the cows and stir them up. I should have left him with Maria and Zeke yesterday instead of keeping him cooped up here all day. "You'll get plenty of company today," I say.

Regarding Susan Shelby's death, I have an idea now about the why of it. Somehow—most likely through Nonie herself—Susan found out that the family money was tainted. Susan decided to blackmail the family and get some of that money. But I wonder why Nonie didn't try to squeeze money out of her family herself.

Now that I have an idea of what happened, I have to figure out the who and the how. Where is the murder weapon? I can't help thinking that if I knew what it was I would have a better idea of who killed Susan. We drained the pond and found nothing but a rusted tricycle, a BB gun, a lot of small kids' toys, and a couple of small animal carcasses.

At headquarters, I can tell right away that Maria Trevino, like Frazier, is put out with me. She greets Frazier readily enough, but her demeanor toward me is frosty. I suspect she's mad that I went off to Tyler without her. And she's probably right—I should have taken her with me. It's not right to start somebody on a trail and then leave them behind. But I'm used to working alone. The fact is we don't really have enough staff to partner up on things. Not routine things anyway, but a murder is hardly routine.

"Maria, I have to apologize for rushing off yesterday without you."

"You don't have to explain yourself to me," she says. Huffy.

"That's right, but I want you to know it was nothing personal. Now, here's what I'd like you to do this morning." I get up and pick up one of the boxes of files left behind by Rodell Skinner from when he was chief of police. "I want you to start going through these files and familiarize yourself with them, and then file them in the cabinets we've got here."

She looks over at the cabinets with narrowed eyes. "I might have known it would come to this."

"Come to what?"

"That I'd be nothing but a glorified secretary."

"There are only three boxes left here. There were six to start with. Who do you think took care of that? It was me and Zeke and Bill Odum. You won't be putting in any time the rest of us haven't put in. And besides, looking through those reports will help you learn the nature of Jarrett Creek."

She nods, but the set of her jaw is stubborn. "Can I ask you something?"

"Go ahead."

"Did I do something wrong the other day when I went with you to the Blake ranch? Did I step out of line?"

"Of course not. You think that's why I didn't take you along yesterday?"

"I wondered."

"Put it out of your mind." I scratch my head, unsure how much to say. "The fact is, I'm not used to having enough manpower—and womanpower—to have the luxury of bringing somebody along on a case."

"Okay, I get it."

I sigh. From her tone I suspect that she might get it, but she doesn't want to show it. I don't blame her for being eager and ambitious. In fact, I admire her for it. But Jarrett Creek is a tough place to contain so much energy to succeed. There isn't that much to do in a small town. Maybe that's why they sent her here, to get her used to the idea that police work isn't an exciting endeavor every single day. Most days it's piddling work, accented with a little spice now and then.

She's not done with me. I see the speculation in her eyes. "I want to ask you something else."

"Don't be afraid to ask anything, ever. You ought to know by now I'm not going to bite you."

She nods. "I've been thinking about the weapon. Has anybody looked around the property? Somebody might have thrown it away, or even buried it."

"I looked close to the house, but I haven't sent anyone to go farther out. It's a big property."

"I know it's a long shot, but nothing came of the dredging. And somebody had plenty of time to take the weapon somewhere and bury it or throw it where they thought it wouldn't be found."

"Or to take it to the lake and throw it in, or drive pretty much anywhere with it and throw it away," I say.

She's watching me closely. "In the academy they told us that criminals are lazy, and that most of them aren't as smart as they think they are. I think it's worth a look around the property."

"Can't hurt," I say. "If you want to put off this filing and search for the weapon, it's all right with me. But don't get heat stroke. And look out for snakes."

She flips her hand at me as if to say snakes don't worry her. She can't hide the sparkle in her eyes at the prospect of some real investigation.

"I'm going out to talk to the Blakes about having the coffin dug up and moved. You can follow me out there, and I'll tell them you'll be walking the property."

She waits while I call the medical examiner's office and tell them that Susan Shelby's family wants the coffin dug up and transported to Tyler.

"Who's going to pay for all this?" T. J. says.

I'm an old hand at this bureaucratic nonsense. "Who do you think ought to pay?"

"The Blakes misidentified the corpse, so maybe it ought to fall to them."

"I'll pass it by them and see what they say. They're already going to be out the money for the coffin. They got top of the line, and Susan Shelby's relatives are going to balk at the cost."

"That's up to those folks. Let them hash it out."

Now it falls to me to go back out to the Blake ranch and present them with a bill for retrieval and transportation of a coffin. I would feel sorry for them, except that they are the ones who claimed it was Nonie, even when they knew in their hearts it wasn't her.

"I suppose I see their point," Adelaide says. "We should bear the expense of digging up the box and sending it to her family since we're the ones who made the mistake."

We're sitting in the kitchen, and Adelaide is coaxing John to eat. "All of a sudden he's off his feed. I swear if it's not one thing, it's another."

It looks to me like he's enjoying refusing the food because of the attention it earns him.

"I sure would like to know what Susan Shelby was doing here," I say.

"So would I," Adelaide says. "John, now if you don't want me to feed you like a baby, you need to eat."

"Would you?" I say. "You mean you don't know why she was here? I think you might have some idea."

At the tone of my voice she jerks her head to look at me. "What do you mean?"

"I've got a theory. Let me run it by you. I think Susan found out a family secret that you didn't want anybody to know—especially the law."

She puts the spoon down. "I don't know what you're referring to."

227

"Then let me clarify. I'm talking about money. The money you and John took to Les Moffitt to invest all those years ago wasn't a paltry sum. And I don't believe it was money that your mamma squirreled away. I think it's money your daddy got from robbing banks."

She laughs, but it's a nervous sound. "Where did you get an idea like that? I don't understand why you don't believe that money came from my mamma. I told you she was frugal and worked hard and put money by. She said she didn't want me to ever have to worry about money the way she did."

"Adelaide, I know what kind of work your mamma did, and there's no way she could have put enough money by for you and John to buy this ranch and raise a family of four and never have to work, much less pour it into investments. And I know John's family didn't have enough to account for that either."

Adelaide is totally focused on me. John has picked up the spoon and started eating applesauce. "I don't care what you think you know. My mamma left me a little money, and I'm eternally grateful for it."

Maybe she's telling the truth as she knows it. Maybe I'm wrong, and Lilah never told her where the money came from and she actually believed it was her mother's savings.

"Let me go at this a different way. You've had a long time to speculate. Do you have any idea why Nonie wanted to . . ." I look at John. He's got his head cocked like an owl watching me. "Why she tried to hurt Charlotte?"

Adelaide is shaking. "Why would you ask me that? What good can come of it?"

"Have you talked to Nonie since you found out she's alive?"

All of a sudden John says, "Where is Nonie?"

"John, she's living in Jacksonville."

"Why doesn't she come home?" John says.

"Because, that's why." Adelaide gathers up John's dishes and takes them to the sink. The dishes clatter as she sets them down hard. She wheels around, hands dripping. "Why didn't she call me when she first got out? Why would she live up there all this time and never call me?"

"Maybe she was waiting for you to make the first move."

"That's ridiculous! I didn't know where she was, did I?"

"We could call her," John says. "Maybe she'll come for a visit."

"He's right," I say. "Maybe you should give her a call." It can't hurt to stir things up between them. Maybe rattling a few cages will open up this case for me.

CHAPTER 30

Back at headquarters I look up Les Moffitt's phone number and give him a call. He isn't answering his phone, so I leave a message for him to call me. I want to check on something he said last time I talked to him. At the time, it didn't seem important, but it might fit into the way I'm seeing things now.

My cell phone rings. It's Trevino. "I found something."

A half hour later I locate Trevino a good way back on the property, out of sight of the house and barn. She has pushed aside some bushes, and we're staring down at a tire iron almost hidden by bushes, with what looks like dried blood on one end of it.

"How'd you spot this?"

She shows me a hefty stick. "I didn't want to poke my hands in where a snake might strike, so I used this to push aside the bushes. And there it was."

I gather it up into the bag I've brought. "I don't know that this is going to do us much good. Probably can't lift a fingerprint off this even if whoever did it didn't wear gloves."

Maria smiles. Her usually morose face is gleeful. "This might help." She points close by to a little pile of sticks and dead brush formed into a circle. Inside the circle is a dried-up cow patty. I get up closer to it, and sure enough there's an imprint of a shoe in it.

"In the dark, whoever threw that tire iron away didn't see where they were stepping."

"Damn good work," I say. "We're going to have to be really careful moving the earth with the print. That's sandy soil on top."

"If we bring the kit out here, I can take an imprint where it lies."

"You know how to do that?"

"I sure do. I'm good at it."

"Tell you what. The kit's in the trunk. I'll stay here while you go get it."

She practically gallops away, pleased with herself. I don't blame her. She has followed basic procedures that she learned in the police academy, while I was too busy depending on the psychology of the people involved. And she's made a success of it. I remember her remark that at the academy they made fun of old geezers like me for thinking they can solve things by knowing people in the town. I thought she could learn a thing or two from me, and now I'm finding I might be prodded to learn something myself.

It takes a while, but she gets a good imprint and finds another one in a patch of soft sand a few feet away.

"It's a small print," she says. "It must have been a woman who did this."

I agree, and the two most obvious women are Adelaide and Charlotte. But it could be that I've missed the mark with the money angle and my original line is right, that Nonie knew someone's weak spot, and she and Susan cooked up the idea of blackmailing whoever it was.

I stop by the house on my way back to the squad car to talk to Adelaide. "I need to know your and Charlotte's shoe size."

"Our shoe size? Mine is eight wide and I think Charlotte's is the same. No, that's not right. She wears an eight and a half. I know that because she and Billy wear the same size."

"They what?"

"Billy has always been embarrassed because his feet are so small."

"How about Skeeter's shoe size?" I say.

"He's got feet like his daddy. They wear something like a size eleven."

On the way back to headquarters I tell Maria the shoe sizes, including Billy's.

"Uh-oh," she says.

We're getting out of the car when I get a call from Les Moffitt. "Sorry, I've been out with a client. What did you need?"

I ask him to hold on while I go into the office. Maria hurries in ahead of me to free Frazier, who greets her joyfully. She tells me she's going to take him out for a walk around the block.

I get back with Moffitt and say, "You told me the Blakes brought money in to invest around twenty years ago. Can you give me the exact date?"

"I sure can. After you asked me, I looked it up. This coming October it will be twenty years ago exactly that John called me."

Early October, shortly before Nonie Blake tried to kill her sister. Has to be more than a coincidence. Very likely she somehow found out about the money, and Charlotte did too. And Nonie was afraid that Charlotte would inadvertently spill the beans to somebody. It chills me that Nonie thought the best way around it was to hang her sister. Doc Taggart said he knew something wasn't right with Nonie when she was a youngster, and he's right.

I call Nonie's number again, and there's still no answer. Probably working late. I consider calling her at Walmart, but on second thought I think it's going to be better if I show up in person to question her— seriously this time. She and Susan Shelby cooked up something between them. Whether it was a blackmail scheme about the Blake money or someone's indiscretion, I'm going to find out. That means another trip to Jacksonville tomorrow, and I intend to take Maria Trevino with me.

It's late afternoon, too late for Trevino to search out matches on the shoe prints. She measures the print and is a little disgruntled to find out the shoes were probably smaller than size eight. She'll get imprint comparisons to find out the possible types of shoes we're looking for. It won't be enough to arrest someone, but it will be good corroborating evidence.

CHAPTER 31

Frazier and I haven't been home ten minutes when Loretta comes puffing in. I blink when I see her, not quite sure I believe my eyes. Loretta has always worn her hair in blinding white, tight little curls, and what I'm seeing before me is completely different. It's now sort of blondish and cut short and straight. I can't help staring for a few seconds until it sinks in that if I don't say something fast—and I mean something good—I'm going to be in a lot of trouble.

"Don't you look cute!" I say.

And as I say it, I realize I mean it. It makes her look years younger and bright-eyed.

"You like it?"

"I do. What made you decide to make such a big change?"

"You know my daughter-in-law, the one I went to Washington DC with a while back? She told me I ought to upgrade my look. At first it kind of hurt my feelings, but I kept coming back to it, so I thought, why not? So Sissy Eldridge and I made an appointment in Houston and we went and got the works. I had a pedicure and a sort of makeover. I even bought some new shoes. For church. Not these old things."

We both look down at her shoes. They look fine to me. "Did you have a good time?" I ask.

"I did. We decided we were going to do it more often. I don't know how I'm going to get Maxine down at the Cut 'N Bob to fix my hair like this, but I think I like it. If it's not too much, that is." She pats her hair.

"I really like it," I say.

I get us some iced tea and we sit out on the porch and I tell her some of what has gone on today—not anything specific, just enough to make her think she's in the loop. While I talk, I keep sneaking looks at her. Who knew a hairdo could make such a big difference? I can't think of exactly the right word. Kind of modern.

"I wish you'd figure out who killed that woman," she says. "Having something like that hanging over the town isn't good."

She asks how Maria Trevino is working out.

"It's a change having somebody there full time. I like her, but I'm afraid she's a little too ambitious to be happy here."

"She isn't permanent, is she?"

"I don't know what the state had in mind. You know how bureaucracy works—they tell you what they want to tell you and hope you can't guess the rest of it."

"If she's planning to stay, maybe it's a chance for you to get out from under the job. I mean . . ." She trails away, and I can't help wondering if she was going to say I'm a little old to continue as chief of police.

I'm glad when she leaves. I'm tired of talking to people and need a chance to gather my wits for tomorrow's confrontation with Nonie Blake. I'm heating up some enchiladas from the freezer when it suddenly occurs to me that Frazier's not around. I haven't seen him since Loretta came. I go outside and call him, but no little dog shows up. My heart sinks. If I lose that dog, Ellen will never forgive me.

I go in and turn off the stove and go back outside. First I head down to the pasture to see if he's snuck down there, but there's no sign of him and he doesn't come when I call. Then I head over to Ellen's. It's possible he decided to check in at home in case she's back. But there's no sign of him there. I ask a couple of neighbors if they've seen him, but no one has.

My heart is heavy when I get back home. It's gotten late, and the sun is low in the sky. I eat the enchiladas, perking up at every little sound, hoping Frazier is back.

It's getting dark by the time I go back out. I feel like a fool walking up and down the streets calling a dog, but I'm desperate. I keep picturing Ellen's face if I have to tell her the dog is gone. And every block I turn onto I'm terrified that I'll see a little dog's body by the side of the road, the victim of a careless driver.

It's almost ten o'clock by the time I give up and go back home. On the porch I give one more half-hearted whistle and walk inside. I had thought I left the light on, but I didn't, so I switch it on as I walk in. And I freeze. Sitting in an armchair in the living room, facing me, is Nonie Blake. And she's holding a gun on me.

"Well, I have to say this is a surprise," I say.

"That's what I was aiming for," she says.

"Looks like this isn't a friendly call. What do you . . ."

"Cut the good old boy crap," she says. She gets up from the chair. "You're coming with me. My car's outside."

She waves the gun—a little snub-nosed revolver—indicating I should go ahead of her, but I stand my ground. "I need to ask you what your plan is," I say. "I'm not inclined to rush off with somebody who's waving a gun around."

"The plan is that I'm going to take you out to my parents' ranch."

"Why would you do that?" She has no intention of taking me anywhere but some lonely road where she can do away with me. It was only a few hours ago that I figured out that she killed Susan Shelby. She must have sensed that I was getting too close.

"No telling what kind of tales you've told my family about me. I need to set the record straight."

"Why do I have to be there? You can tell them on your own."

"I want to get everybody together so I can explain. Then you'll leave me alone. Now let's go."

I'm out of questions, so I'll have to think of something clever before we get to the car. I start toward the door, and she says, "Wait. You have a cell phone on you?" I reach in my pocket and pull it out.

"Throw it over there on the couch. You armed?"

"I never thought it was necessary to carry a gun to walk around my neighborhood."

"I heard you walking around calling somebody. Your dog?"

"A friend's dog. I'm watching him for her and he's disappeared. I'd like to find him."

"He'll come back. Let's go."

I head outside and down the steps, keeping a slow pace, but my mind is racing. I've got to figure out an escape. I stop and turn slightly toward her. "Where's your car?"

"It's down the street. I parked down there because I was afraid you'd recognize it. Turn around and keep moving."

I'm hoping that somebody will be out and about, maybe walking a dog or coming home late, but it's quiet and deserted on our street. Jenny Sandstone's lights are out, and I'm sure Loretta is either watching TV or in bed. There's an upstairs light in a couple of houses, but likely they wouldn't hear me if I shouted—not before Nonie shot me, anyway.

I stop walking again and say, "I thought you and Susan were in cahoots trying to shake down your family, but that's not exactly right, is it?"

She gives a bark of laughter. "No way was I going along with her. She was a fool to think I would."

Stalling for time, I turn toward her with my hands out. "I can't make sense of it though. You knew that your family's money was tainted and you told her. Why? That doesn't sound like a smart thing to have done." I know by now that Nonie likes to be right, and if I suggest to her that she did something that wasn't smart, she'll defend herself.

We're standing in the dark so I can't see her face, but her voice is belligerent. "Remember that picture of me and Susan at the lake? We had a good time out there. At least I thought we did. She acted like we were best friends, and we sat around on the cabin steps and got stinking drunk. It was only later that I realized she was pumping me to find out about my family. I told her things I shouldn't have. It was her fault for being nosy," she says. "Anyway, that's not important. Keep walking. My car is up the way there."

"Whatever you told Susan, she planned to use it to blackmail your family, is that right?"

"I said let's get going."

I turn back around, but I know I'd better not get in that car with her. I've got to think of a course of action. But what? Should I lunge to the side and hope to grab her before she can shoot me? Can I count on her aim being poor? Probably not. She's young and with quick reflexes— quicker than mine anyway. Should I call out for help and then leap at her? She could shoot me five times before anybody could get here.

I stop walking but don't turn around. "Don't do this," I say, raising my voice a little. "It isn't going to solve anything to shoot me."

"Shut up!"

"Can I ask you one thing?"

"What?"

"I think I've figured out why you tried to kill Charlotte and I want to know if I'm right."

"I don't want to hear what you think you've figured out." She takes a step and jabs the gun in my back.

"Ouch!" I say, louder than necessary, hoping for someone to hear me.

"Don't be a sissy," she snaps.

I hear a rustle in the bushes, and I cough to cover up the sound. I hope to goodness somebody has heard what's going on and is sneaking up on us.

"Somehow you and Charlotte found out where your family's money came from and you were afraid she'd blab it. You figured getting rid of her was the only way to protect your folks."

"Very good. Now move it." She jabs harder, and I take a couple of steps forward.

Suddenly I hear a ferocious sound like the roar of a panther, followed by fierce growls. Nonie screams and the gun goes off. I duck, flinching, expecting the bite of a bullet. The growling increases, and Nonie screams louder. I turn to see Nonie on the ground and a blur of light fur on top of her, snarling and snapping at her. Lights start going on in the houses closest to us. "Here, now!" a man's deep voice says. "What's going on out here?"

In the light I see Frazier has clamped down on Nonie's wrist that's holding the gun, and he's trying to wrestle it away from her. My first thought is to go for the gun. If she kills Frazier, Ellen will never speak to me again. Footsteps are pounding toward us, and I throw myself on top of Nonie. I grab her gun hand, dog and all.

By now she's screaming bloody murder. For all I know the neighbors who are charging up to us may think I'm a man who has attacked a young woman. A lot of people go armed these days, and somebody could easily shoot me. "I'm Chief Craddock," I yell. "This woman is dangerous!"

"Samuel! What the hell is going on?" I hear Jenny Sandstone's voice.

By now there are several people surrounding us, and strong hands pull me up. But in the flurry of activity Nonie scrambles to her feet and takes off running.

"Don't let her get away," I yell. "Be careful. She's got a gun."

"No, the gun's here," a man says. He shines a powerful flashlight at the revolver. Frazier is standing over it, tongue hanging out, looking pleased with himself. I grab the man's wrist and turn the light toward Nonie's retreating figure.

"Get her!" I yell.

Young Colin McCovey, who lives next door to Jenny, has come out of his house dressed only in his undershorts and slippers. He takes off after Nonie, with Frazier in hot pursuit. They reach her as she opens her car door. McCovey slams her up against the side of the car. She kicks and hits at him. Frazier lunges at her, barking furiously.

As soon as I get to them, I grab Nonie's arm and say, "Nonie Blake, you're under arrest for the murder of Susan Shelby."

"You can't arrest me," she says. "You don't have any evidence." She struggles to squirm out of my grasp, but McCovey grabs her other arm and she can't get away.

"I've got all I need," I say. "You're going to jail."

I direct McCovey and another man to march her in front of me back to my house so I can get my handcuffs and my gun. We start forward, but I turn and say, "Frazier, come!" He trots back to the house beside me.

CHAPTER 32

"Were you scared?" Loretta has brought berry-filled buns this morning, and we're eating them on the porch. It's barely 7 o'clock, so there's a hint of cool in the air. Fall won't be long in coming now.

"I didn't have time to be scared. Tell the truth, I was more scared that that mutt was going to get himself killed." I have Frazier tied up on the porch with us. He doesn't seem to mind. He's laid out sleeping with his head lolling off the bed I made for him. Whatever adventure he was on yesterday—not to mention the energy it took for him to save my life—wore him out.

"What do you suppose made the dog attack like that? He can't have known what was going on."

"Maybe he heard that my voice sounded nervous. All I can tell you is that I'm grateful for whatever made him do it."

"What's going to happen to Nonie Blake?"

"I'm not sure yet."

"I think this answers the question of whether or not they should have let her out of that institution. She's got a loose screw," Loretta says.

"Now, Loretta, don't talk like that. She's a troubled person and since what she did was premeditated, she's bound not to see the outside of a prison for a long time."

"Or else they'll put her back in that cushy mental hospital."

I get up. "I better head on down to headquarters. Lot to be done today."

After Loretta leaves I get ready, and when I walk out the front door, I say, "Frazier, you want to sleep it off today or are you coming with me?"

He leaps up and barks once. I take that to mean he wants to be part of my day. I untie him, and he trots to my pickup with me. I open the passenger door, and he hops in. I've always liked my cat, but I kind of like having this dog to pal around with. I might consider getting me a dog.

You'd think after Nonie Blake threatened me with a gun last night, she'd be worried, if not contrite. But she greets me full of bravado when I walk into the back room of headquarters where she's being held in one of our two cells. I've brought her coffee and one of Loretta's buns, but she tells me she only eats organic food.

"What does that mean exactly?" I say.

"Nothing that's been processed. Like that sweet roll was made with processed flour. Stuff's not good for you. Not to mention the sugar." Her lip turns up in a sneer. "I don't suppose you have any vegetarian food around here?"

"So happens I do," I say. "I'll be back."

I drive to my house and retrieve a plastic container from my freezer. Last time I had dinner at Ellen's she sent me home with a brown rice, broccoli, and cheese dish. I stick the leftovers in the microwave and head back to headquarters with it. If the dish doesn't suit Madame Nonie, then she'll have to starve. But she gobbles it up.

"We're going to be taking you to Bobtail to the county jail," I tell her when she's done eating. "But I'd like to ask you to clear up a few things first."

"Why are you taking me to the county jail? You have nothing to charge me with."

"Threatening an officer of the law with a firearm is frowned on," I say. "That can get you a fair amount of jail time on its own, let alone the matter of your hand in Susan Shelby's murder."

"That's stupid," she says. "I wasn't threatening you. I wanted you to come with me, and I didn't think you would unless I made you."

It strikes me that Nonie lives in something of a fantasy world in which whatever she wants, she ought to be able to have—regardless of reality. Only somebody with a skewed idea of the way things work would think she could point a gun at somebody—especially a lawman—and get away without some kind of punishment.

I walk out into the outer office, grab a chair, and bring it back to sit down in front of the cell. "Let's talk," I say.

"You can talk all you want to," she says. "I don't intend to say anything."

I was afraid she was going to say she wanted a lawyer, after which I'd have to forego questioning her. But for now, I can proceed. "Last night you said you were going to take me out to your folks' place to straighten out a few things. What was it you were planning to set me straight about?"

She told me she wasn't going to say anything, but by the way her eyes dart to me and away a couple of times, I can tell she's itching to show me how smart she is. If I bide my time, she'll talk. "You think you've got it all figured out," she says, "but you don't."

Not only does Nonie like to be the smart one in the room, but I suspect she likes nothing better than to tell people when they are in the wrong. Maybe I can use that to my advantage. "Why don't I tell you what I think, and you tell me where I'm wrong?"

"Aren't you forgetting something?"

"What's that?"

"You haven't read me my rights."

"You know, it's true, I did forget that. I guess in my old age, I'm getting forgetful." I pat my pockets. "Let me see, now where did I put that card?" I know the rights by heart, but I've got an act to put on. "Here it is, in my wallet."

The door to the back opens, and Maria Trevino steps in, as we'd planned. "You mind if I sit in?"

"Not at all. I'm afraid I'll get something wrong and you can help me with it."

"I'm sure you'll do fine," she says . . . condescending, sounding like she's indulging an old man, part of our plan, although her act is maybe a little too convincing.

I read Nonie the card, and before she can take me up on the lawyer part of it, I say, "Now, I was going to give you my idea of what's been going on, and you were going to tell me where I went wrong."

Nonie has leaned back on her bunk, like she's disinterested in the whole process.

"The short story is that you found out that your folks were living on money that your granddaddy stole."

She snorts. "I don't know where you got an idea like that."

I ignore her. "Here's how it happened. Your granddaddy was a bank robber who managed to steal a fair amount of money. He told his wife Lilah—that's your grandmother—where the money was hidden and after he was killed in a bank robbery, she waited a while and then retrieved the money and moved to Jarrett Creek. She didn't use much of it, or maybe none of it, because she was afraid somebody would notice and wonder where all that money came from. And she wanted to save most of it because she wanted her daughter, Adelaide, to have chances she never had."

She's still not looking at me. "You think you have it all figured out, don't you?"

"Feel free to jump in and set me straight anytime."

"No, I like hearing this story. It's entertaining."

"Adelaide married John and they dipped into the money to buy the ranch. I'd love to have been a fly on the wall when Adelaide told John about the money."

I pause, expecting her to protest, but she's got her eyes closed, leaning her head back. The only indication that she has heard anything I've said is bright-red spots on her cheeks.

"Then about twenty years ago they decided it was safe to invest the money. But they didn't realize how smart you are. You like to do a little snooping, and you found out the secret." I pretend I'm not looking at her, and out of the corner of my eye I see her sit forward. "You found something that told you where the money came from—I'd like to know what it was you found. Did you overhear your folks discussing it, or did you find something in your mamma's possessions?"

"Which was it?" Trevino says. She does a good innocent act. "Did your granddaddy leave a note to his wife and she kept it and then gave it to your mamma? Or maybe you found a newspaper article?"

"You have no idea how far off-base you are," Nonie says. "What is it that makes small-town cops so stupid?" But the fight has gone out of her voice. This is strictly bravado.

"Why don't you tell me the way it was then?" I say.

"Good try. What a pair of idiots!"

"Anyway, what led me to this line of thinking was wondering why you tried to kill your sister," I say.

Nonie sits up on the edge of her bunk.

"She told me that you said the reason you had to kill her was to keep her quiet. I wondered what a little kid might know that you were afraid she'd talk about. After I found out that your granddaddy was a bank robber, it occurred to me that maybe Charlotte was with you when you discovered the source of your family's money. And maybe she threatened to tell—being a child and not understanding how important it was to keep quiet."

Right on cue Trevino says, "Nonie, what size shoe do you wear?"

"Huh?" For a second Nonie looks dazed.

"Your shoes," Trevino point at Nonie's feet. "What size are they?"

"What difference does it make?"

"It's all right if you don't want to tell me."

"I don't mind telling you. I wear seven and a half. What do you care?"

Trevino and I look at each other and nod.

"What?" Nonie's voice is sharp.

"I feel sorry for you, Nonie," I say. "I suspect you really love your family. You were trying to protect them. Weren't you worried after you got put away that Charlotte would talk after all?"

"This is bullshit," she says, but her voice falters. She coughs to cover it up.

"You loved your mamma and daddy so much that you were willing to kill your sister, so of course when your friend Susan told you her fine scheme to come down here and blackmail them, you knew you had to stop her. You even tried to talk her out of it on the phone."

"I don't know where you got an idea like that."

"Skeeter overheard her talking to you. You don't know Skeeter. He's a funny kid. You'd like him."

"Shut up." She stands up, fists clenched at her side. "Why don't you just shut up and take me to Bobtail like you said you would. I don't want to hear anything else you have to say."

"We found the tire iron you used to kill your friend Susan," I say. "Her blood was on it. Unless you were wearing gloves, your prints will be on it, too."

"Tire iron? You can't get prints off a tire iron." She leans sideways against the bars of the cell, arms crossed.

"Maybe, but that's not all we have."

She laughs. "Oh, right."

"Tell her, Trevino."

"Remember I asked about your shoe size? You stepped where you shouldn't have."

"What are you talking about?" Nonie's eyes dart back and forth between Trevino and me.

"You stepped in a cow patty and left footprints when you got rid of the weapon," I say. "Trevino, here, found the imprint."

"That wasn't mine."

I stand up, shaking my head. "What I wonder is, if you're so much smarter than everybody else, why didn't you take the tire iron with you?

You could have thrown it anywhere on the way back home. That was stupid."

I meet her eyes. Her face has gone white. "Yeah? That shows how much you know! Suppose I'd been stopped by a cop on the way home and he looked in the trunk?" She's so outraged that I said she had done something stupid that she doesn't even realize that she has admitted she had the tire iron.

"Why would a police officer do that?" I say.

"You don't know, do you? You don't know how the cops stop you in the middle of the night if you drive a crappy car. They always think you're up to something. Mexicans and blacks are always whining that the cops treat them like shit. But it's not just them; it's everybody. If the cops think you're poor, they'll stop you for nothing."

"So instead of taking the tire iron with you, you walked a good ways out to the back of the property and threw it away, thinking nobody would ever find it. Too bad for you that Trevino is smarter than you."

She looks daggers at Trevino. "Could we get on up to Bobtail? Maybe their cells are a little more comfortable and I don't have to listen to you two rattle on."

CHAPTER 33

Later in the afternoon, after Trevino and I have taken Nonie to Bobtail and processed the paperwork, we go out to the Blake ranch. In the comfort of the sumptuous living room furnished with stolen money, Trevino and I break the news to Adelaide that not only have we arrested Nonie, but we've also figured out the source of the family's income. "Billy is the only one you ever told where the money came from, isn't he?" I say.

"Yes," she says softly. "When he was twenty-one. I shouldn't have told him. That's why he dropped out of college and took up with the rodeo. He said he didn't want anything to do with tainted money. I decided then it would be better not to tell Charlotte or Skeeter."

"Did you ever have any idea that Nonie knew?"

"No. All I can think is that she must have overheard John and me arguing about whether to take the money to someone to help us invest it. We were worried that an investment counselor would want to know where the money came from. It was a bad argument, and I'm pretty sure we wouldn't have noticed if Nonie eavesdropped."

"Maybe it wasn't that. Maybe she found something incriminating. Everyone said she was a snoop. Did you keep something that mentioned the source of the money?"

She drops her head into her hands. "Oh, my Lord. That's how she found out. I kept a letter from my daddy to my mamma telling her where the money was."

"Why did you keep it?"

"For sentimental reasons. When my daddy was killed, I was too young to remember him. In the letter he said I was the apple of his eye, and that if anything happened to him, he wanted me to be provided for. John told me to get rid of it, but I hid it away. I guess I didn't hide it well enough." She gets up from her chair and looks around the room as if wondering how she got in this predicament. "I wish the money had never existed."

Trevino and I get up. "Do you want to tell Charlotte and Skeeter about this, or do you want me to? They'll have to be told. Charlotte may have known at some point, but she doesn't remember it now. And the banks are going to be after the money."

She stares at me. "That money never did us any good. A secret like that eats you up. It just eats you up. I'm glad you know about it now."

She says she'll tell her family herself. "I don't know what we're going to do. We'll have to figure out something. I don't know what we're going to do about John . . ."

I'm ready to leave headquarters for the day when Ellen Forester pops in. I should be glad to see her, but I know she's here to pick up her dog.

Frazier goes nuts with delight. I thought he liked me a lot, but now I see how he acts when he really likes somebody. He leaps as high as my belt buckle again and again, giving out high-pitched yelps, and then dashes back and forth between Ellen and the door. He's ready to go home.

Ellen hears the story of Frazier's bravery and how scared I was that he'd get himself killed.

"I'm glad you're safe. And I appreciate your concern for Frazier." She looks down at him. "How in the world did he know you were in danger?"

"Dogs know that kind of thing," Trevino says in a lofty tone.

After she leaves, Trevino and I look at each other, and I know she's thinking like I am that we're feeling pretty sorry to see Frazier go. "Let me take you out for a meal," I say.

"You don't have to do that," she says.

"You did a good job on the case."

"I'm only doing what I'm trained to do," she says with a stubborn jut of her jaw.

"Let me put it this way. If you were one of the guys, I'd ask you to go have a meal, so what's the difference?"

"You're right."

We spend a couple of hours over enchiladas at the only Mexican restaurant in town. I introduce Trevino to the owner, who treats her like a celebrity.

I find out a little bit more about her, and when we're ready to go she says, "I was wrong about older small-town cops. You know what you're doing."

Small concessions are appreciated, and I tell her I know I can learn something from her, too.

Nonie Blake is cooling her heels in the jail in Bobtail awaiting the results of psychiatric tests and adamantly refusing to talk to the lawyer who has been assigned to her. Apparently Adelaide and Charlotte have been to visit her, but she refused to see either of them as well.

A few weeks later, I have more news about the illicit money to impart to the Blakes, so I drive out there to talk to them. The house feels hollow somehow, and Adelaide and Charlotte tell me that Billy has gone back home.

"Is Skeeter here?" I say. I figure I might as well talk to all of them at the same time.

"Skeeter went with Billy," Charlotte says. "Billy is going to try to get him a job."

Adelaide smiles vacantly, as if they are talking about people she knew long ago. I wonder where John is, but I figure if he were awake, he'd be here.

"Like I told you, I need to update you on what's going to happen to the money Aaron Cousins stole."

"I know we have to give it back," Adelaide says. "But we've earned a fair amount of interest over the years investing, so we'll be okay."

"I'm afraid you need to understand something. I've talked to federal banking authorities, and the banks are going to want the interest on the money as well as the principal."

"But wait a minute," Charlotte says. "They never proved that my granddaddy stole any more than the money from one bank, and that was only twenty thousand dollars."

"It's complicated. Apparently the feds are going to reopen some of the cases of the other robberies and try to prove Cousins did them, too."

"Even if he did," Charlotte says, sounding panicky, "the statute of limitations has run out."

I sigh. I've already been over this with Les Moffitt. He'll explain the particulars to them later, but I felt like it was my duty to break it to them initially. "You may be right, and they may never prove anything, but the banks plan to sue, and the money is going to be tied up for a long time."

Charlotte looks deflated. "I don't know what we're going to do. I guess I'll have to get a job. What about the house? Will they take that, too?"

"The state of Texas protects your house. The banks can't take it, so you have a place to live."

"But you said all our assets besides that will be frozen?" Charlotte says. "How will we live?"

"Like you said, you're going to have to get a job," Adelaide says. There's a new kind of steel in her voice.

"What kind of job can I get?" Charlotte says.

"You'll work that out," I say. "You'll be all right."

"But I've got Trey. And Mamma has to take care of Daddy . . ." Her voice trails away.

"Charlotte," Adelaide says. "Samuel's right. We're going to work this out."

"I talked to Les Moffitt," I say, "and he's going to be in touch with you. He'll help you."

"Of course." Charlotte's voice is full of relief.

I'm not really worried about Charlotte. Moffitt will be more than happy to help her and her family. Charlotte's biggest problem is that she was coddled for so long. There are a lot of people in worse situations. It will take her some time to readjust to having to make a living, but she's smart—she'll be okay.

I'm more concerned about Adelaide. All along, the reason Adelaide didn't put John into a proper facility is that she was afraid he would tell someone their secret. And now that the secret is out, she can't afford to have him cared for in a nursing home, so she'll have to continue taking care of him herself. He's going to get worse and her life will be harder, but oddly enough, today I'm seeing something different in her. Being out from under the burden of her secret, she seems lighter.

The excitement of catching Nonie Blake has died down, and I've completely forgotten the minor task I assigned to Trevino, when I get to headquarters one morning and find her with her feet up on her desk, looking tired but satisfied.

"You're here mighty early," I say.

"No, I'm here late. I was waiting for you to get in before I leave to go get some sleep."

"What were you doing so late?"

"Come on back and find out." She tips her chair forward with a clunk, stands up, and heads for the cells.

I follow her to the back room, and in one of the cells a teenaged boy is sitting on the side of the bunk with his head in his hands. He jumps up when he hears our footsteps. "Chief Craddock, I'm so glad to see you. This lady is crazy."

I glance at Trevino, and she's glaring at him. "How do you figure that?" I say.

"What kind of person would hide in the bushes to catch somebody who doesn't mean anything . . ." His voice trails away.

"Somebody stealing people's flowers," Trevino says. Her voice is stern, but there's something else there, too. Can it be humor?

"Son, what is your name?"

"Please don't tell my folks," he says, hanging his head.

"Name?"

"Doug Wilton. Dougie, they call me."

"Doug, have you got any good reason why you've been upsetting the flower growers in our community by sneaking into their yards at night and cutting their best flowers?"

"I didn't mean to take the best ones. It was dark. How did I know?"

Trevino makes a funny noise, whirls around, and heads for the door. "I'll be right back," she says, and I know she's gone off to laugh.

"You've got a girlfriend, don't you?"

He nods.

"And you wanted to get her some flowers."

Another nod. "I didn't have any money. I didn't think anybody would miss a few stupid flowers."

"All right. Here's what you're going to do. I'm going to give you the names and addresses of the people you've stolen from." I emphasize the word 'stolen,' and he flinches. "You're going to personally apologize to each of them and offer to do two hours of work to make up for it."

"Yes, sir. I can do that. I'll be glad to do that."

I go get the keys to the cell, ignoring Trevino, who is still wiping her eyes. I open the cell. "Now get back home before your folks raise the alarm that you've been kidnapped." He starts to scoot out. "Wait. Don't let me find out you haven't followed through with what I said, or your folks will hear about it."

After he leaves, I tell Trevino that it's important the boy's parents not know about his humiliation.

"You think I don't know that by now?" She shakes her head. "Small towns!"

ACKNOWLEDGMENTS

So many little pieces of information go into making up a novel. Sometimes writers don't even know what they don't know. Information finds its way into books through direct and indirect means. I want to acknowledge the unsung heroes who have passed along tidbits that helped me in my work. In particular, thanks to Lee Lofland and his team of dedicated faculty members in the Writers' Police Academy, to Ruben Vasquez of the Georgetown, TX, Police Department Major Crimes Division, and Dr. Daniel Wescott, Director of the Forensic Anthropology Center at Texas State University.

Also a shout-out to the speakers and panel members of the numerous conferences I have attended over the years. With few exceptions, they give their all to inform and inspire other writers to get it right.

ABOUT THE AUTHOR

Terry Shames grew up in Texas, a vast and varied landscape that still drives her imagination. She is the author of the best-selling Samuel Craddock series. *A Killing at Cotton Hill* was awarded the Macavity for Best First Novel of 2013, and *The Last Death of Jack Harbin* is a nominee for the Macavity for Best Mystery Novel of 2014. She is a member of Sisters in Crime and Mystery Writers of America. Visit her website at www.Terryshames.com.